Never Standing Still

By Anie Michaels

For Becca,

whose tremendous strength and enormous heart defy
words,

but inspire so many of mine.

Prologue

This wasn't how I'd imagined my seventh birthday would turn out. The balloons were great, the Rainbow Brite birthday cake was just how it looked in the book at the grocery store, and even some of my friends showed up to my party.

That part was awesome.

But as I lay in my bed, listening to my parents argue, their yelling only getting louder and angrier, I tried to keep my tears in. They didn't need to hear me crying. I didn't want to cry, either. I'd cried a lot lately and it never seemed to do any good. I startled when I heard a cabinet slam shut as my father's shouts floated down the hallway.

"I just couldn't be here," he said in a growly voice. I imagined him braced against the kitchen counter, elbows locked, head bowed. "The house was filled with kids I don't know and their parents. It just wasn't how I wanted to spend my day."

"It's her birthday, Kevin."

"I know."

"A father should be with his daughter on her birthday."

"It doesn't matter, Alli. She didn't notice that I wasn't here."

I had noticed. But he was right, it didn't matter that he wasn't there. I wasn't surprised. He never seemed to be around, so I didn't think my birthday party would be any different.

I heard a frustrated grunt leave my father and I could picture his hands coming to his hair, scraping it back, leaving it sticking up in all directions. It was what he always did when he fought with Mommy; he pulled his own hair.

"I'm so sick of the same fight. I can't keep having the same stupid argument with you, Alli. I'm not the person you want me to be. I never was."

"So change! You don't have to do it for me, but you *should* do it for that little girl. She's your flesh and blood."

"I didn't ask for this!" He screamed. "I didn't want to be a father. I didn't want to be tied down for the rest of my life. I didn't want this kind of responsibility."

"She's your daughter! Not some obligation! Don't you feel any kind of pull to be *good* for her? To be the kind of man she can look up to?"

"Honestly Alli, all I feel is like I'm tied down, like I'm standing still and can't move. I don't want to stand still anymore."

The arguments weren't new. They fought all the time. I usually didn't have trouble sleeping through it; the rhythm of their voices yelling at each other usually lulled me to sleep. But tonight, for some reason, I heard everything he said. His words shot down the darkened hallway like an arrow and found its way through the crack in my door and hit its target right in my chest.

I held the tears in as long as I could, but when I heard the back door slam shut, my mom yelling at him to never come back, I couldn't keep the tears from falling. They soaked through my pillowcase, but I didn't care. I pressed my face into my pillow so my mom wouldn't hear me crying.

Eventually I stopped crying and listened to the frogs, which lived outside my window in the wet months, when the water would pool outside my bedroom from all the rain. I listened to the frogs and waited to hear the back door open again, signaling that my father had returned. But the door stayed closed, and I never heard him come home.

Chapter One

Ice Queen

"No, listen to me. I can't just make a coffee stain disappear, Ron. I can replace the shirt and have it dry cleaned, but I can't magically make the stain disappear this instant." I rolled my eyes only because Ron was on the phone and not standing in front of me. "Let me grab an extra shirt and I'll bring it out." I walked through the costume trailer, looking for the rack that held the wardrobe for the leading actor. "Okay, I'll be five minutes." I reached up to my ear and pressed the button on the earpiece to disconnect the call.

This job was one of the worst I'd ever lived through. Ron, the director, seemed to always have unrealistic expectations of everyone—not just me. He was always chewing someone out for something completely uncontrollable. It made for a stressful work environment, but the flip side was the cast and crew seemed to bond over his tirades. There was a lot of eye rolling and snide comments going on behind his back, and the fact that no one was spared from his evil wrath meant that everyone could bond over his erratic behavior.

I found the shirt I was looking for and quickly made my way to the set. We were shooting a scene in the park blocks of Portland and the beauty of the area was never lost on me. It was like a little haven in the middle of the city. A place for children. A place for dogs. A place for families and couples. It was the eye of the storm that was Portland. You could come here for a moment to mentally reset or relax. Or, usually you could. Today we'd closed down the majority of the park blocks for filming.

I ran out of the trailer and headed toward where they'd set up the cameras, cutting through the people who were standing around waiting for filming to begin. I made my way to Adam, the leading actor. He gave me a brilliant smile as I approached him and I smiled back, only not as widely.

"Hey, Kals," he said.

"Hi. I've brought your shirt," I said, raising the white shirt, motioning toward him.

"Oh, so you want me to take this one off?" He looked down at his chest and the white shirt, which had a dark brown coffee stain all down the front of it.

"You could go to your trailer," I suggested.

"Well, where's the fun in that?" he asked as he started undoing the buttons at the top of his soiled shirt, giving me a wink as if I should have been excited to watch him undress.

Again, I found myself rolling my eyes. Adam was my least favorite type of actor to work with. He thought every woman wanted to sleep with him. He wasn't exactly wrong, just overly aware of the fact. He was built like a god, with blond hair that just barely fell to his ears and piercing blue eyes. He'd been in a few movies, mainly movies for young adults, but he'd gotten his big break when he'd been cast for a new TV show that had hit it big and garnered a huge fan base.

I'd known Adam for a few years. We'd met when he was still an unknown during a movie shoot, back before he was on the cover of magazines. Before he'd been to award ceremonies. Hell, back before he'd been nominated for any of those awards. He had just been a newbie actor trying to break into the business. He'd been sweet, kind, and even a little shy. Which were all the reasons I'd slept with him once.

Now, I wouldn't touch him with a ten foot pole covered in antibacterial hand sanitizer. He'd found success and turned into a complete douchebag. I could tolerate him though, only because every time he flashed his smarmy smile in my direction, I only had to picture him naked and stifle the laughter. He wasn't as *blessed* as he'd like everyone to think.

"Adam, just put this shirt on. No one wants to watch you stumble through a striptease."

"Oh, really?" His smile grew wider. "I remember a time when you were begging me to take my shirt off." He slowly slid the dirty shirt off his shoulders, holding it out to me.

"Your memory is getting bad in your old age. I distinctly remember begging, but it wasn't for you to take your shirt off," I said as I handed him the clean shirt. "I begged you to put it in, and all you could say was, 'It already is!'" I smiled back at him and tilted my head, trying to goad him on.

I heard a few people around us snickering, but no one looked in our direction or commented.

"Jesus, Kalli," he said as he shoved his arms through the shirt sleeves and started buttoning it up. "When did you become such a bitch?" His angry words stung because I didn't think I was being a bitch. I was just throwing the same shit back at him that he threw at me and every other woman on set.

"Adam," I said, all humor gone from my voice. I hadn't meant to hurt his feelings. "Listen, I'm sorry. I didn't mean to—"

"Don't worry about it," he said, throwing a hand up at me, signaling me to stop speaking. "Ron, I'm ready when you are." He walked away from me, tucking in his shirt, heading toward the director.

Well, shit.

I stood by, watching Adam and his fellow cast members film a pivotal scene in the episode that included some pretty cool stunts. It took a few hours and after every take I ran to Adam and adjusted his clothes, making sure everything was where it was supposed to be and looked the same as the take before, all for continuity's sake. Adam never said a word to me, wouldn't even look at me. I could feel the irritation wafting off him and I did my best to work around it. I was nothing if not professional; well, except when I told the entire crew that Adam Front had a small penis.

When filming was over, I walked back to the trailer and let out a loud sigh, trying to release some of the tension from the last few hours. I moved to the rack, making sure I had everything prepared for the next shoot, and I heard the door open. When I turned I saw Adam standing in the doorframe.

"Can I come in?" he asked cautiously.

"Uh, sure." I was caught off guard by him. I moved toward him and he held his hand up again, gesturing for me to stay put and not come any closer.

"You know, Kalli, when I met you all those years ago, I really liked you. You were funny and sweet, but you always seemed so unobtainable. Untouchable. Then, one night you started responding to me, laughing at my jokes, flirting with me. I thought I'd finally gotten through to you."

"Adam, I'm sorry, I don't really know what you're trying to say."

"I'm trying to point out that even though you think I'm a jerk, that I'm just some guy who slept with you, you're wrong. You slept with me and then an ice cold brick wall went up around you. I couldn't get through to you even though I tried, multiple times. Hell, I'm still trying. Or, I was, until you pulled that shit this morning."

"I'm sorry about that. You know I was kidding."

"I know. It's not important. I'm just trying to tell you that I see you and feel badly for you. You always put up this front, like you're impenetrable. But I know you're not because you let me in once. One night, so long ago, you put down your shield and let me in. I've been trying to get back to that place for so long because I can't stand to see you alone all the time, and I really like you. But you shut me out quicker than I could get my clothes back on." He paused and shoved his hands in the pockets of his jeans. "I guess I'm just trying to say that, perhaps, if you'd stop trying to push everyone away all the time, you'd actually enjoy getting close to someone."

"I am close to people, Adam. Just not you." My words flew out and they were rude, harsh, and pointed. I aimed them at him and hoped they hurt. I didn't need him psychoanalyzing me, didn't need him sticking his nose in my business, and I didn't need him to tell me something I already knew. I *had* let him in and that was obviously a mistake. And if I'd known it would come back to bite me like this, I never would have.

"Yeah, okay, Kalli. I get it. Back to the ice queen. Just remember, if you ever feel like melting a little, or taking down all your armor, you can call me."

"Well," I said as I turned from him, not wanting to see his eyes full of pity staring at me anymore. "Don't hold your breath." I kept riffling through the rack of clothes until I heard footsteps and then the sound of the door closing as Adam left. I exhaled and sagged down onto the bench seat along the wall of the trailer. I hadn't come to work this morning anticipating a verbal smack in the face. The most jarring part of his tirade was the truth he pushed at me, the way his insight reminded me that I was, in fact, damaged. He called it armor, I called it bandages. I was merely trying to manage the hemorrhaging. I couldn't prevent the wound from being torn open.

It had happened years ago.

Later that day, when I found myself walking into Poppy, my mind was reeling with Adam's words, my heart was heavy and I really needed a drink. My eyes immediately saw Megan behind the counter. When she saw me, she smiled her warmest smile and I felt a little of my tension release.

I never really wanted to make friends. Business contacts? Yes. Girlfriends? No. But I'd walked into Poppy, a cute clothing boutique, two months before when I was in Portland working on a movie and met Megan. Her outgoing personality had drawn me to her, and then when I'd met her sister, Ella, I was even more pulled to her. The two of them together offered me a no-questions-asked kind of friendship I hadn't known I'd needed, but by now it was obvious I couldn't get rid of them if I tried.

Besides, their lives offered a reprieve from my personal issues which gave me a kind of escape. Listening to Ella, who'd had amnesia for the last six weeks, trying to recover her life, was not only heartbreaking, but distracting as all get out. If I could lend my ear to Ella and give her half the support she offered me, then I'd do that without question. Being there for her, listening to her troubles, offering some insight—it allowed me to forget all the shit in my life. Plus, her sister Megan was a hoot. I adored them both.

I listened to Megan chat about the customers she'd encountered at the store that day, and when Ella came in, I listened to them talk about Porter. I hoped, deep down inside, that Ella and Porter would figure their relationship out. He sounded like someone worth taking a chance on, and Ella deserved only the best. She was obviously smitten, even if she couldn't remember falling in love with him just weeks before.

Eventually, Ella went home but Megan agreed to get a drink with me. We found ourselves, just an hour later, at Bartini, a trendy martini bar that looked like you had walked into a genie bottle. Lots of jewel-toned fabrics, fluffy pillows, and gold.

"Are you really going to try to keep Ella and Porter from seeing each other?" I asked her because I was insanely curious. I knew Megan and her parents had only good intentions when they kept Porter's existence from Ella, seeing as how she didn't remember him, but now that he'd made his presence known, it seemed like a waste of energy.

"Kalli," Megan said with the sarcastic drawl to her voice I'd become so accustomed to. "You didn't see Ella and Porter when they were together before her accident. There's nothing in the world I can do now except watch with popcorn readily available."

"Really?"

"Yeah. Those two are like the strongest, most electrically charged sexual batteries you've ever seen." She took a sip of her drink, a long island iced tea. "I wouldn't want to stand between them. That crossfire is hot." She laughed a little, swirling the straw in her drink. "Patrick and I were pretty steamy when we first got together, but it was more of an excitement from two young kids just exploring their sexuality. Ella and Porter are, well, more like two very mature people who seem to have found that one person who could light you on fire."

"You think that's a thing? Like, one person for everyone? A soul mate?"

Megan shrugged. "I think that if you find someone who makes it impossible to imagine yourself with anyone else, then what's the point of continuing to search?"

I thought about her answer, but mostly pushed away the idea that someone out there was destined to be with me. I didn't need that kind of pressure.

Chapter Two

It Wasn't Glamorous

I was in my Range Rover, headed North on I-5, when the ding from my Bluetooth alerted me to a phone call from Ella. I pressed the button on my dash and heard the crackling of the phone call connecting.

"Hey, Ella. What's up?"

"Hi! I'm calling to see if you'd like to get lunch today. I feel like I haven't spoken to you in a while and I miss you."

"Damn, I'd love to, but I'm on my way to Seattle. I wrapped yesterday so I left this morning to go home. Sorry."

"Oh." The disappointment in her voice was apparent and guilt crept though me. "Okay, well, do you know when you'll be back in town?"

"I don't know. I don't have any work lined up down there at the moment."

"Oh." I hated the sadness in her voice. "Okay."

"But I'll make sure I come down for a weekend or something when I get a break."

There was a long pause and I knew she was trying to formulate her thoughts. "Just promise me that one day you're not going to leave and never come back?"

"Ella, you're my best friend. I promise I'd never just disappear on you." Even as I said the words I knew they weren't one hundred percent truthful. I might disappear on her. I'd done it before. But things were a little different now and even though the tethers that tied me down were thick and strong, they weren't unbreakable.

She took my promise to heart and I hoped I'd never have to break my word. We spent the next half hour talking about Porter and how much she loved spending time with him, but she still couldn't remember him. I tried to assure her that even if she never regained that memory, she should give him the benefit of the doubt and just take things slow. Get to know him all over again.

"Well, I'm almost home so I'm going to let you go," I said as I exited the freeway in Seattle.

"All right, and Kalli, don't be a stranger, okay? I really do miss you."

"I miss you too, Ella. I'll let you know when I can make it down again."

"Bye, Kalli."

"Bye, Ella." I disconnected and then concentrated on getting home.

Home, for me, was a weird place where I knew I should feel comfortable, but my home was almost like a second identity. I turned into a different person at home; had different goals and responsibilities. And as long as I was there, I transformed into my other self.

I pulled up to the house, parking next to the sedan in the driveway, then grabbed my bags and headed toward the front door. I'd made it halfway up the path when the door swung open and I saw him barreling toward me.

"Kalli! You're home!" Before I could stop him, not that I would, Marcus had me in a tight and loving embrace.

"Hey, buddy. It's good to see you." Marcus was huge at six feet tall, two hundred and ten pounds, and still growing. He was just seventeen and I knew he'd be growing for a few years yet. It still amazed me every time I laid eyes on him. He was mammoth, much like his father had been.

"I tried to tell him to wait inside, but you know how excited he gets when you come home."

I heard Nancy's voice coming from the house and turned my head to smile at her. "It's fine."

Marcus pulled away from me and began his normal, incessant chatter. "Nancy and I went to the park today and she let me ride my bike. Don't worry," he said, rolling his eyes. "I wore my helmet. But then there were ducks and one big goose and it totally chased me on my bike. But I wasn't scared, I just pedaled faster."

"Hey, Marky, I'd love to hear about your day, but let's go inside. Wanna help me carry my bags? You take this one and I'll grab the other from my trunk."

"Sure thing, sis!" he shouted, taking the bag from me and running back toward the house. Nancy followed me back to my car, offering to help.

"He's been amped up all day waiting for you," she said, smiling at me.

"How's he been otherwise?"

"Good, actually. No big issues have come up lately."

I smiled back at her. That was good news. I spoke to Nancy and Marcus nightly when I was away for work, but I was always nervous that I would be missing something important, or something would go wrong and I wouldn't be able to get to him quickly enough. Besides Nancy, who was a godsend, I was all Marcus had in the world. The guilt of working away from him weighed on me heavily, but my job paid really well and it was the only way I could afford the care he needed and deserved.

"Great. I'm glad to hear it."

Nancy helped me lug my bags to the house and once inside I listened to Marcus relive the last six weeks. As I unpacked my bags, he told me about every trip to the park, every movie Nancy had taken him to see, every exciting thing that had happened at school: he was a chatterbox. And I eagerly ate up his words. I wanted to know about his days, how he felt, what he'd done in my absence. When everything was in its place, put away, and organized, we went into the living room to find Nancy reading on her Kindle.

"Nance, you want to take the night off? I think I've got things handled around here, and you deserve a little time to yourself."

"Well," Nancy said with a smile. "How could I refuse an offer like that? There is a movie I've been wanting to see."

"Oh, yeah?" Marcus said, his voice playful. "Why don't you invite Mr. Bob to see the movie with you?"

Mr. Bob was Nancy's longtime man-friend. They were both in their fifties and were the cutest couple ever. But they were both older and set in their ways, feeling no need to be anything more than, well, *friends*.

"You know what, Marky? I think I *will* invite Mr. Bob."

"Mr. Bob and Nancy, sitting in a tree, K-I-S-S-I-N-G."

"Marcus, stop teasing Nancy. I'd be careful if I were you, Mr. Bob might not like you teasing her and he might be forced to hide all your Spiderman toys again." Marcus' face dropped and I could tell the idea of his Spiderman collection disappearing was enough of a threat to stop his assault on poor Nancy. "Now, tell Nancy to have a good time with Mr. Bob."

"Have a good time, Nancy. And tell Mr. Bob to come over and play Monopoly with me soon."

She laughed and as she walked past him she gave his shoulder a tender pat. "I'll give him the message," she said sweetly. "Now, you be good for your sister, and make sure you show her the new song you learned to play on your keyboard." Nancy winked at me as she left the room to get ready for Mr. Bob.

Marcus and I spent the evening watching Nickelodeon, eating pizza, and listening to him bang out "Take Me Out to the Ball Game" on his little battery-operated keyboard.

It wasn't glamorous, but it was the best night I'd had in a long time. There was nowhere else I would have rather been than with my baby brother.

Chapter Three

Isn't He Perfect?

I was sitting at the kitchen table playing Monopoly with Marcus, Mr. Bob, and Nancy when my phone rang in the other room. I jumped up from the table. Knowing Marcus wouldn't halt his game for me, I didn't even bother asking him to wait, but I did jog through the house in an effort to get to my phone quickly. I saw the number on the screen and answered as I walked back to the game.

"Hey, Lucy. What's up?"

"Hi, Kalli. I just got a call from the assistant producer over at Satin Look studios in Portland. They have a high profile shoot this weekend, but just lost their wardrobe manager. What are the chances that you're free for the next few days to take this job? It's a pretty big deal."

"What are they shooting?"

"It's a music video for Lexi Black."

"Lexi Black?" Lexi Black was, arguably, the biggest pop sensation since Taylor Swift or Katy Perry. Her career was on fire, even if her personal, although not so private, life was adding fuel to that fire. She was rumored to have slept with half of the Hollywood music scene, and even left broken hearts all over America when she was on her latest tour. "Don't you think Lexi Black would have access to someone a little more high profile than me?"

"Well," Lucy said with a little too much enthusiasm. I could hear the gossip train coming at me, full speed ahead. "Apparently, when her costume designer fell through the assistant producer at Satin Look recommended you. Lexi looked into some of your work and thought you'd be perfect for the concept of her new video. Bingo, bango, I get a phone call that you're wanted to meet with the director tomorrow at nine a.m. So," Lucy stopped to inhale and let her brain catch up with her mouth, "feel like making a music video?" The smile in Lucy's voice was almost jumping through the phone. I could picture her red lips gliding over her pearl-white teeth. Lucy had never steered me wrong before.

"Well, I guess it's pretty hard to say no when you've been scouted."

"That's my girl. You've worked at Satin Look before, right? You know where to go, how to get there?"

"Yeah, I should be fine. I'll be there at nine tomorrow, bright and early."

"This is big-time, Kalli."

"I'm getting that impression."

"Her last video got forty million hits on YouTube in one week. Forty. Million."

I gulped down a nervous swallow, trying not to let my nerves get the best of me.

"You'll do great," Lucy assured me, even though I'd lost the ability to talk. "Okay, I'll let you go so you can get your shut-eye. I'll check in with you tomorrow. Knock 'em dead, Kalli!"

She hung up before I had a chance to even thank her for the opportunity, and I ended up just staring at my phone in shock. I was going to design the costumes for Lexi Black's new music video. This was huge. Bigger than huge. This was enormous. This was *soon*. I hadn't planned on being away from Marcus so quickly; I'd just gotten home from a job last week.

I shook off my shock, which was slowly turning into excitement, and walked back to the game of Monopoly I'd abandoned.

"Kalli!" Marcus shouted, bouncing up and down in his seat. "Mr. Bob landed on Boardwalk and had to give me all the money he had left! I bankrupted him!"

"That's great, bud," I stammered.

"What's wrong, Kalli?" Nancy asked, concern evident in her voice.

I shook my head. "Nothing's wrong. I just got a call from Lucy. I've been hired to work on the new Lexi Black video."

"Oh my," Nancy said, her eyebrows raising and lips turning up at the corners. "That seems like it would be a big deal."

"Yeah." I laughed as I sat down in my chair, looking down at the measly amount of money I'd acquired with a few properties, but *all* the railroads. That was my thing— the railroads. I didn't like having all my money in one spot on the board, didn't go for the properties. I liked to be spread out, so I bought the railroads. It might not have paid off big, like Boardwalk and Park Place, but I always had at least one safe place on each side of the board. I wasn't afraid to move around. I picked up the dice and rolled, then moved my thimble past all of Marcus' expensive properties and landed on Go. "I have to leave really early in the morning though." My eyes shot to Nancy, silently explaining to her that I'd be gone for at least a few days, apologizing for leaving—again—when I'd only been home for a few days. She reached over and gave my hand a warm and affectionate pat.

"Then perhaps we should wrap this game up. We can finish it tomorrow after your sister leaves for work." Nancy was looking at Marcus as she said the words. "Go get ready for bed and then you can pick a movie to watch in your pajamas."

Marcus grumbled a little, but thankfully made it to his bedroom without much fuss; a small victory.

"I'm sorry, Nancy. I didn't expect to be gone again so soon."

"Don't worry about it, honey. This is your job, and this is a big opportunity. Don't worry about us."

"Yeah," Mr. Bob piped in. "I'll make sure everything's taken care of around here."

I laughed. "Thanks. I appreciate it." I looked back at Nancy. "I'll be back as soon as I can."

"And we'll be waiting, just like we always are." Her smile was sweet, motherly. There were a few times I'd wondered why Nancy never had kids. She took care of Marcus like he was her own, and she definitely cared for me, but I couldn't help but think of how great a mother she would have been to her own kids. I stood up and went to stand behind her chair. I leaned down and wrapped my arms around her shoulders, putting my cheek right up against hers.

"You're the best," I whispered. What I really wanted to tell her was that I loved her, but I never said those words to anyone. Any time I'd ever said those words to someone, they were taken from me. I couldn't even bring myself to say them to Marcus, even though I loved him more than anything in the world. But I justified it in my mind by telling myself that he knew I loved him, that he could feel it from me and *knew* it, even if I couldn't say it.

She patted my arms again, gently rubbing her hand up and down my forearm. "You better go to bed early, Kalli. You've got a big day ahead of you."

The next morning I pulled into the parking lot at Satin Look studios with five minutes to spare. I walked into the lobby, shoulders pushed back, head held high, trying to appear confident and professional, all while I was trembling on the inside. This was, by far, the most important job I'd ever been offered; it needed to go amazingly well.

"Good morning. Can I help you?" The friendly greeting came from a tiny brunette behind a desk and her smile was as welcoming as her voice.

"Yes, hi. My name is Kalli Rivers, and I'm here to meet with someone about the Lexi Black shoot."

"Oh, yes. Hi! We've been expecting you. George is really looking forward to your arrival."

"George?"

"George Lebowitz."

I choked on the breath I drew in, coughing, sputtering.

"George *Lebowitz?*"

The receptionist smiled as if she were used to people freaking out over his name. He was one of the most famous directors in Hollywood. I couldn't fathom why he'd be in Portland doing a music video, but it wasn't up to me to question his motives. Whatever level of nerves I'd been feeling before I walked in the studio, it had been instantly amplified and dread was now coursing through my veins. I could not be working for George Lebowitz.

The woman wasted no time having me sign the standard contract and I looked over all the terms, finding them very generous. Then she slid a credit card across the counter toward me.

"Here is your card for all purchases. Please just be sure to get receipts for all transactions, and return the card when you're done purchasing for the shoot."

I smiled at her and put the card in my wallet.

"Just follow me this way and we'll find him around here somewhere, I'm sure." The receptionist took me back through hallways lined with prints from famous movies and videos, presumably stills from videos shot in this studio. My eyes wandered over the stills and I couldn't help but feel like it was a lot of pressure to live up to. I was beginning to think I'd gotten myself in over my head.

"Mr. Lebowitz?" the receptionist called out as we walked into a huge warehouse. My eyes grew wide as they fell upon George Lebowitz standing in what might have been one of the biggest and nicest sound stages I'd ever seen. The equipment was state of the art, the lighting looked more complex than any I'd ever seen, and the sets that I could see were beautiful.

Yep. I was definitely in over my head.

"Mr. Lebowitz, this is Kalli Rivers, the costume designer you've been waiting for."

My hackles immediately rose and I broke in to defend myself.

"I'm so sorry if you've been waiting long. I was told to be here at nine, I apologize if that was incorrect—"

"No, you're fine," he said, waving away my panic. "Hi, it's nice to meet you." He put his hand out to me, a friendly smile on his face, and I shook it, hoping I hadn't already ruined my only chance at a good first impression.

"Hi," I replied, trying to appear less shaken than I was.

He took his hand from mine and turned abruptly, walking away. It took me a second before I realized I was supposed to follow, so I took a few big steps to catch up.

"Video shoot is tomorrow, Lexi is in the back dressing room now waiting for a fitting, the male talent will be here soon—we're still ironing out all those details." He was walking very fast, and I had a hard time keeping up. Usually I would have a notebook out, taking everything he said down, but he'd caught me off guard and I only had my memory to rely on. I followed him as he rattled off information that I stored away in the "Not Terribly Important" file in my mind as he led me onto an even bigger sound stage.

This one was built with very large steel beams with giant gears hanging from the rafters above. The floor had moving parts and they must have been testing the lights because they were changing from orange to red to yellow. It was all very visually stimulating, definitely not a set that blended into the background. It was almost as if the director wanted the set to be its own character in the video.

"This is incredible," I stammered, my eyes wide, head turning in every direction trying to take everything in.

"Yes, well, it's been quite the production. We're going for steampunk chic meets freak show. So, you'll need to outfit not only Lexi and our lead male, but also a few performers. One of them is a fire breather, so make sure her costume is flame retardant."

"Uh, noted." There was a lot of information.

"All the performers will be here in one hour for a rehearsal, so you can do your work then, but for now you should probably go see Lexi in her trailer. She's been anxious to meet you."

"Oh." That was surprising. Lexi Black was kind of a big deal. I wasn't a total newbie or anything, and I'd worked on a few things that were pretty impressive, but nothing on this level with this caliber of people. "I'll go see her now then."

George gave me some directions and I tried to remember them as I wound my way through the halls of the studio, trying to find the back doors he'd instructed me to exit from. I found them and my eyes fell upon the trailer I assumed was Lexi's. I knocked on the door lightly, hoping I wasn't interrupting anything.

The door opened and I tried not to gasp as Lexi Black stood before me.

I didn't get star-struck often, I wasn't even a big Lexi Black fan, but I couldn't deny the way my lips turned up and my heartbeat raced when she opened the door and looked like every single picture I'd ever seen of her. She was really standing in front of me. A bona fide superstar.

"Hi, I'm Kalli," I said, reaching out to her.

"Uh, duh! I know who you are! I'm so excited to meet you!" She took my hand but didn't shake it, she pulled me into the trailer and once I was standing in front of her, she wrapped her arms around me and gave me a long hug. "I'm so happy you were available for this. Sorry about the short notice. I had to fire my original costume designer; she just didn't see my vision."

"I'm happy to be here." And I was, but I was also worried about what would happen to me if I didn't come up with exactly what she wanted – in twenty-four hours, no less. "I'd like to start with your measurements, if you don't mind."

"No, of course not. Let's get started." She turned around and went farther into the trailer. I followed and my eyes roamed the small space, taking everything in.

It was obviously a premium trailer and looked barely used, if not brand new. Everything was black with stainless steel accents. Even the countertops were black granite. There was a girl sitting at the table, talking on the phone, with what looked to be a large calendar set out, along with a notebook and pen, a tablet, and another cell phone. She was talking rapidly to whoever was on the other line, and her hands were switching between all the tools on the table.

"That's my assistant, Betsy. She's scheduling my tour with my manager, so I wouldn't expect much involvement from her anytime soon."

"You're going on tour?"

"Yes! Oh my gosh, my new album drops next month and then in the spring I'm starting a US tour! Isn't that exciting?"

"Totally," I cried, trying to match her enthusiasm. "So you like being on tour?" I asked as I opened up my bag and brought out my notebook, pencil, and tape measure.

She beamed. "It's so much fun. A different city every night, plus you get to share a bus with your closest friends for months! What's not to like?"

I smiled at her because I didn't know what to say. It didn't sound like much fun to me. Sure, I got around, liked traveling, but moving from city to city every single day didn't really seem like fun to me. And sharing a bus with so many people, stuck with them almost all day, every day? No, thanks.

"Well," I said with a sigh, trying to change the subject. "Tell me a little about the video and I'll get started." I moved toward her and she immediately put her arms up, making a T shape with her body, obviously used to wardrobe people measuring her.

"Well, it's pretty much just one big beauty shoot. No real story line, just really pretty imagery, interesting shots, and entertaining things happening in the background. Oh, and hopefully one really hot guy."

"What's the song about?" I moved around her, wrapping the tape measure around different parts of her body and making notes. She was a tiny little thing. I usually took as many measurements as I could. I wasn't a seamstress by trade, but usually if I couldn't find exactly what I was looking for I could make it. Plus, it was always better to be over-prepared than under.

"It's a ballad about unrequited love."

"Sounds interesting. I can't wait to hear it."

"Well," Lexi said with a laugh. "You'll hear plenty of it tomorrow. Over and over again. I mean, I love my music, but even I get tired of hearing it so much on video shoots."

I mumbled an agreement, furiously measuring and notating.

"George is working on the male lead right now. So it'll be like, a lot of kissing and touching, maybe some bedroom scenes, but basically just me singing a love song to a man who doesn't want what I want."

"Sounds lovely," I commented, not sure what else to say.

"We had one guy lined up, but I wasn't sure he was right for it. I want someone hot, but also someone who won't overshadow me, ya know? I want someone who will make an impact, someone who makes the video better." She paused for a moment and then said confidently, "I want people to watch my video and then call all their friends telling them they *have* to see it."

"Wow, that's quite a tall order. I hope George has good connections." I silently berated myself; of course George

Lebowitz had good connections. I was, undoubtedly, an idiot.

"George is the best," Lexi said, with a somewhat dreamy look on her face. Suddenly it became clear to me why *George Lebowitz* was directing a music video; he was sleeping with Lexi. I tried not to let my realization show on my face; it wasn't my place to judge. I needed to be professional, but she must have noticed the slight raise in my eyebrows.

"It's not really public knowledge, Kalli. We're just so in love and he wants to help me with my career. He's the best man...."

Her voice trailed off as her eyes went soft and her face looked as if she were drugged. She was definitely floating on a love cloud.

"Hey," I said as I stood, done taking measurements. "I'm not here to judge. He seems like a really nice guy. I'm sure he'll get someone perfect for your leading man." I put my tape measure back in my bag and started formulating a plan in my mind for everything I needed to accomplish in the next few hours. "Is there anything in particular you're looking for in terms of your costume? Anything you'd really like for me to focus on?"

Lexi put some real thought into the question before answering.

"I want to look sexy, but not trashy. I don't want people to talk about my body when they're done watching the video. I want them to talk about how beautiful everything is."

"Got it." And I did; I could totally appreciate what she was going for. She wanted to be recognized for her art, not her body.

"I think I've got everything I need then."

"Oh, give your number to my assistant so I can get a hold of you if I think of anything."

I slid a business card with my phone number on it to her assistant who was on the phone with two different people. She gave me a sideways head bob, indicating she understood what it was, and I headed out.

I made it three steps from the trailer and stopped to take a deep breath. This was going to be a crazy day. I pulled my cell phone out and immediately called for reinforcements.

"Hello?" I heard an excited voice answer the phone.

"Hey, Ella. What are you doing? Feel like being my assistant for the day?"

"Oh, yes. Sounds exciting." Ella's voice was chipper and happy, making me smile.

"You at Poppy?"

"Yup. But I can leave, I've got all the girls here today."

"Sweet. I'll see you in ten."

Ella and I spent the next four hours scouring every spot in the city that I thought would be beneficial, including raiding the wardrobe for a hit TV show that filmed in Portland whose costumes I thought would work for the shoot. Luckily for me, I left all my jobs with good contacts and felt comfortable reaching out to people who I hoped would help me.

We were just about to head to one more location when my phone rang.

"Kalli, it's George."

I freaked out for just a moment that George Lebowitz had called my phone, but then responded professionally.

"Hi, George."

"Listen, we've got our lead male and he's on a plane right now heading to Portland. Can you be back at the studio at six p.m. to fit him?"

"Of course," I answered, looking at the clock and gauging how much time I had.

"Great," he said, and then I heard the line go dead. I shrugged. George Lebowitz didn't need to say goodbye to me; I was all right with that.

"Okay, we've got a few hours to get the rest of this wrapped up before I have to meet the male lead."

Ella clapped her hands excitedly. "This is so much fun. I can't believe this is your job, Kalli. You just get to go around and buy clothes and jewelry for people, then you get to dress them up." She sighed. "We've both got really great jobs."

Ella owned a boutique in downtown Portland. In fact, that was how we'd met. I'd seen a dress in the window display of her store that I wanted for a movie shoot.

"We are pretty lucky," I said, giving her a smile. "And thanks for helping me today. This would have been impossible without some help."

"Have you ever thought of getting a real assistant?" Ella asked. She looked over at me as I backed out of my parking space, sipping from the iced caramel mocha she'd snagged from a Starbucks we happened to walk past.

"Not really. I travel so much and sometimes, as this job so clearly demonstrated, I don't get a lot of notice. It's not really a steady kind of job. I don't think I could find someone who'd be willing to just up and leave town at a drop of a hat. People have lives."

"You have a life." I stilled at her words. She was, in her caring, best friend kind of way, asking for information about my life. I hadn't been very forthcoming with her or Megan, and they never pried. In fact, I'd never told either of them about Marcus.

"Yeah, but I can do this part—getting on a plane at a moment's notice or just driving to another state. I've built my life around it."

"Hmmm," was her only response as her lips were still wrapped around her straw.

"Besides, usually for one or two day shoots there isn't a lot of need for an assistant. I'd usually have some more notice and be a little more prepared. And when I get booked for longer shoots, like movies and TV shows, that's when an assistant would make more sense. There's a lot more involved in those kinds of jobs." I was rambling to try and keep the topic of conversation off my life at home.

Marcus wasn't a dirty secret, but he also wasn't a reason for people to feel sorry for me. And he definitely didn't need anyone feeling sorry for him. I only kept him from Ella and Megan because it was easier. Easier than explaining my whole history to them. They'd never meet him anyway.

I shook my head, trying to jostle the thoughts from my brain. Marcus was the focus of my life, all the time. Just because I didn't tell everyone about him didn't mean I didn't love him more than anything in the world.

I realized my fingers were starting to hurt from gripping the steering wheel so hard. I loosened my grip and shook out one of my hands.

"Who do you think it'll be?" Ella's voice broke into my thoughts.

"What?" I asked, confused.

"The male lead. Who do you think it'll be?"

I shrugged. "It could be anyone, I guess."

"Justin Timberlake?"

I laughed. "No, not Justin Timberlake." Well, I guess it could be....

"Why not? George Lebowitz is a big deal. He worked on that one movie with Justin. They could be besties."

"First, I don't think guys can be besties. And second, I think Justin's got bigger things he's working on than a Lexi Black music video shoot."

Ella laughed. "A girl can hope."

"Besides," I said, turning a corner, heading to another upscale costume shop, "Lexi said she was going for an up-and-comer. Someone kind of unknown. I don't think JT fits into that category."

"You're probably right," she sighed.

We both laughed and I felt the tension from just a few minutes ago fading away. I exhaled, letting the last of it go. This was why Ella was my best friend. She didn't care who I was. She accepted me at exactly face value and she didn't expect anything more.

"Okay," I said, staring at my car packed full of the things we'd acquired throughout the day. I checked the time on my phone and then looked to Ella. "Do you think you could drop me off at the studio and then run to Nordstrom for those shoes?"

"Yeah, of course. Do you want me to come back for you?"

"Let's play it by ear. It might make more sense for me to grab a cab and meet you." I waved my hand in the air, not really wanting to make a decision at the moment. I just needed to get back to the studio.

We pulled up to the doors of the studio and Ella got out to switch seats, giving me a good luck hug, and then I watched as she backed out and left. I walked in the front doors again, but the receptionist wasn't there. It made sense, it was getting late. I wandered through the halls, hoping I remembered the way to the correct sound stage. I found my way and smiled when I entered, recognizing the complex set.

Standing in the middle of all the steel beams, with just one light shining down on them were George, Lexi, and a man who I assumed was the male lead.

My boots made a clacking noise as I walked toward them. I pushed my shoulders back and straightened up, wanting to make another good impression on everyone. As I got closer, I had to start stepping over pieces of the set: metal poles, ramps with slight inclinations, and giant gears seemingly buried halfway into the ground.

I was watching my feet, not wanting to fall and make a fool of myself, but when I got close enough to look up, my eyes were caught by the man who already had his eyes on me.

He was absolutely breathtaking. His eyes. My God, his eyes. I'd never seen eyes that color. They were golden, a shiny caramel color. And he was smiling. His smile was heartbreaking.

"Kalli, glad you made it back. We've got our male lead." George was speaking, but I had yet to take my eyes off the beautiful man standing next to him.

"Uh," I stammered. "Hi." I managed to look away from him and focus on George, trying to recover from the humiliating exchange.

"Kalli Rivers, this is Riot Bentley."

"It's nice to meet you," Riot said. Sweet baby Jesus. His voice was deep and musical. I'd never met anyone with a voice I wanted to listen to forever, but his was gorgeous. I looked at him and his hand was out, waiting for me to take it. I swallowed, hopefully silently, even though I could feel my throat working too hard to push down all the sensations building up.

I reached out and took his hand, managing a decent grip. That was something I felt passionately about: a good handshake. I hated it when women just gave their hands and then let them lay there like limp noodles in the other person's hand. Participate in the hand shake, for crying out loud.

Riot had an awesome handshake.

It was firm, warm, and he held on to my hand just a little longer than necessary, which caused an involuntary blush to creep over my face.

"Hi," I said, still shaking his hand. "I'm Kalli."

"It's nice to meet you," he said, his words floating through the air and caressing my skin like silk.

"Likewise," I said as he finally released my hand.

"Isn't he perfect?" Lexi cried, hopping up and down, clearly excited.

"He sure is," I said, making my cheeks burn even more. I heard him chuckle and looked at him as he slid his hands into the back pockets of the soft, worn, with holes-in-all-the-right-places jeans he was wearing, which only caused his washed-until-it's-as-soft-as-a-cloud t-shirt to stretch over his chest, and his biceps to become the most magnificent things in the room.

"Kalli, why don't you take Riot to Lexi's trailer and get all the info you need. We'll wait here. We're still going over a few things for the shoot, but we should be ready to head out when you're finished."

"Sounds great," I managed. I looked to Riot and said, "Shall we?"

"Sure. Lead the way."

I made my way back through the set, still paying close attention so I didn't fall, and then continued to Lexi's trailer.

"So," I said, turning back to him, trying to engage him in light conversation like a professional. "Riot? That's a really interesting name."

He smiled and ran a hand over his jaw which had a delicious amount of stubble covering it. "Yeah, it's pretty unusual. My agent loves it though, wouldn't let me change it for the business."

"It's not a stage name?"

"No, but it sounds like one, doesn't it? It sounds fake and pretentious."

He was smiling, but I suddenly was afraid I'd offended him.

"Oh, no, not at all. It's just not a name you hear all the time. Or at all. I'm sorry," I rambled.

"No, don't be," he said as he laughed. "It's fine. People just hear Riot and they think I'm trying to be some bad boy actor, and I'm not."

"Oh, well, at least your name isn't boring. Mine is pretty forgettable."

"I think your name is beautiful," he said with so much sincerity it made my breath shudder.

"Thanks," I murmured. We made it to the trailer and I opened the door, allowing him to enter, and then followed, plopping my bag on the table. I was surprised to see Lexi's assistant wasn't there, slaving over her calendar. But it gave us more room to work. I pulled out my notebook, tape measure, and a pencil.

"I just need to get some measurements." I looked him up and down, trying to gauge his size. I had gotten pretty good at guessing; sometimes I didn't have the luxury of measurements.

"So, I'm sure you've done this before, it should only take a few minutes."

"No problem," he said as he raised his arms into a T, like a pro. I smiled, partly because he was being agreeable and partly because with his arms raised I could see a sliver of skin just above the waist of his jeans. I wrapped the tape measure around his chest, having to get closer to him so that I could grab it behind his back.

Good God, he smelled good.

"George said you were on a flight here. Where'd you come from?" I made note of the measurement and wrote it in the notebook, moving the tape measure lower.

"San Francisco," he said, looking straight ahead. "I live there because I don't want to live in Hollywood, but it's still close enough that I can make it there in a day if I need to."

"Smart. Hollywood is kind of a different world," I say, looking up at him and smiling. I found it incredibly easy to smile at him.

"I love acting, but I don't love the whole Hollywood mentality. I'm a little more, uh, chill than most people in So Cal."

"Gotcha. I agree. I wouldn't fit in there either."

"Are you from Portland, then?"

I made another scratch on my notepad and then moved to measure the distance from shoulder to shoulder, trying to seem as if I didn't notice all the muscles under the thin cotton of his shirt.

"No, I live in Seattle when I'm not working."

"I've never been there."

"Oh, well, it's a fun city. You know, Space Needle and all."

"And the guys who throw fish are there."

I laughed. "True."

"Maybe someday I'll make a trip to see those guys."

"I'm sure they'd be happy to see you. They might even let you catch a fish."

"They do that?" he asked, sounding almost like a little boy, so excited at the thought of catching a fish being hurled at him through the air.

"Sometimes. But it's usually for a special occasion. It's not something they just let anybody do. It's kind of a big deal."

"Hmmm." He sounded like he was trying to figure out a puzzle, trying to come up with a plan to get them to let him catch one of their fish.

I took a deep breath and knelt to the ground, softly landing on my knees in front of him, trying to keep the blush from my face. I pretended to look at the ground as I closed my eyes and took another hopefully silent deep breath. I'd never had a moment I could remember where I was so flustered by someone I was working with, but kneeling in front of Riot, being this close to him and in such a vulnerable position, had my blood thrumming through my veins.

I looked back up, determined to remain professional, and wrapped the tape measure around his waist.

"How does one become a costume designer?" he asked, softly. I was grateful for his question, glad it took my mind off his body in front of me.

"I went to college, got a degree in costume design," I looked up at him and gave a wink, trying for sassy. He smiled and it felt like a reward, making my stomach flip. I wanted to earn more smiles from him.

"Which college?"

"Art Institute of Seattle. Well, I finished in Seattle. I started in New York."

"Then you moved in the middle of college? Why?"

I wrote a note on my pad and then moved to measure his inseam, hoping to God he didn't see or feel my hands trembling. "Circumstances. Can you drop your arms?"

"Well, that's not vague at all," he said, flopping his hands back down to the sides of his waist.

"How'd you get started in acting?" I was hoping he'd take the bait and allow the change in subject. Luckily for me, he was agreeable.

"I started as a model actually. It was really kind of stereotypical. I was just at the mall with some of my friends and this woman approached me and asked if I'd ever considered modeling."

I wrote down his inseam measurement and tried to gracefully get to my feet. He noticed me start to rise and held out a hand. I took it before I could think better of it and my heart thumped rapidly as he pulled me up off the floor effortlessly. I was on my feet in a nanosecond and his impressive strength was just another tally in the "Reasons Riot is Attractive" column.

"I signed with a modeling agent and after a few shows, and a few campaigns in some popular magazines, people started calling asking me to audition for small roles."

"Sounds exciting," I said as I put my tape measure away. "What size shoe do you wear?" I asked as my eyes flitted to his feet.

"Fourteen."

"Oh, my," I said breathily, then immediately clamped my hand over my mouth.

Riot laughed. "I know, they're huge."

I coughed, trying to camouflage my outburst. This man did nothing but fluster me and I had no idea how to make it stop. The last thing I needed was a bad reference because I couldn't keep my mouth from uttering the most asinine comments about the size of a man's feet. And thinking about the size of his feet only made me think about the size of his…. Oh, for goodness' sake! This was enough. I had to get out of there.

"Well, I think I've got all I need. We should probably get back to George and Lexi." I said, not nearly as coolly as I would have liked.

He smiled at me as if he knew I was flustered and he kind of liked it. Yup. Out of there. "All right."

I packed up my things and walked out of the trailer in a way that would make a bystander think it were on fire. I heard the door close after me, but didn't stop to see if Riot was following or not. I just kept walking until I was inside the studio and found George and Lexi on the soundstage, almost exactly where we'd left them.

"All finished," I said, a little too loudly.

George's eyes met mine and then dashed behind me to where I was sure Riot was standing because I could feel his presence like a heat wave radiating from him, washing over me. It was an unnerving feeling, but also brought a certain warmth I wasn't necessarily opposed to.

"Great. You both know call time tomorrow's at seven?"

"Yes, your receptionist gave me the call sheet. I'll be here."

"Me too." I heard his wonderfully warm and low voice from behind me, sending a shiver up my spine.

"Thanks, Riot, for coming on such short notice, we really appreciate it," George said nicely, but without a smile.

"It's going to be the best video, I just know it," Lexi said with her usual enthusiasm.

"I'm just thankful for the opportunity," Riot replied, with sincerity.

"Okay, we'll see you both tomorrow then."

We all walked to the front of the building and I pulled out my phone to call Ella. George and Lexi both climbed into what I assumed was his Audi, and they drove away.

"You need a ride?" Riot's smooth and dark voice floated through the darkness and I couldn't help but look up at him. Even in the absence of light his eyes shone, the gold color of them almost glowing in the darkness.

"Um, no, I've got a ride. I just need to text her." I pried my eyes away from his to send that text to Ella.

"Listen, I know we don't know each other very well, but I'm not about to leave a woman alone, in the dark, in a parking lot, in the middle of the city."

Ella responded to my text saying she was on her way and would be there in five minutes. I held the phone up to him. "My ride will be here soon. It's no big deal."

"It's a big deal to me. I'll wait with you."

"Okay," I managed to squeak out, his protective comments doing nothing to lessen my attraction to him.

"So," he said as he leaned back against the brick wall of the building, propping one foot up, hands in his pocket, completely unaware that he was embodying every high school fantasy any girl ever had. "How long have you been doing this?"

"Almost ten years. I started right out of college at twenty-one."

"So you're thirty?"

"Ish."

He laughed, dragging his hand over his smile again, then rubbed the underside of his chin with the back of his hand. I couldn't explain why it turned me on, other than the fact that it was the most masculine thing I'd ever seen any man do. Hands, stubble, chin, *fingers*... Jesus.

"You won't tell me how old you are?"

"Gentlemen aren't supposed to ask women their age."

"I guess that's true. I'm twenty-seven, in case you were curious."

I was curious. I tried to let my mind wrap around his age and figure out if I was bothered by the fact that he was younger than me. I determined, in that moment, that it didn't bother me, but I also determined that it didn't matter. His age was unimportant because he was just a guy I was working with. Nothing more.

"Just a baby," I teased.

He laughed and I felt my cheeks bunch up from smiling. His happiness was contagious and I wanted to catch it. "How long are you in town for?"

"Just for the shoot. I drove down this morning and I'll stay until it's done, but then I'll probably go back to Seattle." I paused and looked him in the eyes, still glistening in the darkness. "You?"

"Well, I'm here for the shoot, but I don't have another job until next month, so I only bought a one-way ticket. Figured I'd go back whenever I wanted to. Thought maybe I'd check out the city."

"Portland's pretty great. My friends live here so I come here sometimes when I'm not working to see them."

"Oh yeah? So you'd make a decent tour guide?"

"Well," I paused, "I'm not sure about that. We don't want the blind leading the blind."

"You wouldn't take an extra day to help me out? You don't want me wandering around a strange city by myself, do you?"

"Something tells me you'd be just fine by yourself," I said through a laugh, purposefully looking out toward the road, not wanting to be trapped by his gaze any longer, hoping Ella showed up soon. I knew I'd only be able to deny him for so long.

"I might be fine by myself, but it doesn't mean I want to be alone." His words, which had been playful before, were now serious and filled with hidden meaning. We were stuck in the silence, staring at each other, and when I opened my mouth to relent, to give in to him and promise to spend a day with him, I heard a car pull up. I turned and saw Ella behind the wheel of my Rover. I turned back to Riot, whose face had returned to the playful, at ease expression he'd had since we'd met.

"That's my ride. Thanks for waiting with me."

"Anytime, Kalli. I'll see you later." He didn't move, didn't budge from his stance leaning against the wall, just watched me climb into the passenger seat of my car. "Do you need a ride somewhere?" I asked once I was in the car, door still propped open.

He shook his head. "No thanks. My rental car is here, but I think I'm gonna take a walk and find a bar to have a drink." I smiled and gave him a small nod before turning all the way into the car and shutting my door.

"Hey. Who's that ridiculously handsome guy watching your ass as you got into your car?" Ella asked, ever observant.

"That's the male lead for the video."

"Huh. He'll do," she said with disinterest. I laughed. I figured that next to her boyfriend Porter, any and all guys seemed like they'd just "do."

Chapter Four

Impossible to Turn Away

The next morning I found myself at the studio at seven sharp. I'd been given my own trailer to dress the talent and even my very own assistant for the day, Savannah. She was an intern at the studio who was majoring in costume design at a local university, and she was a dream. I felt spoiled having her, even if she insisted I call her Savvy, which I didn't.

I dressed all the extras first, which was the easy part. They were like background noise, they didn't need to be flashy or impressive, they just needed to blend in. My main focus was Lexi and Riot.

When Lexi came in to be dressed, she already looked amazing. Her make-up was flawless with dark eyes and red lips, her skin pale as if she hadn't seen the sunlight in years. Her hair was tall and teased, looking messy and chaotic, yet tamed below the headband I'd provided for her hair stylist. A pair of old-fashioned flying goggles sat on the crown of her head, and seeing them there, I knew I'd made the right decision. I could imagine the rest of her costume on her and knew the goggles were going to be perfect.

"Hey, Kalli, I'm ready to look amazing," Lexi exclaimed, standing in the middle of the wardrobe trailer.

"Great, let's get started."

Thirty minutes later I was nearly bursting with satisfaction as Lexi stood in front of me in full costume. She not only looked amazing, but she looked the part.

"You nailed it, Kalli. It's outstanding."

I nodded, walking around her, looking for any last minute thing I could do or fix. She needed to look perfect.

Lexi wore a white cotton dress, which hanging by itself on the rack looked sweet and innocent. But I'd imagined it otherwise, and it paid off, because the dress no longer looked like that of a farmer's daughter. It looked a little dangerous and a lot dystopian. The white cotton dress had a sweetheart neckline, but paired with the black, lacy push-up bra, it lost a little bit of its innocence.

I left the top two buttons undone, making the bra just barely visible, but not trashy. Wrapped around her tiny waist were black and brown straps of leather that had silver and brass buckles in the middle, looking haphazard and almost necessary, as if she'd put them there to actually hold her dress up, not just as a fashion statement. The dress wasn't too short, but she did have a garter belt on under it and the straps came down to latch on to thigh-high stockings that had thick black and brown vertical stripes, paired with brown knee-high boots.

She wore black fingerless leather gloves, and had a long silver chain hanging between her breasts with a compass dangling low. I'd also supplied the hair stylist with white, brown, and black ribbons that had been braided into her hair, like little peekaboos poking out from the back.

She looked soft yet hard, beautiful, sexy and every bit the steampunk princess.

The door opened and Riot walked up the small set of stairs. His eyes found Lexi first, and even though she looked like a punk rock sex kitten, his eyes only stayed on her for a moment before they found me. It was when he saw me that he smiled.

"Riot, what do you think?" Lexi asked, spinning in a slow circle.

Riot looked back at her, but then said to me as his eyes met mine again, "You did a great job."

"Thanks," was all I could manage under his appraising eyes.

"Well, I'm headed to the set. See you both in a few," Lexi said, chipper as ever, exiting the trailer.

"You ready?" I asked, turning back to the rack filed with now-empty hangers and his costume.

"As I'll ever be."

I grabbed his hanger and turned back to him, holding it out. "You can dress in the bathroom there," I said, nodding toward the door behind him. He took the costume from me and went to change. While I was trying to regain my nerves, thrown off balance by Riot and his attention, the door to the trailer opened and Savannah entered.

"George wanted me to let you know he wants everyone on set in fifteen."

"No problem. Can you do me a favor and do one last check of all the extras? Make sure all their buttons are buttoned and buckles are buckled?"

Savannah laughed. "Yeah, they had a lot of buckles."

"Yeah," I said as I smiled. "And make sure to check their shoes. I don't want anything left undone."

"No problem," she said, then made her way back to the set. The bathroom door opened and Riot came out. He'd left his shirt wide open and the sight of his bare chest, even just the small part I saw, was enough to make my breath falter.

"Can I leave my clothes here?" He asked, looking around for a place to leave his bag.

"Uh, yeah, sure. Just put it on the couch there," I said, pointing behind him.

When he placed his bag on the couch I couldn't help but notice how well the brown leather pants he was wearing fit his ass. He bent at the waist and I absolutely could not keep my eyes from his rear. When he stood, my eyes darted away and I tried to justify checking him out as part of my job; I had to make sure his pants fit, right?

On set, I watched as Lexi sang and danced, all the while Riot did his job looking sexy in the background. He was wearing some heavy guyliner and, even though I usually wasn't into the look, his eyes penetrated through the smoke and fog of the set, making it nearly impossible to turn away. Part of Lexi's choreography called for her to caress Riot, to walk around him trailing her hand over his partially exposed abdomen, and I couldn't help but want to trade places with her for just one of those takes.

I found myself focusing on unnecessary distractions to keep my eyes from traveling to him, his attraction was that powerful. I was adjusting ties and goggles on extras, checking buttons, Googling 'steampunk chic' and *not* Riot Bentley.

After an hour or so of getting the same sequence from all different angles, George announced we were moving to the bedroom set, and I swallowed hard. I picked up the case I used on sets that had anything and everything I could possibly need on-the-go, sort of like a sewing kit on steroids, and moved with the rest of the crew to the set built just on the other side of the sound stage.

I watched as George gave direction to Riot and Lexi, wondering if he was feeling any splinter of jealousy, telling another man, a younger, arguably more attractive man, to practically dry-hump his girlfriend on a bed.

There was a camera shooting from directly over the bed and as Riot kissed and nuzzled her neck, Lexi sang to the camera about how she knew he only wanted this one night, how she'd do anything to make him stay, questioning what she could do to change his mind. Then, they wanted the steamy shots. George gave direction for Riot and Lexi to kiss, telling them to make it 'almost R rated,' but then gave direction about camera angle and tongue usage, making it all seem very unsexy.

I couldn't keep myself from being uncomfortable. I'd seen people kiss before, but it was something completely different to watch two people kiss like they wanted each other, kiss like there was no one watching, regardless of the cameras and the ban on visual tongue usage.

The music played and they continued to paw and grope at each other, but when George yelled "Cut!" between takes, they pulled away and looked for direction, the two of them acting positively professional. I didn't know if I'd be able to kiss someone like that, and then make suggestions about lighting and prop placement like Lexi was. Riot was ever-accommodating, tilting his head whichever way the lighting director needed, fixing his blocking to make the cameraman happy, also making sure Lexi was on board with all the touching he was going to be doing, asking her for permission to graze her breast with his hand.

No, I could never be a Lexi or a Riot. I could, however, make sure that the wardrobe was on-point.

Hours later and after many cups of coffee, George finally called the shoot a wrap. I sighed deeply, knowing that even though the filming was finished, my job was far from over. I watched as the extras moved to exit the soundstage and I instructed them to head to the wardrobe trailer to leave their costumes with me. One of the girls came up to me with a broken cuff bracelet and before I could tell her to leave it in the trailer for me, George approached us and she scampered away.

"Kalli, great work today. Thank you again for coming on such short notice."

"It was absolutely no problem, my pleasure in fact. Thanks for the opportunity."

"Listen, it's really late and you've already put in more than a day's worth of work. I'm fine with you coming back tomorrow to finish up everything. I know you've still got a few hours' worth of cleaning up and organizing."

"Really? I mean, that would be great."

"The lot is open tomorrow, so you shouldn't have any problems getting to your trailer."

"Thank you. I appreciate it." And I did. I'd much rather grab my purse and hit my hotel than stay there until nearly sunup finishing everything. He smiled then walked away, shouting something to someone across the soundstage. I made my exit, heading for my trailer. I walked in to find chaos. People shedding their costumes left and right, shirts and pants being flung every which way. Being in the costume design business, I was used to seeing people sans clothing, but seeing mostly naked people never got any less uncomfortable for me.

Through all the moving limbs I caught sight of Riot's torso, shirtless and tan. My eyes strained unconsciously to see more, but my mind shut them down, pulling my head downward to look at the floor.

I wove through the crowd, searching for my purse.

"Everyone!" I called out into the packed trailer. "Just leave your costume in the trailer when you're done and I'll be back tomorrow to sort it all out. Thank you!" That was my best effort at getting the message across. I was exhausted and just wanted to go to bed.

I found my purse and snatched it up, then turned back around to make my way out. I was nearly to the door, one hand on it, when I felt a hand wrap around my upper arm. I turned to see Riot's smiling face just a foot away from mine, his strong hand sliding down my arm, coming to rest at my elbow. He urged me forward with a nod.

We made it outside into the very early morning air, and I stopped, turning to him.

"You're coming back here tomorrow?" Riot asked, eyebrows up.

"Yeah, well, I'm exhausted and George said I could clean up tomorrow instead of tonight. So I'm going to sleep." I turned slowly, pointing myself in the direction of the parking lot and Riot turned, then fell into step beside me, walking me to my car.

"Do you want some help?"

"Cleaning up?" I couldn't hide the surprise from my voice.

He shrugged. "Yeah. I mean, I don't have anything to do tomorrow and I was hoping if I helped you clean up, then maybe you'd spend the rest of the day showing me the city."

My steps halted and so did my ability to speak. My mouth opened, urging words to come out, but none did at first. I looked down at the ground, trying to organize all my thoughts. Riot wanted to see me tomorrow? Did I want to see him? I'd just spent the day watching him rub himself all over Lexi. I looked back up only to be assaulted by the boyish smile across his face, hopeful, waiting for my answer.

"Riot," I started, intending to give him some excuse as to why we couldn't spend the day together.

"Aw, come on, Kalli. Don't 'Riot' me." He sounded almost like a child being told he couldn't go outside to play with his friends. "You're gonna be here anyway, and I don't have any place to be, let me help you." He widened his stance, spreading his feet to an unusual distance, bringing his face level with mine. He sounded as if he sincerely wanted to help me and if I was being honest with myself, I could use the help.

"Fine, you can help me. But I can't stay very late, I have to get home eventually."

"Can I at least keep you for dinner?"

My breath snagged in my lungs at his words, gulping at the thought of Riot *keeping* me. I knew he was flirting with me, he had been the day before as well, but I didn't want to lead him on.

"I should probably leave before dinnertime."

"Got a hot date back home?" he asked, his tone joking, but the intensity of his eyes said something else; that he was curious.

"No," I said, trying not to blush. "I just have a life I have to get back to."

"Well, tell you what," he said, standing up straight again, but moving closer to me so that I had to tilt my head back to maintain eye contact. "We'll get you all sorted here, but then I get a tour of the city, and if you have to leave before dinner, so be it. But I'll be spending the day trying to show you such a good time you won't want to."

He sounded very sure of himself, and his confidence was endearing. I narrowed my eyes at him, trying not to smile.

"Okay, you've got a deal, but I'm warning you: I don't give in easily."

His smile widened and I watched a dimple I hadn't noticed before appear, and its effect on me was instantaneous. I inhaled as a wave of warmth rolled through me. Then he brought the back of his hand up and rubbed it on the underside of his chin again, just like he had the night before.

"I'm gonna go," I mumbled, turning toward my car again. I had to get away from him before my body completely betrayed me and melted right in front of him.

"Should I meet you here tomorrow?"

I stopped and looked back to him. "Do you have a ride? I could drop you off at your hotel."

He shook his head. "I found a place close by last night. I'm good. What time should I meet you here tomorrow?"

"Ten sound good? I'd like to get at least a few hours of sleep."

"Sounds perfect. See you tomorrow, Kalli." His voice went soft on my name, but the dimple came out again. Words failed me, so I just waved.

I made it to my Range Rover, but took a few deep breaths before I started the engine. I hadn't expected to be so affected by Riot or his words. His body, sure. But not his words. Perhaps he was just punchy from the long day. I sighed, started the engine, and then headed toward my hotel just praying for a good night's sleep.

Chapter Five

A Wonderful Wasted Day

I walked into the trailer the next morning and groaned. It was even more of a mess than I left it the night before and I was immediately regretting putting it off. I had taken a few more steps in, looking around, trying to formulate a game plan in my mind on how to best attack the mess, when I heard the door open.

Riot stepped in, eyes widening. "Holy shit," he said with conviction.

"Yeah," I said as I placed my bag on the table. "Feel free to back out. You don't have to stay and help with this. It's my job."

"What kind of a guy would I be if I just left you here by yourself?"

I shrugged. "One with better things to do than clean up someone else's mess?"

"Turns out," he said with a dazzling smile, "I've got absolutely nothing better to do."

I simply couldn't help the smile that spread over my face, so I chose, instead, to turn away and focus on picking up the mess.

That's how we spent the next two hours: picking up. We picked up the clothes, hung them on hangers, organized them into categories, then I rolled most of them on the rack back to the studio for their manager to deal with, and then put the few items I'd brought with me in the back of my Range Rover after Riot had kindly carried them out for me.

"Nice ride," he said after he closed the trunk.

"Thanks. I need something big for instances just like this," I said, smiling at him as I held my hand up to block the sun from my eyes. Something about the way he looked just then, the sun shining behind him, only allowing me to see the silhouette of his face, cheeks big from smiling, it made something inside me melt a little. Soften. I could feel something warm spreading throughout me, coating everything that had been solid and cold before.

"Shall we go get the last load?" he asked softly, forcing me out of my state of wonder. I blinked and looked down at the ground, allowing my eyes to adjust to the lack of light.

"Sure," I said quietly, then started to walk past him. He turned to walk beside me and I felt his hand rest at the base of my neck, gently squeezing. After a moment or two of feeling his big, strong hand wrapped around the back of my neck, I felt the warmth leave as he removed it. The loss of his skin against mine left me breathless. I'd never been a huge fan of public displays of affection; I also had always shunned a lot of physical contact. I was usually more annoyed by being touched than anything. But having Riot's hand on me hadn't been even remotely annoying; it had been exhilarating. I tried to keep my reaction to his touch under control, letting out a slow and silent breath.

When we'd finally made the last trip to the car and I was positive we'd gotten everything that belonged to me out of there, I turned to Riot with a smile.

"So, I don't know about you, but I could really use some coffee."

"I'm up for just about anything." He smiled and then gave me a wink. I tried to keep myself from blushing, but it was unavoidable.

"Great." We both climbed in my car and I took off toward the center of the city.

Thirty minutes later we sat on the steps of Pioneer Courthouse Square, coffee in hand, enjoying the sunshine and watching the people pass by.

"This is kind of a cool spot," Riot said just before taking a sip of his sugary coffee concoction through a straw. I'd had to stifle a giggle when he'd ordered his drink. Something about a big, tall, masculine man ordering a triple iced grande vanilla mocha made my eyebrows rise. I'd never met a man who drank anything except straight coffee before. He'd thrown another adorable wink my way and insisted on buying my iced latte.

"Did you ever see *Free Willy*?" I asked between sips.

"Uh, of course," he answered, as if it were ridiculous to even ask. "I was a child of the nineties."

I laughed. "Well, do you remember the opening scene where the homeless kids are asking for change?"

"Yeah," he said, sipping again from his straw.

I made a grand gesture with my hand to the open square and to the light rail track behind me. He looked around, confused at first, but then his eyes went wide.

"Really?" he asked excitedly.

"Yeah. They shot that scene here. This is one of the first places Ella took me when we started hanging out."

"Ella?"

"My best friend. She lives here, owns a boutique just a little ways away. She and her sister Megan are the only reasons I come to Portland so often anymore. Ella loved playing tour guide to me when we first met. She was going through some stuff and couldn't work a whole lot, so when I had free time between work I'd let her show me her hometown."

"She sounds cool."

"She's the best," I said with a sincere smile.

"Well, she's got good taste in friends," he said, bumping his shoulder into mine gently, causing me to smile even wider. Riot was a complete flirt. But he flirted in the cutest, most innocent ways; it was hard to wrap my mind around. I was used to men being really forward, even aggressive. Riot was neither. He seemed sweet, relaxed, and completely in the moment.

"Man," I said, looking up at the sky. "It's getting really hot out." The August sun was beating down on us and there was no shade in the square to protect us. "Ready to move on to our next destination?"

"Lead the way," he said as he stood.

We started walking out of the square and down the city streets, the tall buildings offering shade on the sidewalks.

"So, would your boyfriend be okay with you spending the day with me?"

"Wow, very smooth, Riot," I said, laughing. I looked over at him, noticing the big, shy smile on his face. "I don't have a boyfriend." I paused, wondering how much to divulge to him. "I'm not really the 'boyfriend' kind of girl."

"Hmm. I must admit I'm a little surprised. It seems like someone should have claimed you by now."

"I'm not looking to be claimed," I said firmly.

"No, of course not, I mean, I'm sorry." He turned to me then and looked utterly lost and contrite.

"Don't worry about it. It's not a big deal, I just don't really get involved in relationships."

"So, you don't date?"

"I date, I just don't really go out with someone more than once or twice." I blushed, knowing what my words were implying, knowing I was admitting to sleeping with men on the first or second date, but then never seeing them again.

"Why?"

His question surprised me, but what surprised me even more was the tone with which he asked it. He didn't sound judgmental or like he thought less of me, he simply sounded curious.

I shrugged. "I don't want to be tied down."

"A free spirit?" he asked, now smiling at me, and all the hackles that I'd put up in the last minute went slowly back down.

"Something like that."

"But you'd see someone often if they were just a friend, right?"

I laughed, mostly at the fact that he was being cute again. "I suppose."

"I'll keep that in mind."

We kept walking through the city and as we neared the waterfront, we had to weave our way through the throngs of people gathered for the Saturday Market. Portland had some pretty awesome summer weather usually, but if it was a Saturday and sunny, downtown would be packed. We tried our best to stay together, but eventually people started forcing us apart. Riot was at least a head taller than me so it was easy to keep an eye on him as I tried to keep close. Suddenly, I felt a big hand wrap around mine and then I was next to him, holding his hand. We were palm-to-palm, wandering, eyeing booths filled with people's wares and goods. When I finally saw what I was looking for I tugged on his hand, urging him to follow me.

I walked up to the edge of the fountain, taking in the sight of all the people playing in the water. The fountain was huge, and could easily accommodate the hundred people frolicking in it at that moment. Water spouted straight out of the ground, ten or so geysers, surprising small children and adults alike. The fountain's floor was slightly graded, so on one side water accumulated, making it the perfect wading depth for small children.

There were toddlers holding their mother or father's hands, squealing with excitement over the water, there were older children running around, clearly enjoying the city summer activity, and there were also adults enjoying the water, albeit less enthusiastically. I immediately thought that Marcus would love it and I'd have to see if there was anything like it in Seattle.

"You up for it?" I asked, looking at him, only to see the biggest grin on his face.

"You wanna play?" he asked, turning to me, his voice lower and rougher. His question sent a prickling sensation through my body and I had to work hard to push the reaction down, to not let it steal my breath away.

"Yeah," I responded.

Not letting go of my hand, he started walking backward into the water, grinning at me slyly, as if he had a secret. I couldn't help but return the smile, trying to keep it to just my mouth, but feeling it creep into my eyes and heart. Our eyes locked and I felt pulled to him, which is why neither one of us spotted the giant geyser of water that shot out of the ground between us, drenching us both.

I screamed, trying to push the water out of my face, and I could hear Riot's deep laugh rumbling on the other side of the plume of water between us. I took a step backward, trying to get out of the direct shot, then saw him run around the water, coming up behind me. I squealed as he wrapped his arms around my middle from behind, picked me up, and carried me right into the water.

I wiggled in his arms, trying to escape, but after struggling and writhing, I came to understand that his very strong arms weren't going to let me go until he was good and ready. So, I did what any self-respecting woman would do in my position: I begged.

"Riot, no. Please put me down, please!" He was holding me near one of the bigger plumes of water, teasing me, inching me closer to the strikingly cold water. "Please, please, please…."

"What'll you give me to let you go?"

"Anything!"

"Anything?"

"Anything. Please," I continued begging. Then his mouth was pressed right up against my ear.

"You'll kiss me?"

My breath, which had previously been fast and frantic, stalled in my lungs. I could still hear the laughter of all the children playing around us, could feel the mist of the cool water being sprayed up into the air, but mostly, I felt my heartbeat pounding in my chest. He wanted to kiss me.

"Kal?"

Oh, my. He'd used my nickname. My head was nodding before I realized it and he was quick to respond, setting me down on the ground again, and then placing his hands on my waist, spinning me around. We were chest to chest, my wet shirt pressed against his, and my hands came to land on him. My eyes flitted down to the wet t-shirt hanging on his pecs and my hands absently roamed over him.

His finger came to my chin, tipped my face up to his, and again he was silhouetted by the sun. Then, even though I didn't think it possible, he stepped even closer to me, sliding his hand up my jaw and back into my wet hair, gripping the back of my neck.

He was serious about this kiss.

My hands slid around him, running over his rib cage and I pulled him in to me.

His face moved down, slowly coming closer to mine, his eyes darting back and forth between my lips and my eyes. I couldn't hear anything, couldn't see anything, and was numb to the cold water lapping at my feet. All I was aware of was his hands on me and his mouth moving toward mine. When he was just a breath away, my eyes closed and I prepared to feel his lips on mine.

What I felt, instead, was a wave of frigid water splash onto my face.

I was startled and I sputtered, trying to breathe through the water running down my face. I laughed, only because I didn't know what else to do, but when my eyes opened I noticed Riot was just as startled and drenched as I was.

I looked to my left and saw two small girls, both with empty buckets, staring at us and giggling. I laughed again, because obviously these two girls had doused us with water. Suddenly Riot took off after the little girls, chasing them, threatening in a totally non-threatening way to get them back. The girls were laughing, running away from him, and he was chasing them slowly enough to never catch them. Every few feet he would bend down, scooping up some water in his hand, and throw it in their direction.

It was, possibly, the cutest thing I had ever witnessed.

I stood there, dumbfounded, as Riot, wet shirt and all, chased two giggling girls around a fountain.

He circled around again, the girls screaming and laughing, and as he ran past me, he splashed water at me again. So, I sighed then I took off after him.

We were both spent, soaked, and quiet. We had found a patch of grass right along the waterfront, lain down, and set out to let the sun dry us. My eyes were closed, face warm, and I could tell I had the most ridiculous smile on my face. I remembered Riot's face when he realized I'd joined forces with the little girls, whose names I learned were Gracie and Amelia. We spent the good part of an hour chasing and splashing him before their mom had told them it was time to go. Five minutes into our water fight, Gracie and Amelia's mom had told them to "leave those poor people alone, girls. They didn't come here to play with children." Riot had very politely told the mom that he didn't mind playing, and that he needed help dousing me besides.

So then it was on.

I could hear people on bikes whizzing by, dogs barking, people talking, the heavy footfalls of joggers, and it was a calming symphony. I was absolutely relaxed, carefree, and happy, lying there on a patch of grass in the middle of the city with Riot.

"You almost kissed me," I heard Riot rasp from his spot next to me on the grass. I suddenly went from absolutely relaxed to acutely aware of the zings of electricity his voice sent through me. I *had* almost kissed him, but only because he was about to kiss me, and his lips were so close, and so full....

"So?" I choked out.

"I was just pointing it out. Technically, I think you still owe me a kiss."

"How do you figure that?"

"Well, letting you go was contingent upon the kiss you promised me. I let you go, but you never kissed me, therefore, ergo, heretofore, you owe me a kiss."

"Heretofore?" I giggled.

"Are you laughing at me now?"

I didn't answer, but I did continue to laugh.

"You wound me," he said, pretending to be offended.

"I think that if there's anything that happened today that should wound you, it should have been those two little girls totally owning you."

"I went easy on them."

"Sure."

I heard movement next to me and turned to see Riot rolled to his side, elbow propped up, with his temple resting in his hand, looking at me with a smile in his shiny caramel eyes. "So, do I get to keep you for dinner?"

His expression was so hopeful, he looked as if he were waiting for me to give him a gift. There was a very large part of me that wanted to say yes, that wished to spend the rest of the evening with him discovering things about him, talking with him. But then I realized, with the same feeling as the ice cold water those girls had tossed on us, that if I wanted to learn things about him, he would probably want to know things about me too. I had to draw the line, had to tell him no.

"I don't think that's a good idea," I said, sitting up and drawing my knees up to my chest, wrapping my arms around them.

"Didn't you have a good time with me today?" he asked, sounding a little confused.

I turned my head to look at him. Trying to keep my voice light, I said, "Yeah. I had a lot of fun."

"Then why won't you have dinner with me?"

I exhaled. "Riot, listen, I told you I don't really date people, and I'm not looking for a relationship. I think it would be better for both of us if we just kept this simple. Friendly."

"Friendly," he sighed, then huffed out a breath.

I winced. His ego sounded bruised. "I'm sorry."

He shook his head. "You don't have to be sorry about anything, Kalli. I just really enjoy being around you, but I totally get it. However, there is one thing I refuse to leave Oregon without."

"Oh, yeah? And what's that?"

"Your phone number."

I tilted my head and narrowed my eyes. "Why do you need my phone number?"

He pulled his head back and scoffed. "I have all my friends' phone numbers, don't you?"

I considered his argument. I did have all my friends' phone numbers, but I wasn't sure 'friends' was the correct term for what we were, or what he wanted us to be. But, then again, I couldn't find a good enough reason to deny him. I reached into my pocket and pulled out my phone, unlocked the screen, then handed it to him.

"Don't snoop," I said with a smile.

"I wouldn't dare," he said with mocked insult.

I watched his thumbs move quickly over my screen, then he grabbed for his phone and did the same. He then held it out to me.

"There you go. All set."

"Great," I said, smiling. "So, when do you think you'll go back to California?"

He shrugged. "I'm not sure. I might head north for a bit, check out Canada. I hear Victoria is beautiful."

"I've never been."

"Really? But it's so close to you."

"I travel so much for work that usually when I'm not working, I stay home." Marcus immediately came to my mind. I stayed home to take care of him. If I'd left for home when I finished that morning, I'd have been home with him already. Nancy could have taken a breather. As it were, I wouldn't make it home until late evening, at best. I'd wasted an entire day. But it had been a wonderful wasted day. I looked over at Riot, admiring his profile as he watched a large cargo boat navigate its way under all the bridges of Portland.

His hair had dried in a sexy kind of disarray, brown locks sticking up every which way. The sun was hitting his already tan skin, highlighting the ridges and contours of his fantastic biceps. I could ogle a friend, right? He was so intensely sexy, it was hard to push the sight of him out of my mind. I had to leave. Sitting here, staring at him, wasn't doing me any good.

"Can I drop you off at your hotel?"

He turned back to look at me and smiled, but it wasn't the same smile he'd worn all day. It was a resigned smile, as if he were knowingly giving up. It wasn't any less sexy though, so I stood up, brushing any residual grass from my backside.

"Thanks, but I think I'll be okay."

"You sure?"

"Yeah."

"All right. Well, I guess I'll see you around." He smiled at me, but said nothing, so I smiled back, then turned and walked back toward the square to my car.

With each step, more confusion rolled through me. That had to have been the most awkward goodbye I'd ever experienced. I didn't know what I expected from of him, but he could have at least *said* something. I didn't need him to hug me or give some long, lingering goodbye, but the way I left it felt, well, unfinished.

I tried to shake my irritation off, walking back through the mass of people still shopping in the market. But still, even when I'd made it back to my car, I was upset. I didn't want to have dinner with him, so he just blew me off? It seemed like a jerk move. I stewed about the way we parted halfway to Seattle, then I let out a loud sigh because, frankly, he was still the most attractive man I'd ever met. Jerk or not, the terrible goodbye did nothing to fog the memory of the day I'd spent with him. He'd been fun, interesting, polite, and made me feel like there wasn't anyone else in the world he wanted to spend his day with.

Turned out, his cold goodbye was exactly what I needed to walk away without the dull ache of longing I'd had all day being with him. Then, as I pulled into my driveway, the concrete illuminated by the flood light attached to the front of the house, I realized I'd spent the whole drive thinking about him anyway.

Chapter Six

Another Bandage

It had been two weeks since Riot blew me off at the waterfront, and as much as I tried to forget about him, my mind simply wouldn't let it happen. A few times, I'd even drafted text messages to him. Some of them were friendly, asking if he'd made it to Victoria or if he'd managed to make it back to California safely. Others were angry, asking why he'd acted childishly when we'd parted ways. A few of them, okay, most of them, were suggestive.

I was a twenty-nine year old woman, without a boyfriend or other source of regular sexual gratification, and I hadn't been on a date in months. I didn't do relationships, but I wasn't keen on random hook-ups either. I needed to, at least, get to know a guy a little first. And that was what I was hoping to do with Scott.

I'd met Scott at Starbucks. I was standing in line and he bumped into me from behind, apologizing profusely, smiling wide with his white teeth gleaming at me. He was classic, upper-middle class, blond haired, blue eyed, former frat guy perfect. Well, perfect for a non-committed, one or two night rendezvous.

He was everything Riot wasn't. He wasn't famous, he wasn't tall or dark, and he wasn't occupying every corner of my mind all the time. Scott was exactly what I needed to take my mind off Riot. So, I'd invited him to come out to celebrate with my friends. Ella got her memory back, Megan got a promotion, and I just happened to be in Portland when all the excitement came about and we were going to drink.

I was about to enter the bar when I get a text from Scott.

Hey. Sorry. Something came up last minute. I'll try to make it if I can.

Well, there went my plans for the evening.

It wasn't so much that I needed Scott, or even wanted him that badly. I was just so tired of thinking about Riot, especially when it was obvious, from his lack of communication, that he wasn't thinking about me at all. Couple that with the fact that Marcus had a setback in school the week before, causing all kinds of drama and making me second guess myself about his care, and I needed one night to just check out of my life.

I sighed, but then shook off my disappointment, hoping to rally and not waste an entire evening being mopey.

The bar was packed and the bass was pumping. I could feel the vibrations in my chest and see people's heads bopping along to the beat on the dance floor. I spotted Megan, Patrick, and Ella at a table in the back. Next to Ella was a tall, well-built, dark-haired man who I'd never met before. As I made my way to them he took off for the bar.

I gave Megan and Ella hugs hello and waved at Patrick as he offered me a shy smile.

"Where's your date?" Megan asked.

"He's a little hot and cold, I'm afraid. I invited him and he said he'd try and make it, but I'm not holding my breath."

Ella frowned and rubbed her hand up and down my arm, trying to comfort me.

"Maybe he'll surprise you and show up," Ella offered hopefully. Just after she'd spoken her words, the attractive man came back, handing her a drink.

Ella introduced me to her boyfriend, Porter, and then embarrassingly told me to close my mouth because, good God, he was attractive. Megan had told me time and time again that Ella had caught a good one, but he was spectacular. And also, so obviously in love with her. Since she'd regained her memory they'd been attached at the hip. She looked at him as if he were her everything and it made my heart ache a little and my thoughts found their way back to Riot.

The girls insisted I dance with them, and even though I put up a good fight, they dragged me to the dance floor. Eventually, a few songs in, after downing my first drink rather quickly, I started to loosen up. I pushed out thoughts of Riot, and I even managed to push away the hope that Scott would show up. Scott was just a bandage after all. Just someone to keep my mind occupied and off every emotion Riot seemed to evoke in me.

After a few more songs, and another drink, another bandage made his way to me, pulling me away from the girls, offering to distract me with his body. I let his hands wander, let him feel me, grind against me to the rhythm of the music and I tried really hard to not imagine it was Riot's hands running over the curve of my hips.

Then, suddenly, the part of the night where everyone was merry and carefree slipped away into chaos.

Megan pulled on my arm, turning me away from the guy I was dancing with. "Have you seen Ella?" she yelled into my ear to be heard over the music.

"No," I yelled back. "Where'd she go?"

"She went to get drinks ten minutes ago, but she's not at

the bar and we haven't seen her."

I looked around and saw Porter and Patrick making their way across the dance floor, eyes wide, looking for her. I stepped away from my dance partner, not offering an excuse or a goodbye.

"Let's go check the bathroom," I said, looking at Megan. She nodded and we made our way to the back of the club. I spied a hallway along the wall, but Megan must have seen it too because she pushed past me and ran toward the entryway.

"She's over here!" Megan's voice was pained and panicked.

"Porter!" I yelled into the club as loudly as I could, hoping somehow he'd hear me. I caught his eye when his head snapped in my direction. "She's down here," I screamed, pointing toward the hallway, just as I heard Megan crying out, "Shit, shit, shit!"

The next thirty seconds were a blur of activity. Porter ran past me down the hallway, Patrick came for Megan, then Porter was carrying Ella out of the club. I couldn't help but stand in my spot and watch it all unfold. I had no idea what had happened, but Ella had looked petrified as she'd been whisked past me.

The next thing I knew, Patrick was telling me that Ella wanted me to go home with them, and he wasn't taking no for an answer.

"What about Ella?" I asked. "Is she all right?"

"Let Porter handle it," Megan said. "Ella needs him right now."

I nodded; surely Megan would know better than me.

I walked with Megan and Patrick to their car, climbed in the backseat, and couldn't have felt more like an outsider if

I'd tried. They were murmuring to each other, making comments I didn't follow, and I couldn't help feeling like I was out of place.

"What happened to Ella?" I finally asked, straight out, tired of being in the dark.

"I'm not one hundred percent sure, but I think Kyle attacked her in the hallway."

"Kyle? Her ex-boyfriend?"

"Yeah," Megan said, catching my eye in the rearview mirror.

"Shit," I mumbled. "Do you think she's okay?" I wanted to pull out my phone and call her, wanted to talk to her, hear her voice.

"No, I don't. I don't think she's hurt physically, but I can't imagine she's faring well emotionally."

I didn't bother responding. Besides, there wasn't much else to say. Ella had been put through the wringer for the last couple months. I was glad she had Porter with her. If anyone could help her deal with this, it was him.

The next morning I was woken by Megan. She'd let me crash in her and Patrick's spare bedroom. My head was foggy and pounding from the alcohol the night before, but Megan's voice was urgent so I found myself alert immediately.

"Kal, wake up. We've got to talk."

I slowly sat up, letting my eyes adjust to the light and, well, being awake.

"What is it?"

"So, Ella and Porter are on the phone."

"Okaaaay…."

Megan's voice and face were strained. She was worried about something. "Ella says that Kyle, you know, her ex-boyfriend? Well, she's saying that he's that guy you were supposed to meet there last night."

"Wait, what?"

Megan took in a deep breath, obviously flustered. "She says that last night, while Kyle was attacking her, he said that he was Scott. That he'd been using you to get information about her."

My stomach dropped and my breath caught. My pulse sped up and my eyes darted around the room as I tried to comprehend what she was saying. My mind reeled, trying to remember what I'd told him, what kind of clues I could have given away.

"Oh my God," I whispered. There had been a couple conversations where I'd spoken about Ella and her unusual circumstances. One in particular where I expressed real hatred for her ex-boyfriend whom I'd never met, but told Scott I fully supported Porter when he wanted to go to the police. And, I had told him she'd be at the bar last night. "This is all my fault," I whispered, tears springing to my eyes.

"Kalli, no. This is Kyle's fault. He's the psychopath." Megan sweetly patted my hand, but then stood up and I heard her walk down the hall, still talking into the phone. I could hear her consoling Ella, trying to convince her that I was fine, that I hadn't gone home with anyone, and that I was safe.

Of course, the night after Ella got attacked, she was worried about me. My head fell into my hands and I couldn't help the cries that came out of me. I was a quiet crier, a habit I adopted after listening to my parents fight at night. I could cry without making a sound. So I did. I cried as I got out of bed, as I put my clothes back on, leaving behind the pajamas Megan had loaned me the night before. Then I continued to cry as I slipped out of her house, sending her a text that I had to go and would talk to her later.

I cried until I was well into Washington, nearly halfway home.

When I finally arrived home, exhausted from both lack of sleep and also two hours of crying, I was greeted by Marcus. He enthusiastically hugged me, meeting me halfway up the path, like always.

"Hey, Marky. How are you?"

"I'm okay. I missed you, Kalli. You were gone longer than you said you'd be."

Guilt immediately ripped through me. I had stayed an extra day to see "Scott." Had I just left when I said I would, nothing would have ever happened. I sighed, but tried to smile for Marcus, not wanting him to know anything was bothering me.

"I'm sorry. Something came up in Portland and I had to stay an extra day. But I promise to make it up to you. Let's go inside." He pulled away from me, smiled, turned, and nearly skipped back to the house.

Marcus' spirit was admirable. Even though he'd been dealt a rather rough hand in life, he hardly ever let it affect his mood. I don't know if I'd be able to always be happy if I were him. He could very well choose to be angry or sad, but he never seemed to dwell on anything for long, which I was very thankful for at that moment.

I found Nancy in the kitchen, putting dishes in the

dishwasher. She looked at me with a smile, but it faded when she actually saw me. I watched as her smile dropped away and she reached to turn the water off.

"Marcus, sweetie, can you go put all of your sister's bags in her room for me?"

"Sure thing, Nancy. Then can we order pizza and watch a movie?"

"Of course," she said to him sweetly. She loved him so much; it was so obvious to me and it made my heart ache. He took off down the hall to gather my bags.

"What happened?" Nancy's voice was pained and concerned, and she took tentative steps toward me.

I shook my head, trying to stave off any more tears. I didn't want Marcus to see me upset. "I'm okay. I'll be all right. I just need a few minutes to put myself back together. Take a shower. Shake it off."

"Kalli, you can't just come in here, looking like you've been hit by a bus, obviously been crying, and tell me nothing's wrong. I love you just like I love your brother, and if something's wrong, you can tell me."

"Oh, Nancy," I cried, emotional from her declaration but also because I knew if I told her what had happened, how I'd been dumb enough to fall for "Scott's" lies, how the whole situation had been me trying to escape the very real and very uncomfortable feelings I had for Riot, well, I'd just break down again. "I just keep making mistakes."

"What do you mean?" She gently touched my elbow and urged me toward the table, and I found myself sitting.

"I mean, I keep veering off track, I keep getting distracted."

"From what?"

"From my life, from what I'm supposed to be doing. From Marcus."

"And what is it you feel is pulling you away?"

"I don't know. I just keep choosing men over Marcus. I've done it twice in the last month and now, this time, I really ended up hurting one of my friends." I placed my face in my hands and tried to take deep breaths.

"Kalli, just because you weren't in that car accident, doesn't mean your life was put on hold. Just because your brother needs special care, doesn't mean you have to sacrifice your own happiness. You're allowed to seek out happy."

I shook my head. "I can't do that to him. It was never in the cards for me."

"That ridiculous," Nancy said, now sounding angry. "It's going to take a special man to come into your life, accept everything that is, and continue on your journey with you, but he's out there. I promise." She reached out and took my hand. "Now, tell me, is your friend all right?"

"Yes. No. I don't know. I think so." I huffed out a breath. "Her ex-boyfriend used me to figure out where she was last night and attacked her."

"Oh my," Nancy said, shocked and concerned. "That's terrible."

"Ugh, I know. I feel terrible," I said, the last word coming out on a sob.

"That's terrible *of him*, Kalli. Don't you, for one moment, think you had any part in his decision to be a terrible person. Don't take that on."

I heard her words and tried to take them in, tried to absorb them, but my mind always reverted back to my inner voice telling me that I would never be wanted, not for real, not forever. I'd never met a man who wanted something genuine from me, something permanent. Last night was just a solidification of that notion.

"I really just want to take a shower," I whispered. "I'll be fine in a few minutes. I won't let Marcus see me upset."

"You think Marcus can't tell when you're sad?"

I looked up at Nancy, and I knew the answer to her question, but I didn't want to admit it.

"Marcus is special, that's for sure, but he isn't stupid and he can sense when you're upset about something. Don't belittle him that way, Kalli. He doesn't deserve that. In fact," she continued, her voice no longer chastising, "I bet if you talked to him about why you're upset, about the feelings you're having, he'd be able to offer you some really sound advice."

"When did you get so wise, Nancy?"

"Comes with age, my dear," she said, patting my hand. Her eyes locked on mine for a moment, then she stood and walked to the dishwasher, continuing to load it like I hadn't just poured my heart out to her.

Chapter Seven

Still Waters

After I had a shower, we ordered pizza and rented a movie. It was more of a movie for Marcus' entertainment, so I couldn't help it when my mind drifted over all the events of the last few weeks.

I hadn't heard from Ella the entire day and, even though I didn't want to bother her, I needed to know that she was all right. I took out my phone and sent her a text.

Hey. I'm so sorry about everything that happened. I swear I didn't know Scott was actually Kyle. Are you all right?

I made myself watch the movie and not obsessively stare at my phone, waiting for a reply. It took a few minutes, but I finally felt it vibrate.

Well, honestly, I've been better, but none of this was your fault, Kal. He's a psychopath and would have found his way to me regardless. How are you holding up? This can't be easy on you either.

Of course Ella would ask how I was doing the night after my date attacked her. I ran my hands over my face, frustration with myself grinding into my nerves. I didn't deserve friends like Ella and Megan, wasn't the kind of person they needed in their lives. I had tried so hard to keep my distance from people for so long because I knew once I made connections, something bad would happen.

I'm good. Just glad you're okay.

When will you be back in Portland?

I didn't have a reason to be back in Portland at all. My next job was, thankfully, in Seattle and the next few jobs after that took me to California. Oregon wasn't even on my radar.

Probably not for a while. I don't have anything lined up there in the near future.

Ella's response took a while to come, but when it did, I sighed heavily and my thumbnail unconsciously found its way to my teeth.

Maybe Megan and I will head to Seattle for a girls day.

This wasn't the first time Ella had hinted at coming to Seattle and I knew I couldn't keep brushing her off forever. The fact of the matter was, I didn't see how I could bring them to Seattle without divulging everything to them. Marcus was someone I kept very close to my heart. I didn't tell anyone about him, or his condition, and I didn't bring new people around. The last thing he needed in his life was more people who disappeared on him, and he didn't have the capacity to understand that adults sometimes just weren't around.

The last thing I wanted was for someone to come into my life, meet Marcus, have him form an attachment to them, only to have them disappear on him. It was heartache I could protect him from.

It might be easier for me to just make a day trip down there.

There was another long pause, but she finally responded.

I can't wait.

I took a deep breath, both relieved by her response, but also guilty that this giant omission was beginning to feel more like a lie.

I'm really sorry, again, for everything.

She couldn't possibly know everything I was sorry for, but it made me feel slightly better to type it.

You've got absolutely nothing to be sorry about. Call me tomorrow, okay?

I responded with a smiley face, done talking and not wanting to elicit any more conversation from her. I'm sure she was exhausted after everything that happened to her the day before, and I was very done denying my best friend the ability to get close to me. It hurt keeping her at arm's length, but I'd been so burnt in the past, this gentle sting was no comparison.

I put my phone down and returned my attention to the movie. A couple minutes had passed before I heard Marcus' gentle voice call out to me.

"Kal?"

"Yeah, Marky?"

He rolled onto his side, looking back at me from his position on the floor where he was lying on a pile of pillows. "If Mom and Dad were still alive, would you still be here with me?"

I stared at him for a few moments, trying to string together the right combination of words that didn't break him apart any more than he already was. The easy answer was no. No, I'd be a somewhat normal almost thirty-year-old living on my own, trying to make my own life. But I couldn't tell him that. I also couldn't tell him that if Mom and Dad were still alive, his life would look a lot different too. He'd be getting ready to start his senior year of high school, probably heading off to college the following fall. Everything would be different were Mom and Dad alive.

But I couldn't tell him that. Couldn't put that weight on his shoulders, couldn't tie him down with those thoughts.

"Yeah, buddy. I'd still be here. There's nowhere else I'd rather be than here with you." At least part of my sentence could be true. There was nowhere else I'd rather be than taking care of my brother. It was the least I could do, after all.

A week passed, spent completely in Seattle with Marcus. Nancy was there, of course, it was her home, but I took on the responsibility of Marcus. I always tried to be the caregiver if I was home. I took him to the park to ride his bike, we went to see a movie, and I also took him shopping for school clothes.

The boy had grown three inches over the summer and needed almost an entirely new wardrobe. And even though Marcus was a boy with special needs, he still maintained the stereotypical male aversion to shopping. There was also the added obstacle of treating him the way you would a normal boy of seventeen—letting him pick his own clothes, letting him go in a dressing room alone—balanced with taking his capabilities into account.

So, I let him go in the dressing room by himself, but I stood just outside the door, making sure he was on track and not getting too frustrated. He was known to throw some major temper tantrums if frustration seeped its way into his mood.

Going out in public with him was something I'd gotten used to. If we were just walking through a store, no one really took notice of Marcus; he looked like an ordinary teenager. But if Marcus started talking, that's when people started to notice he was different. I tried not to let the gawkers bother me, because I knew if I let it bother me, it would bother him. So, I responded to him the way I would any child. It was what he needed. To be treated normally.

"How's it going, Marky?" He grunted, then groaned, so I deduced it wasn't going well. "Are the pants too small? Do you need a bigger size?"

"I think so," he sighed, then opened the door. Not only were the pants too small around the waist, they were a good two inches too short.

"Okay, you wait here and I'll go find another pair in a bigger size."

"Can't we just buy the bigger size? I'm sick of trying on clothes." He was whining and I tried not to let it show it grated on my nerves.

"I know, bud. But we have to make sure they fit or else we'll just have to come back another day to return them."

He heaved out a sigh and plopped himself down on the bench in the dressing room. "Fine," he snapped. I chose not to reprimand him about his tone. I could deal with quietly angry Marcus, but didn't want to poke the bear.

I went in search of pants and when I returned I found his dressing room empty. I backed up, trying to remember if I had the right room, and checked the adjacent rooms just to be sure.

"Marcus?" I called out, but heard no response. "Marcus?" I yelled a little louder. Still nothing. My eyes darted all over the dressing rooms, looking for him, listening for any sign of anyone, but they were empty. I walked quickly out to the sales floor, my eyes making broad sweeps, looking for a tall head over everything else. "Marcus!" I called out.

"Can I help you with something, ma'am?"

I turned to see a sales associate with a polite smile on her face.

"I can't find my little brother. I went to get a bigger size and when I came back he was gone."

"Okay, what was he wearing?"

"Uh," I said, closing my eyes, trying to remember. "A blue shirt with white stripes and a pair of blue jeans with white sneakers. He's, like, six feet tall."

"Oh," the woman said with surprise. "I'm sorry, I just assumed he was a child, you looked so upset."

"I am upset. He's seventeen, but he's got the mind of a seven year old." I'd said those words so many times, but they never made me less sad, never failed to remind me of what had happened to him.

"Okay, don't worry. We'll help you find him," she responded, taking only a moment to digest what I'd told her. She took a walkie-talkie out of a holster at her hip and then started talking rapidly into it, giving his description, making sure to let everyone know he was a "special needs teenager."

My eyes kept darting around the store and I walked up and down aisles, looking for Marcus. The sales associate was still with me and I heard chatter over the walkie, other employees calling out that areas of the store were clear. Then, I heard a man's voice over the walkie say that there was a kid answering to the name Marcus in the electronics department.

I turned on a dime and started toward the giant sign overhead that said Electronics and looked down every aisle until I saw Marcus standing in front of a video game console, fingers tapping quickly on the buttons of a controller. I sighed when I saw him and smiled at the man with a name badge that read Tim standing with him, talking him through the video game.

"Marcus, where have you been? I went back to the dressing room and couldn't find you. You scared me to death."

Marcus' eyes didn't leave the screen, but he responded to me. "I got bored. But then I found this video game to play."

I turned to Tim, saying, "Thank you. I should have assumed he would come here."

"No problem. He's pretty good at this game," he said with a chuckle. "I've seen him in here before, but he's usually with an older woman. They usually stop here for a few minutes so he can play the game." He patted Marcus on the shoulder. "You gave your sister quite a scare, man. You gotta stay close to her."

"Sorry, Kal," Marcus said with little conviction, still staring at the screen. I had to laugh because it was so *Marcus*.

"Yeah, okay, well, when you're done with this level we've got to try these pants on." He didn't answer me, but I knew he'd heard me. A few minutes later he stepped away from the controller and looked at me.

"All right, let's try the stupid pants on." We walked past the electronics counter again and Marcus called out, "See ya later, Tim!"

"Later, buddy! Don't give your sister such a hard time."

Marcus waved at him in acquiescence and we continued to the dressing room. He went back into his original room and I heard fabric shuffling around so I knew he was on task.

"You really scared me, Marcus," I said to the closed door of his dressing room. "I didn't know where you were or if you were safe. Don't ever wander away again."

"I'm not a baby, Kal. I can take care of myself." His words were firm and he sounded so much like the seventeen year old teenager he was, but he couldn't grasp his limitations in this way. He would never think of himself the same way I did, and I wasn't sure I wanted him to. I never wanted him to think of himself as handicapped or limited. I wanted, desperately, for him to believe he was capable of anything. But I couldn't have him wandering away, either.

"I know you're not a baby, Marky, but I still need to know where you are. Wouldn't you be worried if I was suddenly missing?"

He was silent for a moment, but then I heard his voice and it was markedly warmer. "I'd be really scared if you disappeared." I smiled just a little, never taking his love for me for granted, but it was also a relief to hear him understand my point of view. "I'm sorry. I won't wander away anymore." He sounded sincere, so I decided it was done and over with.

"Okay, thanks for apologizing. Now, are those pants fitting better?"

"Yup," he said as he swung the door open wide, modeling the new pants. They looked like they fit fine, so I wanted to get out of there.

"Great. Take them off and get dressed. Let's get out of here and grab some dinner, yeah?"

"Oh!" he said excitedly. "Can we get those giant burritos?"

"Sure," I said through a laugh, glad all had been forgiven and we'd avoided a large commotion.

After the biggest burrito I'd ever eaten, and an hour and a half of Monopoly, from a game we'd started three days prior that just never seemed to end, Marcus was in bed, Nancy was out for the evening, and I found myself on my porch with a glass of wine.

I didn't have the best view of the sound, but I could see a little bit of the water and that always calmed me. The beach was nice, but still waters always gave me strength. They were a deception. A fraud. A bluff. They looked like glass, appeared solid and strong on the surface, but in the end couldn't hold you up if you needed it. There was something about the façade of still water to which I related.

I pulled my phone out of my pocket and stared at the screen. Every now and then, when I was quiet and pensive, I thought about calling Riot. But I never knew what I would say to him. I didn't know if I would ask him why he'd acted so strangely, or if I'd ask him if he thought about me half as much as I did him.

Then, all of a sudden, my phone lit up and the ringtone I'd never bothered to change started chiming. The screen said two words and my throat closed up at the sight of them.

Riot Bentley

My finger touched the screen to answer the call, and my arm raised the phone to my ear, but my mouth hadn't gotten the memo yet that it was time to converse.

"How…. What…. How…." I stammered.

"Kalli?"

Oh, God, that voice. That melodious voice that wrapped around me like velvet and chocolate and fire.

"How?" I continued to ponder. How in the hell had he happened to call me at the same moment I was thinking of calling him? After weeks of not speaking. After *never* having spoken on the phone. "You called me," I finally managed.

"Kalli, are you all right?"

"You called me, right when I was going to call you...." My voice drifted away, my mind still not able to compute everything happening. It was too weird. Too coincidental.

"You were going to call me?" He sounded hopeful.

"I was thinking about it."

"I think about you all the time."

Seven words, those seven words, were all it took to stop my heart. My eyes closed, my breath halted, my entire system shut down as if it were trying to preserve the moment. If I never took another breath, I'd never have to let this moment go. I would live and die in his words, his admission that he was just as hung up on me as I was on him.

I finally exhaled and it was loud and embarrassing, making it obvious I'd been holding my breath. I opened my mouth to speak, but before I could get a word out, I heard his voice again.

"I'm in Victoria, I have been for a while, and I was going to head back, was going to drive right through Seattle. I kept telling myself I wasn't going to bother you, wasn't going to force you to see me, but I know if I drive through Seattle and don't at least try to see you, I'll regret it."

"You're driving through Seattle?" This time, it was me who sounded hopeful.

"Yeah," he said on an exhale. "I am. Can I see you?"

"Yeah," I said, sounding just as relieved as he did.

"Okay, if I leave right now I can make it there in about five hours."

I pulled the phone away from my ear, checking the time. "That would put you here at three a.m. Why don't you just sleep there and leave in the morning?"

"I'm not sure I can sleep if I know I'm just going to see you in the morning."

His words were sweet and soft, and I sort of agreed with him. I had excited nerves running through my body and I wasn't sure sleep was something I would be capable of either.

"Okay," I whispered.

"Okay," he agreed, and I heard him start to move, sounds that made me think of him shoving things into a duffle bag, hastily slipping on a pair of shoes. He was coming to me. "Can you text me your address?"

Suddenly, all the excitement left my body and was replaced with fear. My address? He couldn't come to my house. I hadn't thought this through.

"Let's meet someplace else," I said, my voice sounding worried and rushed.

"Someplace else?"

"Yeah, uh, there's a viewpoint where we can meet, look out over the skyline. It's called Hamilton Park."

"You don't want me to come to your house?" He sounded a little hurt and even more suspicious. "Are you married?"

"No! God, no. I'm not married. I just don't think it's best for you to come here."

"Okay, I guess that's valid. I'll see you there in about four and a half hours."

"Thanks. I'll see you there." I disconnected and then stared at my phone for a moment, trying to stave off the freak out I could feel building up inside of me. What in the world had I agreed to? And what did one wear to meet someone at a viewpoint in the middle of the night? Good God, this was a mistake.

I stood up and took my wine back inside, then went to raid my closet. An hour later when Nancy tried to quietly sneak in the front door I accosted her before she made it to her room.

"Nancy, I need you to stay with Marcus for a little while."

"All right, is he awake?" She looked around the house, her eyes looking at the kitchen table and the couch, then back at me with confusion.

"No, he's asleep, but I'm going to be leaving in an hour or two."

"So, you need me to go to sleep and be here when he wakes up, like normal?"

"Yes," I said, pointing at her with an index finger. "That's exactly what I need you to do."

"Okay," she said, crossing her arms. "What's going on?"

"I met someone a few weeks ago, and he's going to be in town in a few hours so I'm going to meet him."

"*He's* going to be here? You're going to meet *him*?"

I rolled my eyes at her. "Yes, it's a guy."

"Who is it?" Her voice turned soft and curious, almost teasing.

"His name is Riot Bentley and he was the male lead in the video shoot I did for Lexi Black."

"Oh," she said, and I could almost see her brain working, trying to piece together all the information. When the last puzzle piece fell into place her eyes widened and fell back to me. "*Oh*...." Now she was definitely teasing me.

"I'm going to go try and sleep for a bit before I go."

"Why are you meeting him at such a strange time?"

"He's driving down from Victoria and didn't want to wait."

"Couldn't wait until daylight to see you?" Her eyebrows raised, lips pursed, as if she was waiting for me to come to the same conclusion as her, waiting for me to catch up with her.

"Don't," I pleaded. "He was going to pass through Seattle on his way back home anyway."

"All right...." She winked at me as she walked to her bedroom door. "If you don't come home or text me by ten a.m. I will send the police to search for your body."

"He's not a serial killer."

She just shrugged in response. Then she went into her bedroom but I heard her voice from the other side of her door. "Ten a.m., Kalli."

"All right," I replied, trying to keep my voice down, not wanting to wake Marcus.

Chapter Eight

It Could Be Wonderful

Three hours later I was sitting in my car, heater and headlights on, waiting for Riot to appear. I hadn't given it much thought beforehand, but the viewpoint was closed after sundown, so the gates were locked. I was parked right outside them and I figured we'd find somewhere else to go once he arrived. I'd left my house and nearly turned around three different times. I couldn't recall another time in my life I'd been so nervous.

Riot had said he couldn't stop thinking about me, but I wasn't sure what context we were meeting under. I wondered why he wanted to see me, wondered if he couldn't imagine being with anyone else, wondered if he found it hard to concentrate on simple, everyday things for thoughts of me. But I also tried not to think of anything, because that made me nervous too.

Headlights appeared around the bend in the road and I watched as a car slowed, passed me, then turned around and pulled up right behind me. Suddenly, I was awash with all the reasons why this was a very stupid idea. The headlights turned off and I saw someone exit the vehicle. I saw the outline of a man walking toward my car and I couldn't take my eyes off him. I couldn't see any fine details, but for some reason I was mesmerized by him.

When he came to my door, I watched as he bent down, and then Riot's beautiful face was filling my field of vision and the corners of my mouth curled up into a shy smile. He motioned for me to roll down my window, and I quickly moved to do so, silently cursing myself for just sitting there like an idiot, staring at him.

"Hey, you made it," I said once my window was down.

"Yeah, it wasn't a bad drive at all." He stood up a little straighter, looking around, then his eyes came back to me. "You wanna go for a walk?"

"The viewpoint is closed. I'm sorry, I didn't even think about the fact that it might not be open. We can go someplace else if you'd like."

"Do you always follow the rules?" His question caught me off guard; no one had ever asked me that before. Especially not with the implication that he wanted me to break them. He had no idea that just by meeting him there I had already broken almost every rule I'd made for myself.

"What are you suggesting?"

"I'm suggesting you get out of the car, walk with me through those gates, and live a little." His smile was radiant, and it reached all the way to his eyes. It was impossible to say no to that smile. So I opened the door, unfolded myself from the car, and shut it behind me, my smile matching his.

"Hi," I said, grinning widely, now standing right in front of him.

"Hey," he replied, his eyes roaming over my face. "Thanks for agreeing to see me." His hand reached out and I watched as it wrapped around mine, palm to palm. The same butterflies that invaded my stomach the first time he held my hand came out from their hiding places and fluttered through me, sending a blush all the way to my cheeks. I was thankful at that point for the darkness that hid my reaction to his hand wrapped around mine.

"Come on, let's go."

He tugged on my hand and pulled me toward the gate. We walked in silence, making our way down the road meant for cars, until we came to the parking lot. Although we didn't speak, my body was alive with his touch. Just his hand on mine caused so many zings of electricity to radiate through me. I was a step behind him, letting him lead the way, and I took the opportunity to admire him. He wore a jean jacket that matched the denim of his pants, with combat boots. The laces were loose, not even pretending to hold the shoes to his feet. I saw a white t-shirt poking out of the hem of his jacket and I also saw a leather cuff bracelet wrapped around the wrist of the hand I wasn't holding. I'd never been with a guy who wore jewelry before, but I couldn't deny the fact that I found that bracelet incredibly sexy.

He led me to the edge of the parking lot where there was a dilapidated wooden fence, obviously meant for looks, not purpose, as it wasn't going to keep anyone away from the ledge if they truly wanted to get close. There were also a few benches, one of which Riot walked straight toward. He sat, then pulled me down to sit next to him, and there was no distance between us.

A few moments of pregnant silence passed, but then he spoke.

"I'm sorry about the way I acted the last time we were together, about how I said goodbye. It was a douche move and I regret it."

He turned his face toward me and even though we were sitting in complete darkness, the shiny caramel of his eyes shone through, and he looked sorry.

"I'm not going to lie, that was really confusing."

He picked up our hands, which were still linked, and brought them to his lap. "I know," he said on a sigh, obviously upset with himself. "I was having a hard time dealing with the fact that I really liked you, but you didn't want to have anything to do with me. I mean," he said, backpedalling, "besides being friends. But I'll be really honest with you, I didn't want to be your friend. I still don't want to be just your friend."

"Riot—" I began, but he cut me off.

"No, I know, you're not looking for a relationship. I remember, trust me. But," he sighed loudly, then looked back to me. "I just can't get you out of my mind."

I was taken aback by his honesty, by the way he seemed to truly be just as caught up in me as I was in him. It didn't feel like we'd spent weeks apart; I felt like we were still on the grass at the waterfront, still just us.

"I'm sorry, Riot. I just can't be with someone that way."

"So, you could sleep with me, spend the night with me, and then just walk away?"

My heart thundered in my chest, listening to him talk about us being together in that way affected me on a base level. It was everything my body craved, but also everything my heart was afraid of.

"I don't know if I could walk away after being with you, Riot. Which is why we can't ever let that happen." I looked out over the city, lights twinkling from far away. I heard him scoff, could tell he was shaking his head.

"I don't understand you, Kalli."

I shrugged. "Not many do."

"But I *want* to. Doesn't that count for anything? Doesn't the fact that I've spent the last few weeks of my life trying desperately to forget about you, only to find myself driving through the night to finally touch you, even if it's just this, just our hands—doesn't that mean anything to you?"

"I'm not sure what it means to me. I don't know much of anything when it comes to you. Just that you affect me more than anyone ever has." So much truth came from me in one sentence. There had never been another man in my life who I wanted so much. I couldn't risk being with him, couldn't trust myself to walk away.

"Can you please, for my sake, tell me why you are this way? Why you won't let anyone get close to you?"

"It's not something I can really explain. I've never tried."

"Could you try though, for me?"

I didn't know Riot from a hole in the wall—not really. He was just a guy I'd met at work and spent one afternoon with. He could have been any number of guys I spent an evening with and then discarded. He was, in reality, less knowledgeable about me than many of the men I'd slept with and then walked away from. But, in that moment, sitting on that bench, with my hand wrapped in both of his, I had the distinct urge to let him in. To tell him what I'd never explained to a single other person before. So, I took a deep breath and decided to take the leap. Even if it was the scariest thing I would ever do, I had the feeling I would regret it if I let him go without an explanation.

"When I was seven, my dad left us. It was my birthday and I'll never forget it. Luckily for my mom, a few years later she met Dave. Dave was her savior, made up for all the crap my real father put her through." I paused, taking a deep breath, unsure of where to go from there. "Dave was as close to a father as I'll ever get. It wasn't a perfect relationship between us, but it was good. He was good. He never made me feel like I was the tagalong to my mom, like he got roped into being a father figure. He was present and he was good to me."

Before I could get the next sentence out, a smile crept over my face. "When I was thirteen, my mom and Dave had a baby. I got a little brother, Marcus." My smile grew wider and I looked out over the viewpoint, taking in the twinkling lights of the city skyscrapers. "I was thrilled to have a baby brother. He was so cute and it was almost like I could play house with him. I got to carry him, feed him, play with him, but then when he cried I could just hand him back to my mom. He was like a real, live baby doll."

I turned to look at Riot's face to find him smiling back at me and he gave my hand a gentle squeeze, almost as if he were trying to encourage me to continue.

"Marcus was the first boy in my world who loved me unconditionally from the very beginning. He was my brother so, I mean, he was kind of obligated, but I swear, Riot, he loved me harder than anyone I'd ever met." I paused, thinking back to Marcus growing up, the little boy he became, how rambunctious he'd been. A small laugh escaped with just the image of him in my mind. "My mom loved me, of course, but when my father left, things were hard for her and I always knew it was my fault she was alone."

"Anyway," I said with a sigh. "When I was twenty, and away at school in New York, my family was in a car accident. A really terrible accident." I took in a deep breath and tried to muster the courage to tell the story I had avoided telling so many times in my life. "They were in the car on their way to the airport to come visit me in New York. They were driving over a bridge and another car swerved into their lane. Dave tried to avoid it, but only managed to hit another car at just the right angle, sending their car over the guardrail and into the river."

"Oh, God, Kalli...." Riot's voice was pained and apologetic. But, instead of listening to him tell me how sorry he was, I kept talking. If I was talking, hopefully I wouldn't cry.

"Dave died instantly, something to do with the force of hitting the car before they went into the water. My mom had injuries from the crash that left her unconscious, so she ended up drowning once the car filled with water. But Marcus, well, a very brave man dove into the water and rescued him." I paused for a moment, looking out over the view of the city, taking just a moment to wonder where that man might be. He'd so drastically altered our lives. So bravely dove into that water and done something I'd be forever grateful for, but I was never gifted the opportunity to thank him or even know his name. He'd wanted to remain anonymous.

"Unfortunately, he was without oxygen for too long and he was left with permanent brain damage." I said the words and I knew they weren't enough; weren't enough to totally encapsulate everything about Marcus and his condition. "He's been through so many years of therapy, and still goes every week, but he's as better as he's ever going to get. He was stunted at age seven. So, even though he's a monster at six foot two and seventeen years old, he thinks and acts like a seven-year-old—a seven-year-old with mental handicaps at that."

"Shit, Kal, that's awful."

I looked back to him, curious about his choice of words. *Awful.* It was, wasn't it? Awful. Most people would say sad, or lucky, or even say it was a *miracle.* But it was awful. For everyone involved, especially Marcus. He didn't know any better, and would never fully understand what the accident had cost him, but it *was* awful. He'd never get to do everything he was entitled to, never live alone, never marry, never have children. But he'd live long enough to watch everyone around him live their lives, stuck and never able to move forward.

I was constantly worried for him, worried that one day he'd realize how much he was missing. He'd come to a place in his life where he realized normal twenty-somethings didn't live with their sisters, didn't need around the clock care from a medical professional, could drive, have a job, have a girlfriend, could be fathers. One day it would all come crashing down around him and I'd have to watch it happen, have to be there to help him through that. But nothing would ever change for him. There would be no progress. He would be stagnant for the rest of his life and so would I.

I was on this ride with him. I was responsible for him and I had been for the last ten years.

"I'm his guardian, Riot. I'm the one who has to take care of him, be around for him, and make sure he's all right. And that's the way it will be for the rest of my life. You can see how that would complicate my dating life."

"Complicate, yes," he said carefully, "but not eliminate. Have you ever given anyone the chance to try and prove you wrong?"

Shivers ran down my spine as his words washed over me, but I shook my head. "Try? Try what? To wiggle their way into Marcus' life and then leave him when they figure out they can't deal? Try to confuse and crush my brother? He's fragile enough as it is, he doesn't need that kind of upset in his life."

"I totally understand what you're saying, Kalli, really I do, but it almost feels like you're punishing yourself and then convincing yourself it's for his benefit. What if you had a child? What if you were just a single mom? Would you swear off men then?"

I stood at his words, now with anger zipping through my limbs, electrifying me. "Those are two different things, Riot. He's not a child, and I'm not just a single mom. He's a mentally handicapped man. He'll be in my care forever. There won't ever be a time when he isn't around. There will be no weekend getaways, no honeymoons, and no vacations. There will never be a time when Marcus isn't *there*. He's a permanent fixture."

"I think that's a little drastic," he said, his voice low, almost patronizing.

"You think it's drastic? You think I'm over exaggerating? You have no idea what you're talking about, Riot. You don't have a clue." My heart was racing with panic as I was beginning to think I'd made a mistake in opening up to him.

"Listen, Kalli, I just think you've put yourself in a box and closed it up tight. And even though someone wants to open it up, to give you a little light, you've decided to make it impossible."

"And you think you're the one to do that? To show me a little light? This has been my life for ten years, Riot. You don't think I know a little more about this than you?"

"Undoubtedly, but you haven't let anyone try. Let me try."

"It's not worth it," I muttered, turning away from him and facing the city again. "I'd let you in, you'd make yourself comfortable, then you'd realize what you'd gotten yourself into and be gone again."

"Now you're not giving *me* enough credit. You've got really low expectations of everyone around you while holding yourself to ridiculously high ones." I heard him stand and walk toward me. "You could at least let me earn the disappointment you've already attached to me. Let me have the opportunity to change your mind about how it could be."

He came to stand next to me, but didn't touch me. "It's not that simple," I whispered, a little ashamed at how broken I sounded. "I can't let you hurt him, I've already hurt him enough."

"Kal," he said gently, his hand gripping my arm, pulling me to him. He brought my head to his shoulder with his other hand, and I went willingly. Allowing myself, for just one moment, to feel him. He stroked my hair while his other arm wound itself around my waist, making sure I was pressed firmly against him.

"I don't know what kind of men you've surrounded yourself with in the past, but I can promise you I'll never intentionally hurt you. And I wouldn't dream of hurting your brother. I can't guarantee everything will work out, but I would never hurt you, Kal."

"It's the unknown that worries me most. The things neither one of us can guarantee."

"You can't protect him from everything. Have you ever considered that by keeping him from being hurt, you might also be keeping him from being happy? I know you're preventing yourself from finding happiness, but what about him? Couldn't he benefit from a healthy relationship with a man? Couldn't you both? It doesn't have to be dangerous or hurtful, Kalli. It could be wonderful." His words were whispered against my ear, his hand stroking slowly down the back of my neck, smoothing down my hair.

His words were weapons against every piece of armor I'd ever put up, and my defenses were crumbling around his voice.

"We could be so wonderful," he said, his voice so low and pleading.

I'd never heard anyone mean what they said as much as he did in that moment. He believed, with every fiber of his soul, the words he was saying to me; I could feel it. In that instant, like a lightning strike, I was convinced to believe him, to let him in, even if it meant heartache down the road. I simply couldn't keep myself closed up anymore. He'd pried the lid off the box and now that I'd seen his light shining in, I wanted out.

I pulled my face away from his shoulder, slowly moving to look him in the eye. His caramel eyes shone back at me, searching mine for any indication of where I was headed or what I would do next. My gaze fell from his eyes and wandered down to his lips, and I let myself remember how lush they'd looked that day at the waterfront. Even now, with the moonlight illuminating them, they looked inviting.

"Don't forget your promise," I whispered, my eyes darting back and forth between his lips and eyes.

"I'll never do anything to hurt you," he said again, still a whisper, but adamant.

"Kiss me," I breathed out, my voice shaky and low.

He paused for a moment, tilted his head slightly, then slowly moved his mouth closer to mine. I watched his eyes as he moved closer still, silently begging him to be the man he claimed to be. Willing him to not make me regret that moment. Pleading with him to make me whole again, to show me how to be the person he saw me as.

When his lips met mine I expected heat, fireworks, sirens, something. But what I felt was relief. A strange, yet absolutely wonderful, feeling of respite came over me. For just that instant, I was weightless. I was suspended in time, feeling his lips against mine and nothing else.

Then, just one moment later, the heat came. As his lips brushed over mine, the friction built and the warmth rolled over me, stinging along my spine, trembling in my hands. His hand moved to the back of my neck, just as it had that first day we'd worked together, and he gripped me there as his tongue teased the seam of my lips.

Without permission, my mouth yielded to him, opening, inviting him in, and a moan escaped me when he took that first hesitant pass with his tongue.

With one hand on my neck and the other cupping my cheek, he pressed into me, taking more from me in one kiss than I'd ever given anyone with all of my body. He licked, nibbled, tasted and took. And all I could do was give myself over to him. I could hear his breath pulling in heavily through his nose as our lips passed over one another's. I felt his fingers flex against the skin of my neck, and after a minute or two, his erection pressing hard into my belly.

My hands found their way to his narrow hips, sliding around his waist to the back of him. I gripped his shirt beneath his jacket, digging my fingers into the fabric, trying to bring him as close to me as possible.

We stood at this abandoned viewpoint, just us and the city, sharing a kiss with the sky. The kiss never tapered, never waned. It built and burned, and soon his hands moved down, floating over my body. They moved over my shoulders, down my arms, and then to my waist. His hands wound around me, the feeling of his big hands moving over my skin making my breath hitch in my lungs and my heart pound with need.

He was so tall that my neck was stretched, arching to meet his mouth with mine, my toes stretching to bring me closer. When his arms became tight around my waist, I yelped as he lifted me, bringing my face level with his. He moved backward and I trusted him to carry me, and in one swift movement, he swung my body and caught the back of my knees with one arm, the other arm cradling my back, mouth still assaulting mine, still kissing me as if this were the last time either one of us would ever kiss again, and we were going to make it last.

We lowered, me still wrapped in his arms, mine wound around his neck, and I slowly realized he'd brought us back to one of the benches that lined the viewpoint. We sat and he placed me on his lap, my rear on the bench with my legs draped over him. With his hands free, not needing to hold on to me anymore, they moved up and into my hair. The kiss, up until this point, had been the perfect blend of heat and anticipation, but in this instant it changed into almost reverent.

His tongue gently danced with mine, his thumbs softly caressed my cheeks, the backs of his fingers trailed gingerly down the sensitive skin of my neck. My body was verging on sensation overload and all we were doing was kissing. I wanted to push myself, to push him, to make the most of our kiss.

I pulled back slightly and, as if he were drawn to me, unable to break away, his mouth simply moved to my neck, splaying kisses wherever his mouth found purchase. With his lips pressed up against one particular spot below my ear, groaning, I moved my leg over his lap to straddle him. Once I was seated on him, feeling the erection that was pressed against me earlier, I heard him growl as he placed his hands on my hips, holding me down firmly against him.

"I've thought about touching you like this for weeks, Kalli," he mumbled against my neck. He pulled his face back and his gaze met mine. "Ever since that first time we met, and you knelt in front of me in that trailer, I couldn't help but picture my hands on you."

His words made my breath catch in my throat, my pulse hammer in my chest, and every part of my body below my belly seize up, clenching with anticipation. I remembered that moment, remembered how mortified I had been to blush while kneeling in front of him. Knowing he'd felt it too, that he'd been just as affected as I had, made any last reservations I had about him and us melt away.

My hands found their way under his t-shirt and I moved them slowly up the skin of his abdomen, taking every chance I could to feel the ridges of hard muscle as my hands rippled over them. Simultaneously, his hands trailed down from my hips, down my thighs, all the way to my knees, and then back up again. Only, on the way up, they slid around to the back and rounded my ass, pausing once the fleshiest part was cupped in his hands. He pulled me against him again, eliminating any space between us, causing me to gasp at the jolt of pleasure that concentrated in my core.

His mouth found mine and I was lost in him again. His hands slid up my back under my shirt as he kissed me, and I thought about the fact that we both had our hands on the skin of the other, thought about the need I felt to touch him in that moment, to use my hands to connect with him. I had never experienced that with a man before. When I was physical with anyone, there was one goal: to orgasm, to release, to forget. But somehow I knew that with Riot, if we ever got the chance to be together in that way, it would be drastically and markedly less one-sided.

I wouldn't be using him simply to escape, or for pleasure—although I'm sure there'd be enough of that to go around. I got the distinct impression that sex with Riot would be an experience in uniting. Whatever happened, it would happen to both of us because the two of us were there sharing something together. A uniqueness I'd never experienced before.

Kissing Riot on this bench in the middle of a deserted parking lot wasn't a race to get each other's clothes off. He didn't want to take me on that bench. He simply wanted to feel me, and I took the opportunity to feel as much of him as I could.

When the kiss finally slowed, and Riot's hands moved back up to my shoulders, pushing my hair away from my face, he pulled his lips from mine with just a few tender kisses as if he wasn't ready to let me go just yet.

I opened my eyes and saw that dawn had just barely broken, and the sky was painted with orange and pink watercolor hues. Suddenly, without his arms pulling me close to his body, I was cold.

"Hey," he said, one hand coming up to frame the side of my face. "You all right?"

I nodded silently, biting my bottom lip, avoiding his eyes.

"Hey," he said, more insistently this time, using a finger to draw my chin up so our eyes met again. "What's all that about?"

I shrugged, trying to hide a smile and the blush I could feel creeping up my chest. "That was really nice."

An adorable half-grin came over him and his eyes twinkled. "Babe, that was a lot of things, but I could think of many adjectives besides *nice* to describe it."

I slapped the bulging muscle of his bicep, noting that I'd probably hurt myself more than him, and laughed. "You know what I mean."

"I do," he said, his sweet smile returning as he leaned forward, kissing me gently once more. "As much as I'd love to stay here with you, I think we both need to get some sleep."

I exhaled, then nodded. "Yeah."

"Can I see you tonight? Bring you dinner? I'd love to meet your brother."

My stomach dropped at his request and all my hardwired defenses snapped to attention. I had *never* brought a man to my house before. Riot must have noticed my panic because he instantly started trying to soothe me, one hand coming to my face as he said gently, "Hey, don't shut down on me now, Kalli. I just want to meet him. And I want to see you. And as beautiful as you look right now, with the sunrise behind you, your hair all crazy from my hands, I'd like to see you when I'm not exhausted from driving all night. I'd like to see you in your home, with your family."

"Okay," I whispered, trying to maintain even breaths. This was something I wasn't used to; letting a man in, allowing him access to parts of me that I always kept private, kept safe.

Chapter Nine

His Irresistible Charm

That evening, when my doorbell rang, I opened the door to find Riot standing on my porch, looking just as sexy as he had every other time I'd seen him. However, this time he had a gleam in his eye I hadn't noticed before, but recognized as pride when he stepped forward and kissed me square on the mouth before I'd even opened the door wide enough for him to come in.

It was a short kiss, but it was hot and just a little bit wet, with the slightest hint of his tongue against my lips.

"Hi," I said as I smiled at him.

"Hey. I promise I won't kiss you in front of your brother, but I wanted to get one in, you know, just to ease the pressure." His smirk was evident and did nothing to tamp down the wave of arousal his kiss caused.

"Kalli, who's at the door?" Marcus' voice roared through the house. He was playing his Wii and couldn't be bothered to get up, so his deep voice echoed down the hall.

"Sorry, he's in the family room, can't be bothered to leave his video game." Before the words had made it past my lips, Riot's mouth was on mine and my back was pressed up against the door. His hands were full of pizza and a six-pack, but his hips worked just fine pinning me back, and his mouth was aflame against mine. My hands ran up the front of him, enjoying the landscape of his chest as I went, and I wound them around his neck, feeling the soft hair just at the nape.

"I decided," he said between small kisses, "to take advantage of him being in the other room. I promise it won't happen again."

My hands retreated, again loving the feel of his chest as they moved down his front, and I slid back down to rest flat on my feet.

"There can be no more of that," I said breathily, not helping me sound convincing at all.

"Pizza," he said as he lifted one hand. "Beer," he said, gesturing with the other.

"Great. Marcus loves pizza." I waved my arm out, indicating he should come all the way in the house, and closed the door behind him. I led Riot back to the kitchen and started grabbing plates and forks. I looked up when I heard big clomping footsteps coming down the hall, knowing Marcus was on his way into the kitchen. I took a deep breath and then looked to the doorway. When his big frame came into view, I gave him a reassuring smile.

He saw me, smiled, and then his eyes found Riot. His smile faltered a little, which caused my heart rate to skyrocket, but within a few seconds it was back to normal and he was making his way into the small dining room attached to the kitchen.

"Marcus, this is my friend Riot. He was in that music video I worked on, remember?"

His eyes squinted a little, then opened wide. "Yeah, you got to kiss that pretty girl, Lexi Black."

Riot laughed a little, then moved toward Marcus, holding out his hand. "Great to meet you, Marcus."

"You're friends with Kalli?"

"Yup."

"She doesn't have any friends," Marcus said, matter-of-factly.

"Marcus, stop it. I have friends," I said, blushing, trying to recover from the embarrassment his words caused.

"Then how come you never have them over? Riot is the first person you've ever brought home." Marcus stopped talking and noticed the pizza box on the table. "We're having pizza for dinner? Awesome!" And just like that we'd moved on.

"Riot brought it, wasn't that nice?"

"Thanks!" Marcus exclaimed, obviously excitable about food.

"No problem, your sister said you liked pizza."

"Kalli, my favorite show is going to start soon. Can we eat in the living room?" I winced on the inside. I usually tried to keep the food in the dining room as Marcus was a spiller, but I didn't want to put him in a bad mood and thought, honestly, that the television might offer a buffer between all of us.

"Sure, but your plate stays on the coffee table, Marky. No pizza sauce on the carpet."

"Deal," he yelled, already halfway down the hallway.

I exhaled loudly, relieved that Marcus not only seemed unfazed by Riot's presence, but that Riot also seemed to be at ease. Warm hands wrapped around my arms, pulling me back into a strong chest.

"That went well, I think," he whispered against my ear. I nodded. "Do you want a beer?" he asked as he backed away from me.

"Sure." I watched him move around my kitchen, looking for glasses to pour the beer into. He looked comfortable, which only made me feel *more* comfortable. I turned back to the table, pulling slices of pizza out of the box and putting them on plates. Riot grabbed one from me and gave me a wink as he left the kitchen, heading toward the living room. I listened as Riot placed the plate on the coffee table, saying, "Here you go, buddy." Then I heard Marcus' response of a simple, "Thank you."

When Riot came back into the kitchen he walked past me to grab the glasses and looked at me expectantly. "I'll carry these if you grab the plates."

"All right." This was all going a little too well; it was feeling a little too easy. I followed him down the hall and as he sat on one side of the couch, I sat down on the other.

"Here you go," he said, sliding a glass my way, then picking up his pizza and taking a bite.

I sat on the couch, eating my pizza, waiting for *something* to happen; for Marcus to realize there was a stranger in the house and throw a tantrum, for Riot to decide he actually wanted nothing to do with my brother and me, that we were too much to take on. But both of those boys just sat there, watched TV, and ate their pizza. I gave myself a mental shoulder shrug, and decided to try and relax.

"Are you using a fork?" Riot's voice called me out of my haze.

"Um, yes?"

"Who eats pizza with a fork?"

"Kalli does," Marcus piped up. "She's weird about some stuff. Always eats pizza with a fork." He didn't turn to look at Riot while he spoke, but the humor in his voice was apparent.

"I don't like pizza grease all over my fingers," I said in my own defense.

"She's also a half-drinker," Marcus supplied.

"A half-drinker?" Riot questioned with a laugh.

"Yeah, she only drinks half of whatever she has. She'll never finish an entire can of soda. She always leaves it half full."

"Okay, well, that's true," I admit, shrugging. "There are exceptions to that rule though. Coffee and beer," I say, lifting my glass to my lips with a smile. "Can't waste either of those."

"Huh," Riot said, just before taking another huge bite, sounding like he'd just tucked a little piece of information away about me, as if he put it in his pocket to pull out later and think about.

"If you used a fork, your pizza might last you more than three bites," I said, laughing at him.

He looked puzzled. "Pizza isn't a delicate food, babe. You're supposed to eat it with your hands and without napkins. It's best that way."

My eyes widened at his term of endearment, my gaze shooting over to Marcus, waiting for him to react, but he didn't. I raised my eyebrows at Riot in warning, but all he did was take another giant bite, all while smiling.

After we'd all had our fill of pizza, Riot asked Marcus about his Wii and then I watched as the boys played two hours of Mario Kart. For a while, I stayed close, making sure Marcus was comfortable. But after forty-five minutes of Riot gently probing him with questions about school, how he spent his free time, and endless superhero comparisons, I began to think that they would be fine on their own for a while.

I stood and started cleaning up our mess from dinner, which led to me doing the rest of the dishes left over from the day, which sparked my interest in the laundry. Before I knew it, an hour had passed and the boys had been alone the whole time. I walked back into the living room to find them both in the exact position I'd left them in, only both looked much more relaxed and they were laughing loudly.

"Hey," I said during a lull in their laughter. Riot's head turned to me, as did Marcus', and I couldn't help but laugh at their matching expressions. They both looked a little frazzled and a smidge irritated that I'd interrupted their game. "Marky, you've got half an hour until you need to get ready for bed."

His shoulders slumped but he turned back to the game with an, "All right." I spent the next thirty minutes sitting on the couch, watching as the two boys played their video game. Riot was surprisingly good with him, congratulating Marcus when he won a round, not being terribly obnoxious when he lost. It was a new feeling to see Marcus with a man, besides Mr. Bob, and having fun. There had been so many instances in the past where new experiences and changes in routine had thrown him over some proverbial edge. But Marcus seemed to really take to Riot.

When his bedtime approached, Marcus politely said goodnight to Riot.

"There's a new game coming out next month and you can use characters from your favorite movies in the game. Kalli said that she'd get it for me. You should come back and we could play it together."

"Sure thing, buddy. Sounds great." Riot clapped Marcus on the shoulder and we watched as he headed down the hallway toward his bedroom. Riot turned to me with a smile, eyes gleaming.

"He's a good kid."

"He is," I agreed. "You were smart to go the video game route."

"I used to play a mean Mario Kart. It was like riding a bike." He stood up from the floor and came to sit by me on the couch, closer than we had been earlier, and his smile changed from amused to sultry. My heart quickened at this new smile and his closer proximity. He turned his body and faced me, still smiling, still making my breath hitch. His hand at the back of the couch reached up and gently fingered a tendril of my hair, twirling it around, pulling tenderly, then tucking it back behind my ear, making every part of my body tingle. "What was your favorite thing to do as a kid?"

I had to swallow down all the swirling feelings he was bringing out of me with his gentle touches and smoldering looks. I coughed a bit, trying to use my 'I swear I'm not totally turned on by you' voice.

"Well," I managed, swallowing again. "After my dad left, it was just me and my mom for a while so I didn't really get a normal childhood. Mom was always working, and I was either with a babysitter or home alone. My mom didn't like me to play outside if she was at work, ya know, in case I got hurt or kidnapped or whatever, so I mainly just stayed in my house and read or drew. I think that's where my love of fashion and design came from, actually. I would read all these books and then imagine what the characters were wearing and draw it." I laughed to myself as a memory surfaced; something I hadn't thought of in years. "At one point, my entire room was wallpapered in drawings I'd done of costumes. I was particularly fond of ball gowns. Dresses really. Anything fancy." I blushed as I realized I was rambling, but Riot was just staring at me with his sexy caramel eyes and I couldn't think about dresses anymore. All I could do was look into his eyes and smile like a fool.

His finger came up to the skin of my neck and started making tiny, slow circles there, causing my head to fall to the side. I was enjoying his touch entirely too much.

Suddenly, we heard the front door open and we both leapt back from each other, like high schoolers caught in a bedroom with the door closed. My head turned to look down the hallway and I saw Nancy walking toward me, her cheeks flushed and eyes bright.

"Hi, Kalli. Have a nice evening?" she asked, just before she rounded the corner and saw Riot sitting on the couch. "Oh, my." Her hand came to her chest and her eyes didn't even try to refrain from running up and down his body. I rolled my eyes at her blatant appraisal. "Hello, I don't believe we've met. I'm Nancy." She took another step toward Riot and held out her hand to him, smiling all the while.

"Hi, my name's Riot Bentley. I'm a friend of Kalli's."

"Ah yes, the friend who drove through the night to see her," she said, her smile shifting to mischievous. "I'm glad to see you made it safely."

"It was an interesting drive, but totally worth it," he said, winking at me and not even trying to hide it from Nancy. They were both being incorrigible.

"All right, you two, knock it off." I stood up from the couch, trying to hide my wide smile and went to make sure Marcus was on track to get to bed soon. The entire time I was helping Marcus, I could hear Riot and Nancy chatting in the living room. I was too far away to hear their words, but every now and then I heard Nancy's laughter, so I knew he was using his irresistible charm on her.

Once I'd flipped off his bedroom light, I shut Marcus' door and made my way back to Riot.

"Where's Nancy?" I asked as I found Riot all alone.

"She said she was headed to bed. Come here," he said, crooking a finger at me.

I walked slowly toward him, but yelped quietly when he grabbed my arm, pulling me down onto his lap.

He was so large. It was impossible to not feel small when he wrapped his arms around me and pulled me into him. It was an instinct I didn't know I possessed to snuggle into him. I'd never been a snuggler. I'd been a 'Hit It and Quit It' kind of gal. I wasn't ashamed of my past with men—I didn't feel there was anything to be ashamed of—but I'd definitely skipped the parts where intimacy was involved. And sitting on his lap with his arms wrapped around me, his heartbeat thumping just below my cheek, well, it felt intimate as fuck. But it also felt right, which was just as alarming.

After a few minutes I looked up at him to ask him when he had to head back to California, but his lips found mine before I had a chance, and I was okay with that. He kissed me, just like he had at the view point, and I eventually found myself straddling his lap again, my body searching for the friction it craved.

My hands cupped his jaw, feeling the stubble of his beard which had been growing for a few days, imagining the scratch of his skin on other parts of my body. His hands found my ass again, and somewhere in the back of my mind I tucked away that little observation, thinking perhaps Riot Bentley was an ass man.

He pulled away, his mouth landing at the base of my throat, kissing down, stretching the neck of my shirt, all while his hands found their way under it, skimming up my belly. He was moving toward second base and I was *so* ready to feel his hands on me, when suddenly he pulled back. His lips left my skin, his hands left my shirt, and my eyes shot open as I gave him a confused look.

His head was leaned back on the back of the couch, eyes closed, breaths heavy.

"Are you all right?" I asked, my fingers coming to touch my lips that felt raw and used, thanks to his stubble.

"Yeah," he said, rubbing his hand over his face. "That just got really intense."

He must have seen the confusion on my face, or the hurt, because honestly, I was feeling both. His hands came up to cup my face and he pulled my forehead to his lips, pressing a kiss there.

"Kalli, we don't have to rush into anything. I'm not in any hurry. That doesn't mean I don't want to be with you, *trust me*, I do. I just don't think this is the right time. Ya know? And I don't know if I'd be able to stop if I went any further. If I got my hands on you, I wouldn't be able to stop for anything."

This was weird. I'd never been told to wait before. Never been turned away.

"So, you want to sleep with me…," I said, my voice trailing off as I tried to work through our situation in my mind. "But, you don't want to sleep with me tonight." I looked to him for confirmation and his eyes were narrowed.

"I want, *desperately*, to sleep with you, Kalli. I want to spend hours on your body, and I plan to, but not tonight. Your brother's down the hall, your, uh, Nancy is down the hall, too. It's not the time or the place. Plus, we've got plenty of time to figure all this out."

I listened to him, and knew he was right, but it was still strange to me to have a man turn me away. I sighed and continued on with my original question I'd tried to ask before we'd made out on my couch.

"So, when do you have to go back to California?"

"I have to leave in the morning, early. In fact," he said, as he pulled his phone out of his pocket, jostling me as I still sat square on his lap, "if I'm going to get any sleep, I should probably head back to the hotel. I've only got about seven hours before I have to be on the road again."

I tried not to let my inner pout show, but I was letting the pout fly free in my mind. I hadn't seen a whole lot of him while he'd been in town, but it was more than enough to give me a taste of what it would be like to have him around all the time. I couldn't help but feel I was going to miss him, which was something I would need to get accustomed. So many new feelings came with Riot.

So, instead of pouting, I swung my legs off him, stood up, and offered him my hands to help him up. With a smile, he took my hands and hoisted himself upward, bringing himself to tower over me again, but he only let go of one of my hands, still holding the other. This time, he laced his fingers through mine and I couldn't help the blush or the smile that came over my face. I was like a teenager, butterflies and all.

"You're sweet when you smile," he said, brushing a thumb over my now-pink cheek.

"I don't remember smiling more than I have in the last twenty four hours."

"I'll take that as a compliment," he said, slowly bending down to place a quick, chaste kiss on my lips. I didn't bother responding because every word I thought to say sounded remarkably like gibberish as all my circuits were going haywire.

He walked to the door, pausing with his hand on the doorknob, looking back at me.

"I had a really great time with your brother tonight. He's pretty awesome."

I nodded, afraid if I opened my mouth the lump forming in my throat would fall right out.

"I'm hoping you'll want to continue what we've got going here, Kalli. I know I'm headed back to California, but I really hope we can talk and get to know each other better." He bent at the knees, bringing his face level with mine, and I couldn't help but smile at him for it. "I want to know everything about you," he whispered.

"I'd like that," I whispered.

"Great," he said, a smile shining across his face, lighting him up. "Can I kiss you goodbye?"

"I'd be a little upset if you didn't," I confessed.

His hand, which was still holding mine, wrapped around to my back, pressing our hands just above the curve of my ass, pulling me into him, and our lips met as if they were drawn to each other. He kissed me hard and deep, my hand finding his hair, and his tongue sliding over my bottom lip before he pulled back and walked away without another word.

Chapter Ten

I Want to Be The One

The next morning I woke up to a text message waiting for me from Riot.

Hitting the road. The last two days were incredible. San Francisco seems very far away at the moment.

I smiled at his words, but knew the distance would do me some good. After he left the night before, I had tried to evaluate the situation with a rational mind, tried to think of the obstacles in our way, the problems we would encounter. I didn't want to go into it with rose-colored glasses; I wanted to be realistic. I had to be. I wasn't some single twenty-year-old girl with her first real boyfriend. I was a thirty-year-old woman, with a job, and—for all intents and purposes—a child. I had responsibilities that I needed to maintain. I couldn't let some butterflies in my stomach derail my life.

But as the smile spread across my face, all my reasons to rein myself in flew out the window and my fingers began furiously responding.

Drive safely. San Francisco is pretty far, but it's a short plane ride.

I had no idea why I sent him that. I wouldn't be getting on a plane to see him any time soon. Instead of overanalyzing, I flung my covers off and headed toward the bathroom, wanting to start my day to keep my brain occupied.

And that's how the next six weeks of my life went. Riot and I texted and talked constantly. Even if he had very little time, he called me every night. I found myself, at the end of the day, looking forward to his calls, longing to hear his voice, to tell him how my day had gone. If I was at home, he'd Skype me and talk with Marcus. They'd have manly conversations about superheroes and videogames, while Nancy and I rolled our eyes at each other.

All the talking let us get to know one another, without the pressure of his sexy face and irresistible body. Although, there were a few times the conversations drifted toward the sexy.

Send me a picture. I miss you.

I'd sent him selfies a few times since we'd been talking. I'd never dared to send him anything racy, but something about the way he asked made me confident that he wanted to see something besides my smile. I got out of my bed, stripped out of my frumpy pajamas, and put on a black lace lingerie set I'd bought a while back, but had no real reason to wear until then. I lay in my bed, bent one knee up, and positioned my phone right above my head, aiming downward. I snapped the pic, then turned it quickly to check the outcome.

I gave myself a satisfied shrug, surprised the first try had turned out acceptable.

The picture was faceless, but caught my entire body from the chest down. I fiddled around with a few filters until I found the most flattering effect, then sent him the file, biting my thumbnail while I waited for a response.

When my phone finally pinged with an incoming text, I couldn't get to it fast enough.

Fucking hell, Kal. You can't send a man a picture like that when he's eight hundred miles away!

I wore a ridiculously huge smile.

Sorry. You asked for a picture.

Yeah, but damn, baby. What the hell am I supposed to do with that?

Send me one back.

You don't want to see me right now.

Yes, I do.

It took a few minutes, but my phone pinged and my mouth gaped open when the picture popped onto my screen. I swallowed, but it was difficult, as my mouth had gone dry. Riot sent me a picture of himself wearing only a pair of black boxer briefs. He was in a pose much like the one I'd picked for my picture. But instead of my soft curves and creamy complexion, he was all hard muscle and tanned skin. Good God, his abs were like speed bumps. All eight of them. His thighs were massive and well defined, and he had just the right amount of chest hair.

The most interesting part of the picture, however, was the part of his body between his abs and his thighs.

The hand that wasn't holding the camera was gripping the waistband of his underwear, right below his navel, and pulling the fabric down. *Down.* Low. There was an obvious bulge, but nothing was visible except just the base of his cock, which was also covered by the most delicious manscaping. It was the happiest trail I'd ever seen in my life, and I immediately started to regret our text conversation.

I was suddenly very hot, squirming in my bed, and very alone.

You're right. This was a bad idea.

I bit my thumbnail as I waited for his reply. I was startled when my phone started ringing, Riot's name appearing on the screen. My finger came up, trembling slightly, swiping to the right to answer. I put the phone to my ear, but said nothing, could form no words.

"Kal," he growled, his voice low and raspy.

"Yeah?" I tried to reply, whispering, just air moving through my lips.

"Fuck, Kalli, I hate that you're so far away." He was groaning, my name falling from his mouth with such angst, with need. I couldn't help but picture his hand moving under his briefs and my eyes fluttered closed at the thought, my breath catching. It was ironic that he thought I was far away, because in some ways, I'd never felt closer to someone than I did in that moment. "What are you doing?" he asked, his voice so rough, he almost sounded angry.

"Lying in bed," I managed.

"Touch yourself."

"Ri," I groaned, a blush spreading from my chest upward. "I've never...," my words trailed off, my brain partially malfunctioning.

"You've never touched yourself?" I could hear the smile in his voice.

"No, I mean, I've never had phone sex before."

"Hmmm…," he groaned again, and the pulsing between my legs became almost painful. "Well, we could stop and hang up, but at this point, I'm doing this with or without you, and I'd much rather do it with you, babe."

Oh. My. Fucking. God.

"Okay," I breathed.

"Good girl," he said, the smile still evident in his voice. "Now, why don't you take off your bra and panties? I want to know you're naked."

I put my phone down and with still shaking hands quickly did as he'd asked. My hands fumbled and I ended up giggling nervously, but calmed myself before I picked the phone back up.

"Okay," I whispered. "Done." There was a pause. "Now what?" I stifled a laugh. I was nervous and uncomfortable, unsure of what was supposed to come next.

"Are you laughing?" Riot asked, his voice no longer smiling. It was dark, almost menacing, but ridiculously sexy. My laughter died immediately.

"No," I answered.

"Good. Now, look down at yourself and tell me what you see. Paint me a picture."

"Um, I'm still lying on my bed, just like in my text, but now I'm naked." Surely, my naiveté when it came to being sexy over the phone should have turned him off, but his raspy voice continued, so I listened.

"What do your breasts look like, Kalli? I've imagined them a thousand times. Tell me what they look like."

How does one go about describing one's own breasts? My brow furrowed. "Riot, maybe this was a bad idea. I'm not very good—" I was cut off by his voice.

"Just look at them and tell me about them. Please," he said, softly. I was a sucker for his politeness, it seemed. So I took in a deep breath and then looked down at myself.

"Well, they're not small, but not too big. Just right, if you ask me."

"I agree," he whispered. "What about your nipples? What color are they?"

My heart stopped when he said 'nipples.' I swallowed hard and my eyes closed. "I don't know, I guess they're a pinkish-brown."

"Fuck, I bet they taste delicious."

Holy.

Crap.

My pulse was beating exclusively between my legs, thumping, pounding, aching. Without hesitation my hand found my breast, gently squeezing, relieving some of the pressure from my core. "Oh, God," I moaned unintentionally.

"Are you touching yourself now, Kal?"

"Mm hmm," I muttered.

"Where? Tell me."

I was torn between being humiliated and being ridiculously turned on. I didn't want to talk anymore; I didn't want to say anything else. But I did want to listen to him. I wanted to do whatever he told me to, just to hear his reaction, so my libido won out.

"My breast. I'm touching my breast."

"That's fan-fucking-tastic," he growled. "What does it feel like?"

"It feels amazing. It's soft and full. Warm too." My fingers pinched my nipple and I moaned louder, biting my bottom lip to try and keep my sounds muffled. A current of electricity ran from my breast straight to my core, arching my back off the bed. My heels drew up, bending my knees, and my hips arched. "Ri," I cried quietly, wishing so badly he was there.

"I know, baby. Shh. Can you move your hand lower?"

I didn't even think about it, my hand just slid smoothly down the valley between my breasts, over my torso, past my belly button, and when I reached the edge of what little pubic hair I had, my breath caught.

"Riot," I quite nearly whined.

"God, Kalli, my hand is on my dick and I so wish it were you. I'm so hard for you, but my hand isn't what I want. My body wants you so bad."

His words urged me on and my fingers slid lower. When they smoothed over my clit, my lungs contracted, a sharp breath pulling in, and my legs jolted. All my nerves were on high alert, like a rubber band stretched too thin, waiting to snap.

"Where is your hand, babe?" he groaned.

"Inside me," I whimpered as I slid two fingers all the way into my depth, gasping.

"Are you wet?" he asked. And even if I hadn't been, after hearing him ask, it would have been inevitable. His deep voice rolled over the words, like rough silk. Silk that had been torn and abused. It was so fucking sexy.

"I'm so wet," I moaned, quietly.

"Shit, Kal. Fucking Christ. Imagine it's me. I'm there, and my hand is inside you, pumping in and out. My mouth is on you. I'm kissing your stomach, moving up to your breasts. I can't get enough of you. Are you with me?"

"Yes. I can feel you touching me. It's so good, Riot." My hand found a rhythm, blissfully slow, and achingly shallow, just enough to tease. Then my fingers moved up to my clit, circling, then back down again. It was both incredible and yet entirely unfulfilling because I wanted it to be him.

I slowed my own ministrations and listened to him on the other end of the phone. His breath was falling heavily, and every few seconds I heard him give a shallow grunt. I could also hear his hand working over his erection and the image I conjured up in my head made my body convulse with pleasure. My hand went back to work, sliding in and out of me, but I made sure to listen to Riot; I wanted to hear him when he came.

"Are you thinking of me?" I asked him, my voice hardly a whisper.

"God-fucking-yes I'm thinking of you," he growled.

We both got to a point where words weren't necessary, all I needed was the sound of his breath, hot and ragged against my ear to bring me to the brink. My hand found a quicker, deeper pace, a rhythm and cadence that matched his breath, trying to sync to him however I could. It wasn't until my slick fingers put that cadence and pressure on my clit that I found my release. I groaned loudly, back arching off the mattress, knees splayed wide, head thrown back as far as possible. It was an earth-shattering orgasm, lasting so long, I worried Riot would think I'd hung up as I'd dropped the phone mid-spasm.

When I picked it up again I could hear he still hadn't finished, and the sounds he was making nearly had me reaching south again.

"Oh, fuck," he growled. He took deep breaths in, held them, and then exhaled quickly. "Christ, Kalli, I'm almost there."

I had no words to urge him on, couldn't think of anything to say because my body was still in overdrive, still buzzing from my orgasm, even more aflame hearing him so close to coming. Finally, I heard a long groan and then silence, followed by heavy breaths. Eventually, after we'd both regained our senses, he finally spoke.

"You there, babe?"

"Yeah," I said quietly, rolling from my back to my side, suddenly very conscious of my state of nakedness. I was very rarely naked unless I was showering. To lie naked on my bed wasn't something I was accustomed to.

"Are you all right?"

"I think so, are you?"

"Yeah," he said softly, and I could imagine his hand running over the stubble of his jaw, making me smile. "Listen, Kalli, I'm sorry. That shouldn't have happened like that. I took it too far." He sighed loudly and my heart nearly stopped because, although unexpected, I didn't regret what had happened. If anything, it just made me miss him more than I already did.

"I'm not sorry," I said, trying not to sound hurt, but failing. "You sounded like you enjoyed yourself. What's there to be sorry about?"

"I did enjoy myself, but Kalli, God, the first time you came for me I should have at least been there. I'd give anything to see you like that. I want to be the one to make you feel that way, and not over the phone."

"Oh," I replied, a little shocked by his words.

"Yeah, *oh.*" I heard rustling on his end and pictured him standing up from his bed, perhaps walking through his house. One of the few times we'd Skyped, he'd taken me on a virtual tour of his apartment in San Francisco. From what I could tell, it looked small and very much like a man lived there alone.

"Kal?"

"Yeah?"

"When's your next break between jobs?"

"I leave tomorrow and I'm out of town for two weeks, but then I've got a few weeks with nothing lined up."

"Okay," he sighed. "Can I come to Seattle to see you when you get back? I'm dying here, Kal. I thought it would be easier to be away from you, but it's just getting more difficult." He laughed a little. "I probably sound like a huge pussy, but I just want to see you. Like, I honestly just want to lay with you in my arms."

The tingles that floated through my body at his words caused a shiver to run along my spine. I had never spent the night with a man. I was more of the 'pounce then bounce' variety of woman. But the idea of spending a night wrapped in Riot's strong arms brought about more emotions than I was capable of dealing with. Of course, there was Marcus to consider. I'd never slept with a man, and he'd never woken up to a man in his house.

Regardless of the sleeping arrangements, my answer to his question was simple.

"Yes," I said, relief coursing through me at the thought of seeing him again. "Yes, please, come to Seattle. I would very much like to see you."

"You'd very much like to see me?" he asked, sounding a little wounded. "Babe, be prepared. I'd very much like to reenact what just happened between us, only next time we'll use each other's bodies. You all right with that?"

I swallowed hard, arousal lodging in my throat. "Um, yeah," I replied, meekly. I tried to push ideas of logistics out of my head, tried not to focus on the worry that sprung up, and tried to just let myself feel the excitement of knowing Riot would be in Seattle to see me in just two weeks.

Chapter Eleven

A Little Broken

"Nancy, do you have everything you need?" I yelled from Marcus' bedroom, trying to make sure I had everything in his bag from my mental list. Sometimes Nancy and Bob liked to take Marcus on trips with them, so I wasn't unaccustomed to packing a bag for him, but it was hard to concentrate on the task at hand when I knew Riot's plane was in the air, heading toward Seattle.

It had been eight weeks since we'd seen each other. Eight long weeks. All of which I'd spent trying to contain the feelings that were growing. I kept trying to lid them tightly; keep them shoved down in that part of me to which I never let myself have true access.

But I couldn't deny the fact that my body was anxious to be near him. He'd made so many promises of what he would do to me when we finally were reunited, told me all the ways he wanted to use my body. So, naturally, it was all I could think about.

"I think we're ready to go, dear," Nancy called from the living room, startling me from the Riot-induced haze I found myself in often. I zipped up Marcus' bag and carried it to the door where he and Nancy were waiting.

"All right, Marky. Your suit is in there, along with your toothbrush and toothpaste. Change of clothes, pajamas, and a towel." I handed him his bag then pulled him into a hug. "Be good and listen to Nancy and Mr. Bob, all right?"

Marcus rolled his eyes at me, but agreed nevertheless. "I'll be good."

"See you in a few days, then."

"Don't worry about a thing, Kalli. He'll be just fine. Enjoy your weekend," Nancy said, and I didn't miss the wink she threw at me before she closed the door behind her.

I let out a nervous breath, grabbed my own bag, and then left, heading for the airport.

My Range Rover was parked at the arrivals turn-about and I was trying to wait patiently for Riot to come from the direction of the giant revolving doors.

I was a mess of nerves. I was taking deep breaths to try and calm myself down, but the butterflies in my stomach and the constant roller coaster I seemed to be riding kept me from achieving any kind of peace.

Then, when my eyes finally found him, everything that had been going haywire in my body halted, and I was just left smiling and bouncing lightly on the balls of my feet.

He looked like the epitome of a bad boy walking through the airport doors. He was all tight white shirt, blue jeans, combat boots only half-way laced up, and aviators. My entire body tightened at just the sight of him. But then his eyes found me, he smiled, and I melted.

He was carrying some sort of rucksack over his shoulder, the t-shirt deliciously tight over his biceps, and his smile was just for me.

I tried not to look like a giddy fool as he neared me, but I could not contain the happiness which was radiating from me.

When he made it to me, he dropped his bag on the concrete next to his feet, and then there was no distance between us, no space at all. He pulled me to him with his big hands on the sides of my face, but I definitely went willingly.

And then his mouth was on mine. There was no hello, there was no awkward I-haven't-seen-you-in-two-months hug; it was the kiss to end all kisses. His hands went directly into my hair, then slid down my back as his tongue begged for entrance into my mouth.

I wrapped my arms around his neck and let him in—in every way I possibly could. It was impossible to keep him out, and what's more, I didn't want to.

When he pulled away he was smiling.

"Hey," he said, out of breath, voice ragged.

"Hi."

"I'm really fucking glad to see you."

"I gathered that." I giggled as he kissed me again. His arms came around my waist and he picked me up off my feet, bringing our faces level, kissing me again. When he put me back down he didn't let go right away, but moved his face into the crook of my neck and just held me. "I'm glad to see you too," I whispered into his shoulder.

When we finally managed to pull away from each other, he bent down to grab his bag and I led him to the back of the Rover, opening the trunk.

"So, I have some plans for us, if you're cool with not staying in Seattle." I gave him a hesitant smile, hoping he didn't have his heart set on sticking around Washington.

"I couldn't care less where we are, Kal. I just want to spend some time with you."

I let out a sigh, still trying to acclimate to having him right in front of me. "Okay, well, my best friend decided to elope, so she's out of town with her new husband. But his mom called and said there was something up at their house at the beach. Something about the alarm panel battery being low, so the company keeps calling her about it. But she has no idea how to change it, so Ella asked if we could go down to the beach house and fix it." I gave him a hopeful smile, and pushed up on my tiptoes to give him my best eyelash bat. "We get to stay at their beach house for the weekend," I added, hoping it would seal the deal.

"Kalli, really, I don't care where we are. Sounds fun."

"Okay, but it's, like, a five hour drive."

"Kalli, get in the car. We're going," he said with a laugh, which caused me to laugh.

I made it to the freeway and once we were on the straightaway he reached over, took my hand, and pulled it to his lap, lacing our fingers together.

"Are Marcus and Nancy meeting us there?"

"Um, no," I said, trying not to sound nervous. "Actually, Nancy and Mr. Bob took Marcus to the water park for the weekend. So, it'll be just us."

"Ah ha," he said, catching on.

"I'm sorry, is it too soon? I mean, people don't usually go away together for a weekend on their third date. We can go back if you want, or I can go by myself. I totally understand if you want to back out." I was rambling because I was nervous, and words were spilling out of my mouth so fast I couldn't have stopped them if I tried. Riot's hand reached up and cupped the back of my neck, gently massaging me there.

"I *want* to spend the weekend with you, and as much as I like Marcus, I'm actually really glad he won't be there."

"Yeah?" I asked, turning to look at him, trying to keep the blush on my face from overheating me.

"Yeah," he said, leaning toward me to place a kiss on my temple.

And the butterflies were back.

He wanted to be alone with me.

Why did Riot Bentley make me feel like a nervous teenage girl? Why did he cause all the tingles and nerves I'd always associated with inexperienced women? I'd had my fair share of men—hot men at that. Actors and rock stars. I'd slept with some men who went on to be very big deals.

"Okay," I said, trying to smile and not seem like the bumbling fool I felt like. "So, how was your flight?"

"It was good. I got a window seat and I was able to look over my new script for a bit," he said, moving his hand back to mine, pulling it onto his lap again.

"You brought it? That's exciting. Do you need help memorizing lines or anything?"

He chuckled. "Maybe. It's not that big of a part, so it shouldn't be too difficult."

"Hey," I said, turning to him. "It's still prime-time TV. Don't sell yourself short. This is a big deal."

And it was. Riot had landed the role of a new recruit rookie cop on a very popular network drama. He'd told me about the audition the day it happened and had felt confident that the casting director liked him and, sure enough, he'd gotten the role. It was just a three-episode deal, but the producer had mentioned something to him about it possibly extending. Riot had been humble, yet excited, when he'd told me about the job. And, for once in my life, I was excited for someone else, too. I was so proud of him. And, truly, I couldn't wait to see his handsome face on my TV.

"I just don't want to get ahead of myself. I want to do good work on this and then maybe they'll give me more episodes."

My eyebrows drew in and I frowned a little. "Would you move to LA if they gave you a contract?"

He shrugged. "I don't know. I've thought about that. I guess it might make sense to move down there if they were to write a part for me. I couldn't afford to live in both places."

"That makes sense." I wasn't sure why it bothered me to think of Riot moving farther south. He was already a plane ride away; it didn't change anything really. But I couldn't shake the feeling of slight panic that came over me when I thought of him being farther away than he already was. He already felt a little unattainable.

"You should come to San Francisco one of these days," he said, smiling at me. "It's a beautiful city. There's tons to do. Marcus would have a blast."

My heart lurched at the mention of Marcus. What kind of twenty-seven year old Hollywood actor dated a woman with a mentally disabled brother, and at every turn, was amazingly considerate and thoughtful? There were times, especially over the last eight weeks when all our communication was limited to the phone, where I had to remind myself that no one was perfect; that Riot wasn't flawless. Eventually, he'd have to show me the part of him that would drive the wedge in between us. It was those thoughts that kept me up at night.

I knew eventually the other shoe would have to drop. I just couldn't anticipate how much it was going to hurt when it finally happened. My mind flashed to the night my father left and all the tears I'd cried, and my throat started pinching.

I tamped down the emotion, not wanting to taint our weekend with the inevitability of our separation.

"Hey," he said, sweeping the pad of this thumb over the back of my hand. "You all right? You got quiet and far away all of a sudden."

"Yeah," I replied, trying to sound cheery. "I'm fine, and I think Marcus would love to visit San Francisco."

"Well, we'll have to plan for that," he said, giving me the world's sexiest smile.

We continued on our way to Lincoln City, the five hour drive not seeming that long, as we never hit a lull in conversation or an awkward silence. One would think, after spending eight weeks on the phone, we'd have run out of things to talk about, but not once did we scramble for words.

On top of the fun conversation, Riot made sure his hand was always touching me somehow. Whether he was holding my hand or resting his on my thigh, he was always connected to me somehow. At one point, for many miles, his hand rested on the back of my neck and every once in a while, he lightly trailed his fingers across the sensitive skin there. Goose bumps prickled my skin and shivers ran down my spine. It was hard to concentrate on anything when his hands were on me.

It had been a very long time since his last visit, since his hands had been on me, but my body remembered him and was begging for more contact.

It was early afternoon when we finally drove past the sign welcoming us to Lincoln City. I pointed out a building just inside the city limits.

"See that building right there? That's Porter's mom's bar."

"Porter is your friend's fiancé, right?"

"Well, husband since two days ago, but yeah."

Riot looked out the window, focusing on the sky. "We're a long way from California," he murmured.

"Welcome to the Pacific Northwest," I said through laughter, watching him eye the dark gray clouds in the sky. "It's probably going to rain the entire time we're here. Sorry," I said, my laughter tapering off.

"I don't mind being indoors." He used his dark, low, and gravelly voice which did nothing to keep my blood from pooling in my core. I inhaled deeply, trying not to let him see that his words had such an effect on me.

"Well," I croaked, then swallowed, blushing because it was so obvious I was flustered. "We can get the battery on the alarm fixed and then have dinner at Tilly's, then we can rent a movie or something."

"Sure," he said, all the while smiling as if he knew a secret.

So I gave up. He was obviously trying to get a reaction out of me. "You're terrible," I muttered. He squeezed my knee in response.

When we pulled up to Porter and Ella's house, Riot let out a loud whistle.

"Your friend owns this house?" he asked, obviously impressed.

"My friend's husband *built* this house. With his own two hands."

"It's massive!" he said in disbelief. "There's no way...."

"You've never met Porter. Trust me, it's possible."

Riot scoffed. "If you know a man who could build this house *himself*, I don't want to meet him. I would melt into a pool of emasculated mush around him, I'm sure."

"First," I said through my laughter. "Porter, although very masculine, is not a jerk and it's not like he walks around carrying logs on his shoulders or something. Second, he is madly, deeply, and irrevocably in love with his new bride. You have absolutely no competition in Porter."

"You don't think I could carry a log on my shoulders?" he asked, straight faced.

"You're ridiculous," I said, still laughing, as I got out of the car.

I walked up to the door, unlocked it with the key Ella had graciously given me months ago with instructions to 'use the house whenever you want.' I'd never been there before without Ella or Megan, but I knew the lay of the land and the house was magnificent.

Once inside the door, I turned to see Riot walking up the steps carrying both our bags.

"Oh, thanks," I said, not used to men carrying my bags.

"No problem. I mean, they're not logs or anything...."

"Oh, my God," I cried, laughing again. "Shut up about the logs." I rolled my eyes and tried to take my bag from him but he wouldn't let me get close enough.

"Just tell me where to put them," he said with a smile.

"Follow me." I led him up the stairs to the second floor. I stopped at the first door on the right. "So," I said as I stepped into the room. "There's this room." I swept my arm out like a model from The Price is Right. "There's an attached bathroom and partial ocean view." I motioned to the one picture window. "There're also two more rooms down the hall, but neither of those have bathrooms or pretty views." When I turned back to him, I was surprised to find him just inches away and closing in.

I yelped as his hands gripped my waist, easily picking me up and tossing me onto the bed. When I stopped bouncing, I was pressed into the mattress by his body.

"I don't want to talk about bedrooms, Kalli. I just want to feel you, underneath me, in a bed." His hands found my wrists and he pulled them up above my head, clasping them both together with just one of his huge hands. "I've been dreaming of getting you beneath me for weeks, Kalli. Months if I'm really honest with myself. Ever since I watched you walk onto that soundstage."

"Well, it looks like you got your wish," I said breathily as I stared into his caramel eyes.

"Did I?" He sounded sullen all of a sudden, and I couldn't help but become concerned. But before I could say anything to him, his lips were lowering to mine and my eyes were closing in anticipation of the contact.

When his lips met mine, my body went pliant and obedient, and he melted into me. My knees drew up around his waist, he settled into me, and I welcomed him. My body molded around his, needing every bit of contact he offered. His left hand still pinned my wrists above my head, but his right hand came to my waist, his fingers brushing the skin just underneath the hem of my shirt.

His hand inched up, his mouth moved over mine, tongue swiping past my lips, his deep voice growling a moan into me. When his hand came to barely brush the edge of my bra, I froze. My heart started beating rapidly and my breathing quickened. Both were too fast, both were uncomfortable. As quickly as my lungs were working, my breath was shallow and I couldn't get in enough air. I started to panic. I pulled on my wrists and Riot quickly got the message and released me.

Once my hands were free, I pushed him off me and rolled over, finally feeling like I could take a deep breath. I sat up, putting a shaking hand to my face, trying to simply regain any semblance of calm.

"Kal, what's wrong?" Riot asked from behind me.

I couldn't answer so I just shook my head. His hand came to my shoulder and the panic that had started to subside slammed back into me, so I pulled away and tried to stand.

"Kalli, what's going on?" he asked again; this time the worry in his voice was thick.

I couldn't listen to his voice, couldn't hear his concern, so I stood and on wobbly legs made my way to the bathroom and shut the door behind me. Once inside, I took a few more deep breaths and started to feel the panic ebb a little.

I filled the little cup by the sink with water and took a sip, closing my eyes for just a moment, trying to figure out what in the world had gone wrong.

I startled when there was a soft knock at the door.

"Kalli, I'm going crazy out here. Are you all right?"

"Yeah," I replied, but my voice was shaky and weak. "I'll be out in just a minute." I gripped the edge of the counter and stared at myself in the mirror. I couldn't help but wonder what in the world was wrong with me. I'd wanted Riot for weeks now. Long, torturous weeks we'd spent dancing around the idea of being together. Phone sex had only happened the one time and after that I felt like anything besides actually being with him would pale in comparison, so I'd never let our phone conversations go that far again. But, man, we'd teased each other. Talked each other in circles with what we'd do to each other, how much we were longing to just *be together*. And now that he was here, in the next room, a room *with a bed*, I'd managed to have my very first panic attack.

What in the actual fuck?

My head dropped. I was clearly crazy. Who pushed a man like Riot Bentley off her? I took a few more deep breaths. I looked to the door and I knew he was on the other side waiting for me. My eyes closed and all I saw was Riot over me, pressing me into the mattress, and my breath hitched in my throat. I snapped my eyes open and shook my head, trying to shake off the visual.

I opened the bathroom door to see Riot standing squarely in front of it, arms crossed, chest out, eyes worried, and jaw tensed.

"Are you all right?" His words were curt and sharp.

"Yeah," I answered meekly.

"What happened?"

I moved forward and thanked him silently for stepping aside and letting me pass into the bedroom. I eyed the bed again, the comforter obviously mussed from us, but I couldn't let my eyes linger there, so I moved to the window to look out at the ocean and the sun setting on the horizon.

"I'm not sure," I said, resting my palms on the wide windowsill. "All of a sudden, it was just all... too much, I guess."

"What was? I was? I'm sorry, Kalli. I didn't mean to push you—"

"No, it wasn't you. You didn't do this." I took another deep breath. "There's something wrong with me," I said, wiping away a tear that had suddenly appeared from nowhere, without warning. "There are fundamental things wrong with me, Riot. I shouldn't have let you get this close; shouldn't have given in to it." I turned just slightly and saw him still standing between the bed and the door. "I'm sorry."

"I'm still really confused. What exactly is it that you think is wrong with you? 'Cause, to me, you seem pretty fucking perfect."

His words sliced through me, causing more phantom tears to run down my face. "You can't keep saying all these nice things to me, please. It only makes it harder."

"Makes what harder?"

"Walking away from you."

"Listen, I understand if you need to take things slower. I get it and I'm sorry. I can take it down a notch, Kalli. I swear I can, and I will. But you're not walking away from me. I won't let you. Just talk to me." He sounded so sure, but also a little broken. He took a step toward me but I held up my hand to stop him. I couldn't be any closer to him.

"I'm not made for this," I gasped, trying to hold on to air that was slipping away from me. It was something I'd known about myself all along—my entire life—but in that moment, it hurt more, cut deeper, than it ever had. And I could only determine it was because I'd never wanted to be with someone as much as I wanted to be with him. "I can't give myself to anyone, and when we were kissing me and I felt your hands on my skin, all I wanted to do was give you all of me." My hand came to my chest, as if the weight of my own hand could stop my breaths from panting in and out of my lungs.

"That doesn't make sense, babe. I want you, all of you. You don't have to be afraid of me, of us. If you want to be with me, then *be with me*. Pushing me away, punishing yourself, will only end up hurting us both. Can't you see that?"

"I couldn't do that to you. Couldn't tie you down that way. Couldn't tie myself down. I don't want to be still, Riot. I can't *just be*."

He looked at me with sad eyes for what seemed like hours, just staring, hardly blinking, but not speaking. When he did finally move, it was his head that fell forward as he took in a deep breath. When he looked back up at me, he was resigned.

"All right then. Let's get that battery fixed." He turned and walked out the door, and I heard his footsteps moving down the stairs.

Chapter Twelve

In Too Deep

It had been a painfully awkward drive to the small hardware store in Lincoln City, but once I'd shown Riot the panel that needed repairing, he'd taken to the task silently and hadn't once said a word to me. I tried to be helpful, to offer assistance, but he'd politely snubbed me, just shaking his head.

I was being torn directly down the center. Half of me wanted to reach out to him, tell him I was willing to risk everything to be with him, while the other half of me was sure I'd made the right decision of pushing him away.

I was sitting in a magician's box, cut in half, and Riot was standing over me, saw in hand.

How would I ever put myself back together?

I'd made my way onto the porch, looking out at the sky, listening to the waves—not visible for all the trees—wrapped tightly in my favorite comfy sweater. I heard the door open and looked over to see Riot walk out, closing the door softly behind him.

"Battery's all installed."

"Thanks for that," I said, turning back to the sound of the ocean.

"It's not a problem." His words sounded a little sad.

"Do you, um, want me to drive you to the airport? I can drive you to Portland, or back to Seattle even. Your choice."

"My choice?" he said with a sharp bite to his words. "You'll give me a say? That's kind of you."

I opened my mouth to apologize, to tell him I was sorry for everything, more than he could ever know, but no words came out and I was left with my mouth gaping open.

"Listen, as far as I'm concerned, I could really just go for a beer. My flight doesn't leave until Sunday night from Seattle, so perhaps we could just try and spend the evening here and go back to Seattle tomorrow." He paused, still not looking at me. "I think I'd like to go to that bar you showed me on our way in to town, but I get it if you don't want me to take your car, so I can call a cab."

"Is it all right if I go with you?" It was painfully uncomfortable here in this house, so I figured leaving with him, going someplace neutral, might ease the tension. "I mean, I'll stay here if you'd prefer, and you can just take my Rover. You won't be able to get a cab out here."

He sighed, but then spoke. "Just let me wash my hands and grab my jacket."

Twenty minutes later we walked into Tilly's, and the level of noise was overwhelming. There were people laughing, chatting, yelling across the bar at each other; but everyone was happy and smiling. It was a real slap in the face and a reminder that Riot and I were existing in a very awkward bubble.

I let my gaze roam around the restaurant and I finally locked eyes with Tilly. It took just a moment for her to register it was me, but I saw her face light up when it clicked, and I watched as she excused herself from behind the bar and made her way toward me. I'd only actually seen Tilly a few times over the summer, on random days when I'd met Ella and Porter at the beach for a day, but she was always welcoming and that night was no different. She came to me, arms open, and wrapped me in a hug.

It was instinctual to let myself relax into her embrace. Tilly was the mom of all moms and I didn't have mine anymore, so when Tilly hugged me, I let her. And I let myself feel it. When she pulled away, after many more seconds than a normal acquaintance hug would last, it was still too soon.

"Riot," I said through a breath, "this is Tilly. She's Porter's mom."

"Nice to meet you," he said to Tilly, reaching out to shake her hand. "Porter is the guy who just married your best friend, Ella, right?" he asked me.

At the word married, Tilly's expression became pained for just one moment, before a beautiful smile spread across her face.

"Those kids are in a lot of trouble for running off to get married without me," she sighed, obviously trying to hold back a tear or two. I reached out and rubbed my hand up and down her arm.

"I have a feeling a lot of people will be giving them guff when they get back," I said, trying to comfort her as best I could.

"Yes, well, I suppose as long as they're happy and plan on giving me a grandbaby soon, I can't complain. They're obviously very happy, and I love Ella, so I'm beyond ecstatic." She took in a deep breath and then smiled at Riot. "It's very nice to meet you. Any friend of Kalli's is more than welcome here." He smiled back at her and nodded in greeting. "Are you kids here for dinner?"

"Yeah," I said, rocking back on my heels, trying to pretend everything between Riot and me wasn't fucked up.

"Great, follow me. I'll get you a good booth."

We sat and Tilly left us to go back to her job. With cold beers sitting in front of us and dinner ordered, we were left to combat another awkward silence. Right when I'd built up enough nerve to try and talk to him, my phone rang. When I pulled it out of my bag I saw it was Nancy.

"I'm sorry, it's Nancy, I have to take it."

He nodded, then put his beer bottle to his mouth, taking a long pull, and I tried not to stare at his Adam's apple as it dipped low when he swallowed. I mentally berated myself for being turned on by something so strange, but God, it was sexy.

"Hey, Nancy, how's it going?"

"Just fantastic, honey. We just wanted to call before we settle in for the night. Would you like to talk to Marcus?"

"Sure," I said, smiling immediately, listening to Nancy tell him that I was on the phone, then rustling.

"Kal?" He sounded tired.

"Hey, bud. Did you have fun today?"

"Yeah, this is an awesome place. There's even a huge water slide! I must've went down it, like, a thousand times."

"That sounds awesome. What are you doing right now?"

"I'm in my pajamas, getting ready to watch some TV in my tree fort bed."

"Your bed is a tree fort?"

"Yeah, it's huge and made of big tree trunks and I'm on the top! I'm not even scared to be up high."

"Wow. That sounds cool. Tell Nancy to take a picture with her phone so I can see it when I get home."

"Okay. Hey, is Riot with you?"

"Yeah," I answer, a little confused as to why he was asking.

"Can I talk to him?"

"Um, let me see if he's available." I held my hand over the phone and whispered to Riot, "Marcus wants to talk to you. Do you want me to tell him you're busy?"

Riot's face pulled back as if he were offended, then he just held his hand out. I placed the phone in his hand, kind of feeling like a scolded child.

"Marcus?" Riot asked into the phone. "Hey, buddy. I heard you're at a water park for the weekend. That's awesome." He paused and I could hear the excited murmuring of my brother on the other end of the line. Riot's gaze was on the table, but I couldn't help but look at him, watch him as he listened to my brother talk about his day. "Do you get to go swimming in the big pool again tomorrow?" he asked, then listened again. "Well, tomorrow you should see how long you can hold your breath. Does Mr. Bob have a watch?" Pause. "Yeah? Cool. Have Mr. Bob time you. I bet you can't hold your breath underwater for twenty seconds," he said, daring my brother. Then he laughed, still looking down at the table, his beautiful smile reaching all the way to his brown eyes.

My breath caught watching him and my heart ached. Somehow, over the last two months of being apart, I hadn't realized how much I'd grown to care about him. It was safer when he was far away, when he was just an idea or a voice. But when he became tangible, when his hands moved over my skin, the fear seeped back in. It was easier, two months ago, to be with him, because I hadn't cared that much about him. He was just a guy to whom I'd been attracted. But now, with so many weeks of texts, calls, emails, and late night conversations between us, I couldn't deny that I so much more than *liked* him. I was falling for him.

"Okay, buddy. Be good for Nance and Mr. Bob, all right? You'll have to tell me tomorrow how long you could hold your breath for, all right?" He smiled, then said, "Bye, bud." Then he ended the call and handed me the phone back. I looked at it, a little offended that my brother hadn't wanted to say goodnight to me, but not concerned enough about it to call him back.

"Thanks for talking to him. I'm sure you made his night."

"I'm not a jerk, Kalli. I care about Marcus; why wouldn't I want to talk to him?" He let out an irritated breath and ran the back of his hand under his chin, the sounds of his stubble scraping along his skin sent tingles directly to my core, sent shivers through me and I wanted to hear that stubble rough and scraping against my skin. "Just because you've decided to push me away, it doesn't automatically erase everything that's happened between us. I still care about you and about Marcus."

"I don't think you're a jerk. I've never thought that about you. Please don't be angry; this is hard on me too. You don't think I'm confused?"

"I don't know *what* you are because you won't talk to me, Kalli. You open up more to me when I'm two states away than when I'm right in front of you. Why is that? Why are you closing up and pushing me out?"

"I don't know," I whispered.

"Well, that's a lie," he said softly. "You might not know the right words, but you know how you feel, and I wish you would tell me."

I was silent for a minute, my heart thundering in my chest, trying to find the courage to tell him anything. When I finally was able to put some thoughts into words, his eyes were soft and he listened.

"It was easier when you were far away," I said first, my voice quiet, but still loud enough to be heard over the bar noises. "You felt less threatening when you were just a voice on the phone." I noticed he tensed at my words and I panicked a little, not wanting to offend or hurt him. "Not, like, physically threatening. More like an emotional threat. This isn't making any sense," I said dejectedly, pulling my hand through my hair.

"Please keep going. I want to hear what's going on inside your head, Kalli. It doesn't have to change anything. I'll still go back to San Francisco and leave you alone if you want me to after this, but I think we owe it to each other to be honest about it."

I took a deep breath and went on. "It hadn't occurred to me how much I'd started to care for you until you were here, in front of me, touching me. I knew I was excited to see you, excited to be with you, but nothing could have prepared me for how I would feel when you put your hands on me in that bed. It was really scary."

"Scary how?"

"Scary because I'd never felt that way with anyone else. I'd never let a man touch me and thought about not letting any other man touch me ever again. Because anyone else's touch would pale in comparison to yours. I'd never been in a position of needing anyone, and I knew if we were together, I'd need you."

"It's okay to need someone, baby. Or to want them, even. That's normal." His voice was so soft and comforting. He reached across the table and took my hand. I let him hold it, let myself feel this thumb brushing over my skin. But eventually, I continued.

"Here's the thing." I took in a breath and it shuddered, nerves and years of pent up sadness finding their way to the surface. "The only man I've ever needed left me." Before I could even feel the tear slip down my cheek, Riot had moved to my side of the booth, his arm was around me, and he pressed his lips against my temple. I leaned in to him, just like I'd wanted to a million times since I'd pushed him away, and let myself melt against him. "When you were in California, it was easier. You were there, I was in Seattle. We were already far apart. There was still something left between us. And I guess it was space, but it was also sex. I don't know," I whispered, pressing my face into his neck, my mind growing tired of thinking all the heavy thoughts.

"No, I get it. I think it might have been easier for you to open up to me because I was on the phone and not right in front of you. If I'm in front of you, I can turn my back on you. But Kalli," he said, pulling away and putting his finger under my chin, lifting my face toward his. "I'm not going to turn my back on you. I couldn't. I'm in too deep."

"What does that mean?" I whispered.

He was quiet for a moment, his eyes searching mine. When he finally spoke, he did it as he ran his thumb across my bottom lip, watching it trail across my skin there. "Think of it like this: there's a rope between us, tying me to you, wherever you go—I go. And if I go one way, you come with me. Does that make sense?" he asked, still looking at his thumb on my lip. I nodded slightly, mesmerized by his touch and his words. "So, when we're apart, do you feel the pull of the rope?"

I nodded again, because I did. I felt it all the time, but only in this moment, with his face so close to mine and his arm so snug around me, did I recognize it for what it was— a connection.

"That's me, tethered to you. That's us. Together." He leaned down and pressed a kiss against my mouth, sweet and soft. "You can fight it if you need to, but it doesn't change the fact that I'm still tied to you, and you to me. You're mine."

In that moment I wanted nothing more than to let my guard down and give in to him, allow myself to just let go.

"It's not that simple," I said.

"Why not? What's complicated about it?" he asked, his hand moving to push a lock of hair behind my ear, then resting on my neck in *his way* that made it hard for me to breathe.

"Marcus."

"Marcus isn't a complication," he said immediately, his gaze never faltering from mine. "Marcus is your brother and I get that."

"He's not just my brother; he's my responsibility. I can't just jump into a relationship with someone and jeopardize him that way." My voice was shaky and adrenaline started coursing through me, coming to my brother's defense.

"Hey, hey, hey," Riot whispered, bringing my body closer to his, pulling me in, recognizing my panic. "I'm not trying to upset you. I just want to talk about it. Whatever you decide I'll deal with, but just talk to me."

"Our lives are already not optimal. My job keeps me away from him a lot of the time. And I don't know what I'd do without Nancy, but she's not his mom. He's not her responsibility. I can't spend time away from him to be with a man."

"I've never asked you to spend time away from him."

I thought back to our times together and realized that since I'd told him about Marcus, he'd been very understanding, and even a little bit wonderful.

"Listen," I said, pulling my body away from his, trying to get some distance from his touch. "I can talk all I want and I feel like you're going to have an argument for every point

I'm trying to make. That's all well and good, but it doesn't make the way I *feel* go away. And I feel scared."

He looked at me, stone still, not even blinking. When he finally moved, it was his mouth saying, "There's nothing I haven't already said to try and convince you to be with me. I'm not going to abandon you, and I'd never hurt you. And Marcus isn't a deal breaker for me. He's a perk." He continued to look at me, then shrugged. "That's all I've got, Kal. I'm offering myself, any part of me that you will take."

We were interrupted by the waitress bringing our plates to the table and another awkward silence ensued as we started to eat.

"I'm sorry. I didn't mean for our dinner to become so serious with heavy conversation. Can we just, I don't know, forget the last twenty minutes for a while and talk like people who aren't in the middle of a huge decision?" I asked, hopefully. I might be terrified of getting my heart broken by Riot, but I knew I could always talk to him. We'd had weeks of seemingly endless and fun phone conversations. Surely, we could do a dinner.

"Sure," he said easily, a slight smile coming across his face. "What should we talk about?"

"Will you tell me about your family?"

"All right. There's not a whole lot to tell. My mom left Lebanon when she was eighteen to study art in France where she met my father who was there backpacking the summer after he graduated from high school." He took a pull from his beer and I made myself look away; I didn't want him seeing me ogle him. "So, they spent four days together, and when it was time for him to leave and move on to his next stop, she went with him. They've been together ever since."

"Wow, that's really romantic," I said wistfully.

He shrugged. "You'd think, right? But they're just like any other married couple, I guess."

"Do you ever visit your family in Lebanon?" I'd always admired Riot's tanned skin and stark black hair, and now that I knew where it came from, it was even more appealing.

"Not really. I went there once when I was really young, but after my grandparents passed there wasn't really a reason to go anymore."

"You mentioned once you have a sister, right?"

"Yeah. Halah."

"Wow, that's a gorgeous name."

Riot laughed. "My dad, who grew up mostly in the eighties, thought Riot was a perfect name for a son—you know, the optimal anarchist. But my mom drew the line in the sand when it came to her little girl. She picked a Lebanese name, and it was even a little bit on the edge of acceptable names for a girl, so my dad agreed."

"How old is she?"

"She's twenty-four."

"And where is she?"

"She works on a cruise ship."

There was never an answer to a question that surprised me more than that one. "Excuse me?" I said through a laugh.

"Yeah." He laughed too. "A few years ago there was an article in the paper for job openings on a cruise ship. She thought it would be fun, she applied, and she's been cruising the Caribbean ever since."

"So, she just floats around on a cruise ship? Doing what?"

"She's kind of like an activities director. So, people who want to *do stuff* on a cruise ship have her to thank. I think she teaches a lot of the physical activities on the ship. She does rock climbing, Zumba, water polo. Stuff like that. She's a mover."

"Sounds like it," I laughed.

We sat in silence for a few minutes, both of us picking at our meals, the waitress bringing us both a second beer.

"So, tell me," Riot said between bites. "What are Marcus' plans after high school? Do you guys ever talk about how he'll spend his time when he isn't in school all day?"

I nod, then took a sip of my beer. "I don't know if *he* fully grasps that next year he won't be going to his school anymore, but I'm fully aware of it. Some of his teachers he's been with for a while have suggested I let him age out of high school by letting him go for a fifth year, but I'm not sure. There are some community programs at the community college I could get him into, like art classes he could audit. Other than that, I don't know." I pulled my hair around to one side of my neck, just needing something to do with my hands, a little uncomfortable with the topic of conversation. Change was not something Marcus was comfortable with, so in turn, neither was I.

"I didn't mean to stress you out," he said thoughtfully. "Let's change topics." He thought for a moment, his face serious and pensive. "Would you rather… cut off your own finger with a butter knife or watch a semi-truck run over your leg slowly fifteen times?"

Despite the abhorrent visuals that ran through my mind at his words, I couldn't help but laugh at his approach. "What in the actual hell did you just ask me?"

"You heard me," he laughed. "What? You've never played Would You Rather before?" His eyes were alight with amusement, his boyish smile back with a vengeance.

"I can't say that I have."

"It's simple. You just pick two really terrible things and then ask the other person which they'd rather do."

"Um, okay, that's pretty demented."

"Well, I think it originated in the male mind, so that's pretty good for an explanation. Now, pick one."

Three hours and two beers each later, Riot and I were still laughing. Our earlier argument and disagreement had been laid to the side and we spent our evening simply enjoying each other. Patrons of the restaurant had long since left and we were watching Tilly and her night crew close up shop. One of the waitresses turned the radio on overhead and a top forty station played through the speakers.

"So, you'd honestly let a dog lick fish guts off your face rather than eat a rotten apple pie?" Riot asked me, his face a little red with the effects of beer and smiling.

"Yes," I said with surety. "One doesn't include me eating anything nasty, so I'll take it." I picked up my beer and took the last sip. Riot, who was still sitting next to me in the booth, took the empty bottle from me, placing it down on the table top softly.

"Would you like another? I think we could bribe the owner, even though it's after closing," he said with a wink. Tilly had been by our table numerous times, never pressuring us to leave, inviting us to stay, actually.

"I better not. But I should probably drink some water."

"I've got it," he said, hopping up and taking our empties to the bar. I watched as Tilly smiled at him, then looked back at me. She filled a tall glass with water and slid it across the bar to him, all the while talking to him about God only knew what. He finally backed away from the bar and headed back to me.

As he was walking, some of the lights shut off, leaving only the flood lights. Riot walked back to the table and I simply couldn't keep my eyes off him. The swagger with which he walked, the way his shirt stretched across his chest, how his jeans were hanging low on his waist; it was all too much to take in and I found myself holding my breath.

He set my water in front of me, but didn't try to sit down. I brought the glass to my lips, eager for something to occupy my thoughts and distract me from his body, which was a little too close at that moment.

I heard Tilly's voice coming from behind him, loud and lovely.

"All right, kids. I'm going to take off. All you have to do is turn off the radio and make sure the door latches behind you."

"Wait, Tilly, we can leave." I moved to grab my purse and started scooting out of the booth.

"Don't be silly, it's early yet. Use the pool table, drink some more water, have fun," she said, smiling.

"Um, all right. If you're sure?" It was a little strange that Tilly was going to leave us in her restaurant after closing, but she was too convincing to give a good argument. She winked and then walked out the door.

"See, we were able to salvage the evening just fine," Riot said, laugher in his voice.

"I suppose you could say that, although, I think I know more about the inner workings of your demented mind than I'd like to." I took another sip from my glass and then looked up at him, his caramel colored eyes twinkling back at me, the low flood lights making his already dark skin look even darker.

"Can I ask you a serious question?"

His voice was suddenly not full of laughter as it had been just seconds before, and I swallowed hard, my body reacting to the new way his eyes were looking at me.

"Sure."

Chapter Thirteen

Simply Together

"Wanna dance?" he asked, holding his hand out to me, palm up.

"Here?" I asked, looking around. "No one else is dancing."

"That's because no one else is here," he said, laughing again. "Come on, Kal. Dance with me."

His eyes were sparkling, even in the dim lighting of the bar. I couldn't say no to him, but his gaze left me speechless so I was unable to say yes either. I answered by placing my hand in his. He led me to the middle of the restaurant, which wasn't exactly a dance floor, but I wasn't complaining because he was holding my hand. He placed my hand on his shoulder and one of his hands landed on the curve of my waist; his other hand clutched my free one, lightly holding it against his chest. I swallowed, trying not to think about the firmness of his chest beneath his t-shirt.

A slow piano started a new song; a sleepy rhythm and a soulful voice filled the empty bar. We started swaying back and forth to the beat of the music.

"You're a good dancer," Riot spoke softly as I tried to avoid his gaze.

"This isn't dancing, really. This is rhythmically stepping side to side," I answered, smiling a little. His response was to pull me a little closer and pull my hand into his body, curling his fingers around mine as far as they would go.

Then he started to add a little spin in our steps, leading me in gentle, tiny circles.

A percussion dropped in with the piano, adding dimension and a heartbeat to the song. I listened for a moment to a man singing about tomorrow bringing better days, about letting go of yesterday. I felt the words deep down inside of me, but was more aware of Riot's hands sliding from my waist and flattening against the small of my back, pulling me closer into him. My hand automatically freed itself from his grasp and moved up his chest, joining my other hand at the nape of his neck. His free hand moved down my side, caressing me as it traveled over my body. I was alight with the electricity he moved through me. His hands were like lightning rods; a storm was brewing in that bar and his hands were going to be the end of me.

Every part of me was buzzing with his energy and I was pressed up against him, soaking it up, relishing it.

When we stepped to the beat of the music, our hips punctuated the syncopation. His leg wound up between my knees as we continued in our electric circle.

"Are we dancing yet?" he whispered in my ear.

"Yes," I stammered, dropping my cheek against his chest. The song grew louder, the singing fuller, more soulful. I felt the music in my bones, but couldn't tell if it was the song that had my heart thundering in my chest or the way Riot's hips pressed into mine as our dance continued, or the way his hands were no longer staying still, but wandering across my back. One hand traveled dangerously close to the curve of my bottom, the other tangled in the hair that fell down my back.

I gasped at the feeling of his hand owning me. He knew he was breaking me down, cracking away the glass walls I'd put up around me. With every sway of our hips, with every breath I felt feather across the skin of my neck, I was sure he could feel me crumbling. I knew that after this I wouldn't be able to push him away again. I knew he wouldn't let that happen. I was never going back to that place. Not after I knew, for sure, what it felt like to be pressed against him like this.

I gripped his shoulders hard when his hands pulled my hips into him, pulled me closer to him. His thigh between my legs, my heat burning up against him, was overwhelming.

"Riot," I gasped, wanting to bite into his shoulder to keep myself level, but resisting.

"Kalli," was all he said in response. I'd heard him say my name a thousand times. That time, that moment with his hands on me and every part of me throbbing for him, my name falling from his mouth was the most beautiful sound I'd ever heard.

His hands slid up my back, over my shoulders, up my neck to cradle my face. My eyes stayed closed. I was afraid to open them and see him, worried he wasn't as affected by this as I was.

"Look at me, Kal," he demanded and I couldn't refuse. My eyes opened slowly, and I was met with eyes that looked just as electrified as I felt. "Stand still with me," he said just before his mouth came softly to press against mine. I couldn't help but cry into him for everything I felt with just one touch of his lips on mine. His hands were grasping at me, pulling on any part of me he felt, and I just let myself go with him.

"Do you feel that, Kalli? That rope between us?" He pressed those words into my neck, saying them between kisses laid on my skin there, my head tilting back to let him have his way. "I'll tie you up so tight, baby."

I knew what he was asking, what he wanted from me, and in the back of my mind I was in agreement. I wanted so badly to let go of all my fears and let him keep me safe. But the most prominent thought, the one I could grasp firmly a hold of, was that I wanted him to take me. I wanted him naked and I wanted him over me.

He must have sensed the urgency in my kiss because the next thing I knew, Riot had lifted me up, my legs wrapping around his waist, and he was walking through the bar. My hands were on the back of his neck, and his were both planted firmly on my ass. I kissed him with all the reckless abandon four beers allowed me, biting down gently on his bottom lip.

He growled through the kiss, attacking me back with his own teeth. The kiss was wet and sloppy, but it was also hot and unrestrained. It was everything I needed in a kiss at that moment and then some.

I felt him lean over and then I was on a hard surface. My hands went down and my fingertips rubbed against the unmistakable felt of the pool table. Once I was safely atop, his hands roamed free, moving anywhere and everywhere they wanted: around my waist, to my thighs, up my belly, under my shirt, over my bra. They were everywhere and nowhere, weightless and heavy, feather-soft and rough.

He climbed up and over me, forcing me to lie back, and my hands naturally found their way under his shirt to grip the hard muscle there. My legs instinctually found their way around his waist. As my legs captured him, he lowered his hips and our centers were deliciously pressed together, the friction there maddeningly and intensely arousing.

"You're lying to yourself if you can't admit you want me," Riot whispered against my skin as he ran his mouth over me. "Everything about your body right now gives you away. The way your breath is panting," he said, pressing a kiss just above my collarbone. "The way your fingers are digging into my skin." His mouth moved up and he nibbled on my earlobe as I tried to stifle a moan. "Even the way you smell right now tells me you want me," he said right against the shell of my ear.

I swallowed hard and tried to keep an even keel, tried not to give in to him so easily, tried not to forget the reasons we could never be, even if he was right and *we* was all I really wanted.

"Do you want me?" he asked, his hand skimming over my breast. All I wanted was for the layers of fabric between us to disappear. I wanted him inside me, all over me, around me—any way I could get him. And I didn't have the self-control to lie out of self-preservation anymore.

"Yes," I rasped.

"Yes?" he asked, running his nose up from the hollow of my neck all the way up my chin.

"Yes. But not here." I looked in his eyes and silently pleaded with him to get me back to the house, take me in a bed, and make me forget I had a million reasons to send him away.

"Let's go," he said, swiftly lifting off me and grabbing both my hands, pulling me off the table and to a standing position in one strong jerk. He held one of my hands, and strode toward our table, pulling me along behind him. He walked past the table, swooping in to grab my purse and jacket, but never stopping, and continuing toward the door.

He continued right out the door, and I had the presence of mind to grab the handle and make sure it shut tight behind us.

"Riot, the radio. Tilly asked us to turn it off."

"She'll understand," he responded curtly. He walked hurriedly through the mostly empty parking lot, finally stopping next to the passenger door of my Rover. "Keys," he barked at me.

"Are you angry?" I asked, digging in my purse for my keys.

"No, I'm not angry. I'm in a hurry and I'm worried if I take too long you'll change your mind and I'll miss my one chance to be with you."

I looked up at him and saw the fear in his eyes, the worry. He wanted this, me, and felt like perhaps I might slip right through his fingers again. My hand reached out and gripped the front of his t-shirt, pulling him toward me. I fixed my eyes on the wrinkles in his shirt, trying to have the courage to tell him how I was feeling.

"I think, for one night, I'm going to give up on pushing you away. I can't do it anymore. I can't fight it."

"Can't fight what, exactly?" he asked, running his hand down the back of my hair, gripping it at the end, and pulling it gently, urging me to look him in the eye again.

"Can't fight the feeling that my body was made to fit yours, fight the urge to let you do things to me that will push me further than anyone ever has, or fight the way my body reacts to your touch. And I want to feel you touch me everywhere."

His grip on my hair tightened, and my head leaned back even farther as I watched his face dip down to the crook of my neck.

"And you're saying I can only have you for one night?" His voice was low and had tiny explosions prickling over every inch of my skin.

"It's all I can promise," I gasped as his lips made contact, then his teeth, nipping at me.

"God, I want so much more, Kalli, but I'll take whatever you'll give me."

He took the keys from my hand and I heard the horn beep and the locks click. He opened the door and motioned for me to get in.

"You're not driving my Range Rover," I said, laughing at his ridiculous notion.

"Babe, you've had four beers."

"*You've* had four beers."

"I've also got eighty pounds on you."

"But—"

"Kalli, get in the car. Four beers over four hours isn't enough to impair my driving."

I narrowed my eyes at him but relented. "Fine. But you should know, I don't let anyone drive my car," I huffed as I hauled myself into the passenger seat.

"I bet I can convince you to do a lot of things you've never done before," he said, winking, then closed the door. I watched him as he walked around the front of the car with a cocky smirk on his face.

He managed to drive back to the house with no help from me. At the beginning of the drive his hand found its way to my knee. His hand was hot and I could feel its warmth all the way through the denim of my jeans. Slowly, as we made our way through the mostly empty streets of Lincoln City, his hand migrated north, and so did the heat.

By the time we made it back to the house, his hot hand was practically between my legs and I was mere seconds from shamelessly rubbing myself against it. Somewhere in the back of my mind, I stowed away the fact that Riot was a master of anticipation. It had started months ago, and now we were erupting with all the sexual frustration we'd hidden away. I hadn't readied myself for the storm that seemed to be Riot, but he was coming for me whether I was prepared or not.

He put the Rover in park in front of the beach house, then got out and came around to my side, and opened my door. He reached in, wrapped his arms around me, and picked me up. I shrieked, then clasped my hands around his neck, holding on even though I knew he had me.

"I am not nearly drunk enough to warrant you carrying me into the house," I complained. In actuality, any buzz I'd had disappeared on the dance floor, replaced by need and want.

"I agree. I'm not carrying you because you're drunk."

"So, why aren't my feet on the ground?"

"I didn't want to give you a chance to run away from me again. I'm not letting go until I'm finished with you."

"Oh," I said as my breath caught in my lungs. He looked at me for just a moment more, but then his eyes moved to the door and he used the hand under my knees to unlock it. He kicked it shut behind us, then made no delay in heading for the stairs. He walked up them as if he weren't carrying a person in his arms and I went a little more breathless for it. I couldn't keep my eyes off his face, couldn't stop looking at him. He was, of course, watching where he was going, but I was soaking up the opportunity to stare unabashedly at him.

He turned into the bedroom we'd originally found that afternoon, our bags still lying on the ground, kicked that door shut as well, and then walked to the bed, stopping for nothing.

He approached the bed and climbed on with his knees, making his way to the headboard, and gently placed me down so that my head landed softly on a pillow. He pulled his arms out from underneath me, but never lost contact.

He moved so his body was between my legs, one hand on my belly just slightly under the hem of my shirt, the other hand planted near my face keeping him just a few inches above me. He leaned in and pressed his mouth to mine, but it wasn't needy. It wasn't the kiss I expected after all the buildup during the drive over. It was sweet and a little innocent.

He sat up, one hand still on my skin, moving up and down my front, just teasing, while the other hand reached into the back pocket of his jeans. He pulled out his wallet and dropped it on my stomach. With his free hand he flipped it open then reached inside and pulled out four condoms, still attached to each other. He used his mouth to rip one off the strip, tossed the remaining three on the night stand, then took the one from his mouth and left it right next to my pillow.

"You've come prepared," I said, my voice raspy and a little shaky.

"I've been waiting for this for a long time."

"Have you? Two months isn't a terribly long time to wait."

His hand moved up to the side of my neck then moved into my hair as his mouth descended on mine again. *This* was the kiss he'd silently promised me on the pool table and in the car; this kiss was nothing but need and want. Heat and fire. His tongue swiped through my mouth, intent on tasting every piece of me.

Both hands now gripped my shirt and he broke the kiss to pull it over my head. His kiss continued, but moved off my mouth, over my chin, and down my throat. When his mouth stopped between my breasts, his forehead rested against my chest and he uttered quietly, "I've waited my whole life for this."

We were frozen, only his breath moving against my skin now ablaze with his touch.

"Riot," I finally whispered, unsure how to proceed. His words were huge, they meant something huge, and he'd said them against me. His lips had said those words against my skin. Even the most meaningless sentence became sacred when pressed against skin. So, how could I ignore what I'd heard, what I'd felt him say into me?

"Don't. Don't push me away. Don't use my words against me. Just let me love you the way I want to. You said you'd give me one night. You never said it had to mean nothing."

He wasn't looking at me. His face was still pressed against my chest, but I could hear the way his voice was shaking, feel the way his fingers were gripping me a little tighter. My hands went to his hair, running my fingers through it, trying to soothe him even a little.

Riot had never been anything but completely honest with me, and in that moment, I had nothing but honesty for him. He'd earned it and I deserved it. I deserved to have this moment with him where we were both fragile and vulnerable and open.

"Hey," I said, trying to urge him to look at me by placing my hands on the side of his face. "Look at me." It took a few seconds, but he eventually brought his eyes to meet mine. "It doesn't mean nothing." I whispered. "You've never been nothing to me, Riot. You're so much more than what I've lead you to believe."

He slowly came back to me, kissing me, laying all his weight on me. This was, possibly, our first completely honest kiss; the first time we kissed with no pretense, no bullshit, and no expectations. The first time his lips touched mine and I wasn't worried about how I was going to forget the way they felt against mine, or how I was going to push him away when things got too deep. No, this was a kiss that communicated exactly how I felt about Riot, and I could feel all of his emotions as well.

He rolled off me, pulling me with him, until we were both lying on our sides and then he started unbuttoning my jeans. This started a sort of domino effect of clothing being removed, and clothes were shed as if a tornado had swept through the room. He was pulling off my pants while I was tugging on his shirt. I was pushing my socks off my feet with my toes while shoving his pants over his hips. With his lips still pressed against mine, I arched my back and reached behind me to unclasp my bra, removing it and tossing it on the floor next to the bed.

And just like that, we were naked.

There was no slow build up, no anxious reveal, and no awkward 'does he like the way I look without clothes on' moment. It was quick, hasty, rushed, and perfect. It was also a relief. A relief to finally be bare with him, bare *to* him. My naked skin was pressed up against his and we were simply together. Having his bare skin touching mine gave my body the same satisfaction as a loud and heavy sigh, as if I'd been waiting for that contact my whole life and finally, it was happening. I didn't realize my body had been waiting for this.

He was still pressed up against my side, his leg thrown over mine, and his hand began to wander over my body, trailing from my neck, down over my breast, past my navel, causing involuntary shudders. When his fingers gently parted me, softly teasing the most sensitive area of my body, he finally spoke.

"Are you all right?" he asked, still trailing his fingers just outside of my opening, causing my toes to curl into the mattress with anticipation.

I nodded urgently, silently begging him to simply undo me, to touch me where I'd been craving the feel of his hands for weeks. When his fingers slipped into me, he kissed me at the same time and all I could do was release a moan into him. His tongue moved to the same rhythm as his fingers, and the effect was maddening. He pushed in, then pulled out, so lazily that my mind was screaming at him to quicken his pace, to do something more than tease me.

My hips began to meet his hand at every thrust, trying to elicit more from him, to take more than he was willing to give me. Finally, his fingers moved into me and stayed pressed inside, and his mouth came away from mine.

"You're perfect," he said, his mouth just a hair's breadth from mine, his fingers reaching far inside me, then stroking upward. He held my gaze for a moment, watching me writhe beneath his hand, then his gaze traveled down my body, watching his hand work me over.

I gasped at the sensation, his fingers moving over my g-spot so intensely, so acutely, every muscle from my belly button down was tense and moving toward rigid. My knees drew up and my hands reached out and wrapped themselves around his bicep, simply looking for a way to ground me to him. He was going to push me over the edge quickly, I could tell. My body, primed for this for weeks now, was simply not going to last much longer without giving him what he wanted.

Just when I was at the very rim of my orgasm, about to plummet into bliss, he pulled his fingers away and slowly stroked my wetness, up and down. The abrupt change in sensation and tempo had me reeling, keening, and nearly panicked. My body both loved and hated what he'd done; loved the way his wet fingers felt against the hot, warm skin of my labia, but hated the absence of the wound-tight feeling in my core. The feeling was like picking up a music box and turning the dial on the bottom. You turn and turn, and slowly the dial becomes more difficult to move, harder to twist, until you get to a point where it simply won't turn anymore and you feel like if you were to turn it just one tiny fraction more it would burst and fall apart in a million miniscule fragments. That's what it was to have Riot's fingers inside me—like being wound to the point of fissure. Only, just when the glorious point of fracture approached, his fingers retreated, along with my orgasm.

As he used his fingers to lazily spread a trail of my wetness all around my opening, his mouth found my nipple, pulling it in and sucking hard. I mewled, of course, because my body didn't care about pretenses or politeness around Riot or his mouth and hands. My body simply wanted to find that place where he was going to give me that ultimate high. So when he used his mouth, no matter where, my body was going to agree—quite loudly.

"I could never have imagined how hot it would be to see you like this," he said, his mouth still pressed against the swell of my breast. "You're so needy," he mumbled, taking my nipple in his mouth again. "I want to give you whatever it is you need."

My response was another moan.

"Tell me what you need."

"I need you back inside me," I managed, but only out of necessity. My words barely audible because my body would have performed any number of miracles at that moment to only get him back to the place where his fingers made my world fall away.

"Like this?" he asked as he slid two fingers in again.

"Mmm…," was my response.

Then his fingers worked inside me while his mouth took my nipple again, and his free hand found mine and our fingers laced together. His hand worked faster, gradually speeding up and applying more pressure until I was crying out and writhing on the bed. His mouth pulled away from my breast and his face lowered to mine, our gazes locking as I panted and brought my hand to his face, holding him there so I could see his caramel-colored eyes as I finally reached my peak.

That familiar ball of tension built in my core, radiating outward, tingling all the way down to my toes. My breath hitched, my heart thundered, and then the wave of release swept through me.

"Yes," he growled slowly. "That's it, baby." He slowly pumped his fingers in and out of me, letting me fall back down to him from my high. "You're so beautiful when you come," he said, his lips moving down my throat again as I was still trying to return to normal. "I can't wait to feel you around my cock, gripping me, clenching like that."

He pulled his hand from me, then rolled back on top of me, settling between my legs. He kissed me again, this time slow, but deep. When he lifted from me he was holding out the condom.

"Would you like to do the honors?" He was smiling and I couldn't help but smile back.

I took the condom from him. "Lean back," I whispered. He did as he was told and sat back on his ankles. When I moved to sit up I realized that in our haste to become naked I hadn't gotten a good look at him, so I let my eyes wander while I had him at my disposal. His tanned skin looked good in moonlight and his body was simply covered in muscle.

My eyes fell to his cock and my breath caught in my throat. He was gorgeous and perfect, just like I knew he would be: long, thick, but not overwhelming. I reached my hand out to touch him, wanting to feel him without the barrier of the condom. My fingers shook, but when I reached him I confidently wrapped my hand around him and slid all the way down to the base.

He groaned and I smiled, liking the idea that I was making him feel good.

"You've got a great dick," I said as I stroked him up and down.

"He's never steered me wrong," Riot said, his eyes closed, head tilted back, obviously enjoying the attention. I swirled my thumb over his head, spreading the milky precum around, watching his face as I touched him. His eyes scrunched closed and he moaned, but then his hands were on my shoulders and his eyes were looking right into mine. "Kal, I've got to get inside you, like now."

I smiled and opened the condom then rolled it down his length, which was even fuller and firmer than before. Once he was covered, he quickly pressed me back into the mattress, one hand gripping me behind my shoulder while the other grabbed my ass and hauled it up toward him.

"Are you all right?" he asked again, his eyes full of affection and concern. He was asking for permission and it was adorable. I wanted every part of him in that moment: his sweetness, his roughness, his ownership. I wanted to be everything to him. But all I could do was bite my bottom lip and nod.

His eyes flitted down to my sex, and I watched as he lined himself up with my opening. When his eyes found me again, they stayed on mine as he slowly pushed into me, inch by inch, until he was so deep I thought he'd found a way to bore into my heart. Once he was all the way in, filling me, stretching me, I let out a sound that was half moan, half sigh, and my head fell back with pleasure.

"Holy fuck, Kalli. You're perfect. It's perfect. So fucking sweet." His head was shaking back and forth, as if he didn't even believe the words himself, couldn't wrap his mind around the way it felt. But it was perfect. I'd never felt so *right* with someone before, and all he'd done was enter me. All we were, in that moment, was a connection. But it was perfect.

After a few blissful moments of just feeling each other, he slowly pulled out, all the way to the tip, then slid back in, groaning the whole way. "I knew it would be good,

Kal. I knew it would be amazing. But I never thought it would feel this way." He continued to pump in and out, slowly building up speed and tempo.

All I could do was grip him, pulling him closer to me, hoping that at the end of everything I would still be whole and the totality of me would still be intact.

Riot might have been the most present lover I'd ever had. He was constantly talking, checking in, and whispering things to me, at me. I couldn't always respond because, well, Riot. But his words never ceased to affect me.

"God, it's good," he rasped.

"Do you feel how perfectly I fit inside of you?" he groaned into my neck.

"You're everything," he whispered against my lips just before kissing me.

He pushed me higher and higher, using my body to get the most perfect fit he could find, listening to my body and its reactions, handling me, molding me to him.

It was when he turned me onto my side at the hips, both legs together and pressed into the mattress, with his hands pinning my shoulders down, as he thrust quickly into me, that I found my release. And while usually I felt my orgasms from the waist down, this one gripped me in my chest and shot outward, causing my back to arch off the bed and a loud moan to rip from me.

"Shit," he groaned, taking long strokes through me. "I'll never get this image out of my head. I'll never be able to forget what you feel like, wrapped around me, squeezing me as you come."

His words did nothing to help calm me, but I didn't have time to think about that because suddenly he pulled out, grabbed my hips, and flipped me so my stomach was on the bed. Then he lifted my hips and my knees naturally found their footing under me. In no time at all he was back inside me, gliding in and out, hitting new spots, and I found myself on that familiar climb again, my core tightening around him.

Then I felt his front against me, and his arms wrapped around my shoulders as he pulled me up to him so that we were both kneeling on the bed. My back was up against his front, and his hands snaked around my body, one coming to rest over my breast, the other finding my clit, and his mouth was at my ear. Every single sense was overwhelmed. I could only hear his breath and his words and he pumped his hips up, thrusting forcefully into me. My skin was hyperaware of his, where we touched, when his skin moved against mine. Each nerve ending was in shock and begging for reprieve, but it felt too good to stop. The musky scent of us swirled around me and my eyes watched his hand furiously rub against my clit, asking me to come again. When I licked my lips the tang of salt was there.

"I'm going to come again," I managed, the build-up too intense.

"I know," was his response, and it drove me that much closer to the edge. "I'm going to come with you this time."

I groaned, both at his words and the images they conjured up in my mind, but also at his hard, thick cock stroking in and out of me at such a bruising pace. It was glorious. My hands reached back and fought to hold on to anything I could grasp; his shoulder, his hip, I was trying to stay grounded in him. I was moaning continually, my cries punctuated by his thrusts, and I was inching closer and closer until finally I felt the heat ignite in my core and every muscle seize up.

"I'm coming," I cried, although I wasn't sure my words were audible; it was very possible I hadn't said anything at all, or that I was mumbling incoherently. All I knew was I was on the precipice and he was dragging me over.

"Fuck." Riot's voice carried throughout the bedroom as he groaned and growled, pumping into me as my orgasm flashed through me, reaching every last part of my body. I knew he'd finished coming when his hips stopped pumping and his voice had quieted, and it was all I could do to reach out and press my hands against the wall behind the headboard to keep myself from falling forward and breaking our connection; I wasn't ready for that yet.

His hands moved slowly all over my body: around my hips, up my back, over my shoulders. He shuddered, then slid out of me, sinking to the bed and pulling me backward on to his lap. I was limp and lifeless, still not fully in control, my hands reaching for support from the wall, his lips moving kisses up my spine.

"I can't wait to do that again," he said against the skin of my back.

It was all I could do to laugh and collapse on the bed. He followed me, landing on his back, removing the condom, then tying it off and dropping it to the floor.

"I don't know if that's possible," I said, but it sounded more like a sigh. His arm pulled me to him, spooning me against his sweat-slicked body. Usually, at that juncture, I'd pick up my clothes, get dressed and make excuses as to why I had to leave. I'd lied about meetings, having to work early, girlfriends having emergencies; you name it, I'd lied about it. All to avoid what was happening in that moment with Riot. Intimacy. Closeness. Emotions. Permanence. I'd avoided those at all costs before, but right then, in his arms, I wouldn't have left for anything. I wanted nothing more than to lie in that bed and soak him in. I wanted to let his arms fall around me, hold me close, and snuggle in. Spend a night asleep in his arms. Spend a morning making love again, and in the sunlight, too. "I'm not sure that's something we can recreate." I sounded more wistful than I intended and inwardly cringed at the sappiness of my words.

"Maybe not, but I'm more than willing to try," he responded, his voice mirroring my own, full of warmth. He sat up suddenly and pulled the comforter down beneath us, then lay back, arms open wide, splayed against the crisp sheets. "Come here," he whispered.

There was absolutely nothing I could do except go to him. My head naturally found its way to the crook of his shoulder and my arm draped across his chest. Lined up like that it became painfully obvious I was much shorter than him, as my feet only reached his shins.

I smiled because I liked feeling small next to him. It brought unfamiliar feelings of security, and instead of pushing those feelings away, for once, I decided to let them stay and keep me company as I fell asleep wrapped around the only man who I'd ever let in that deep.

Chapter Fourteen

Make it Official

I woke the next morning to the smell of bacon and the sound of Riot softly saying my name.

"Kalli, baby, wake up. Time to eat."

My eyes fluttered open and I focused on Riot's handsome face hovering just above mine, his boyish grin turning up the corners of his lips. I stretched under the covers, noticing my body ached, but not uncomfortably so. It was a good ache.

"Hey," I garbled sleepily. Then my eyebrows furrowed and my mouth turned into a pout. "Did you make bacon?"

"I did, indeed," he said, laughing and sitting back, holding a plate out for me. I sat up and brushed my hair back from my face, then leaned against the headboard. The plate he handed me was covered with scrambled eggs, bacon, toast and hash browns. The sight of the food, coupled with the wonderful smell, kicked my hunger into overdrive and I realized I was starving.

Riot walked around the bed and picked up another plate from the table on his side and slid in next to me, careful not to spill his food. Then he picked up his fork and started eating as I watched in a state of shock.

We were going to eat breakfast in bed, yet another thing I'd never done with a man, and he was going to act like it was the most natural thing on the planet. He noticed my slack jaw and wide eyes.

"Do you not like your eggs scrambled?" he asked with a full mouth, which should have been repulsive but came across as adorable.

"Um, no. I mean, yes, I like my eggs scrambled. What…." I closed my eyes for just a moment to gather up my thoughts and get them in line. "Where did all this food come from? Ella and Porter haven't been here in a while and they don't usually keep food like this in the house."

"I drove to the grocery store," he said, shrugging, then piling another forkful of food into his mouth. I tried not to notice his lips as the fork was pulled back through them.

"How'd you know where the grocery store was? I'm not even sure I know where it is."

"I saw it when we got into town, and again last night as I drove us home."

"You drove *my Rover* to the grocery store? While I was sleeping?"

He had the audacity to laugh at my outrage.

"Chill out, babe. Your food's getting cold."

I narrowed my eyes at him, but couldn't argue with the growls coming from my belly, so I picked up my fork and started eating. I managed to tamp down the groans that I wanted so badly to release at the taste of the food, not wanting to stroke Riot's ego any more than necessary.

"So, what would you like to do today?" he asked between bites.

"Well," I said just before swallowing. "We could stay in Lincoln City, go to the beach, or walk around the waterfront. Although, it's really not being-outside-at-the-Oregon-Coast weather. We could drive back north and stop in Portland and do something there, or we could go all the way to Seattle and figure it out later."

"Or...," he said, a smile coming over his face. "We could stay here, naked, and watch movies between all the sex."

"All the sex?" I asked, laughing. "You think this is like some sort of buffet?"

"That is a very interesting proposal."

I scoffed. "It's not a proposal."

"I think you'd let me make you into a buffet if I really wanted to." His voice dropped low and I tried to ignore the blush I felt creeping over my face.

"You're being more than a little ridiculous."

"So, what'll it be? Driving all day, or movies and sex?"

"Are those my only options?"

"Those are the only *good* options."

"I choose option B then," I said, just before taking a bite of bacon.

"I'm sorry," he teased, holding his hand up to his ear. "What was that?"

"Oh, my God! I choose movies and sex!"

"That's my girl," he said with a bright smile, leaning over and quickly placing a kiss on my lips.

"You're incorrigible."

"People have called me worse. You have, in fact."

"Well, I meant every word."

"Where was this mouth last night while I was inside of you?"

I choked on my bacon. "Excuse me?"

He shrugged. "You always have a lot to say, but last night you were noticeably quiet." He wasn't looking at me, but I could see his face was worried. He might have been using a playful tone, but he was being quite serious.

"Well," I started. "I was a little too, um, overcome to be talkative. I'm sorry, is that bad?" I had never, not once, had a next-morning check-in about the status of the sex the night before. I had no idea what we were doing, or what answers he was looking for.

"No," he said hesitantly. He rubbed the back of his hand along the bottom of his jaw, making my skin tingle. "I just wanted to make sure you enjoyed yourself as much as I did."

"Ah." I nodded. I picked up a piece of toast and took a small bite, still at a loss as to what I was supposed to say to him. How much information was I supposed supply? I wasn't even sure I knew everything I was feeling. All I *did* know was that being with him was, hands down, the best night of my life. But surely I couldn't tell him that.

"Ah? That's all you're going to give me?"

"I thought last night was incredible," I mumbled quietly. The bed shook slightly and I saw him inching closer to me.

"Incredible?" he asked with a smirk, taking my plate from my lap and placing it on my bedside table.

"Um, I wasn't finished with that," I said, watching my food drift away from me.

"You're hungry?"

His voice was suddenly back to the sexy tone he'd used on me the night before and my body took notice. I swallowed and then replied, "Yes."

"All right, here's the deal: you answer my questions and I'll give you your food."

"Okay." I agreed because there was no way I could have said no to him; my body was already submitting to simply the vibration of his voice.

"How many times did you come last night?"

I blinked rapidly at him, eyes wide. "Excuse me?"

"You heard me," he said, his cool and sexy voice taking on a playful tone.

"You couldn't keep count?" I raised my eyebrow at him.

"Of course I counted, I just wanted to see if our numbers were the same, wanted to make sure you didn't sneak one past me," he said with a wink.

"Does that happen to you often? Women come and you aren't sure? Cause that's a pretty big indication that she actually *didn't*."

"You came once around my fingers and twice around my cock. I know you came because each time I could feel your pussy gripping me, feel your wetness seeping from you, and your toes curling—each time."

"Oh," was all I could manage, because holy shit, that was hot. Not the part about me, but the part about him and what he felt and how, based on the way he was looking at me in that moment, he really fucking liked the way I came.

"Yeah, oh. Were there any I missed? Any quiet ones? Ones that felt like tremors instead of earthquakes? 'Cause the quiet ones can be fun too."

"Um, no," I croaked, and then swallowed, trying to clear my throat. "Just the three."

"Hmm," he said, reaching past me and grabbing my toast, holding it up to my mouth. His eyes didn't leave mine as I leaned forward slightly, taking a small bite. "Now," he said, after putting the toast back. "Before I ask you the next question, I should probably let you know that last night was not something I'm taking lightly. I know we talked about it not being serious, and it just being one night, but I'm hoping I convinced you to reconsider."

"Um, that's not exactly a question," I stated nervously, knowing exactly what he was alluding to, but trying to buy a little more time.

"You're right, my apologies. The question is, did last night make you want to amend your previous statements that *we* couldn't happen?" He motioned with his hand in between us.

"Riot, look." I sighed, unsure of even what I was trying to say; there was so much going through my mind. "Last night was wonderful," I said, putting a hand up on the side of his face, feeling that same stubble he'd run his hand over just moments before. "But I'm no good at this part. I don't know what we're doing."

"We're eating breakfast," he said, deadpan, causing me to laugh.

"No, we're sitting in bed all post-coital and post-spoonage, and you're trying to ask me if I want *more* than what I thought I wanted."

"Do you?"

"Yes! Of course! I always have on some level, but that doesn't mean it's something that is feasible. You and I are living very far apart, and I still have Marcus, and my job, and I just don't see how last night changes anything."

"I'm not looking for much to change, Kal. I'm not talking about anything more than us, or you, admitting that this means something. That we're together. I want to call my girlfriend, I want to send her flowers, and I want to miss her and think about her all the time and get on planes to visit *my girlfriend*."

"So, you want a commitment?"

"You'd be all right if you knew that when I got back to San Francisco I slept with some random chick?"

The sudden swirling of my mostly empty stomach answered that question before the resounding "No!" came from my mouth.

"Then," he said softly, soothing a thumb over my chin, "can't we just make it official?"

"Have you slept with someone else? Since the last time I saw you?" I was suddenly very curious about the idea of him being with another woman. I knew it was a possibility, but I'd tried not to dwell on it. Now, however, I was very anxious to know the answer.

"Of course not," he said, his hand moving back into my hair and resting on the back of my neck. "Have you?" he asked nervously. I bit my lip and shook my head slightly. He exhaled and leaned his forehead against mine. "What are we doing?" he whispered. He sounded pained, as if our conversation was actually hurting him, and that bothered me. I didn't want him to hurt in any way.

"I don't know. All I know is that the way I feel about you scares me. I've never felt this way about someone and I've never felt the need to be *with* anyone like I do with you. I don't know how it's supposed to work, and I don't know, specifically, how it can work between *us*."

"I'm not asking you to rearrange your life, I'm just asking to be allowed in. I just want in."

His voice was so low and needy. His hands gripped me as if he were afraid I'd drift away if he let me go.

"You're in it, I promise you are. And I'd love to be your girlfriend," I said with a tiny, shy smile. His lips came to mine and I could feel his smile against my mouth. My heart lifted at the idea of making him happy. He pulled away and his hands found the sides of my face. "But I need your help, and your patience. I've never done this before and I know I'm going to mess up, make mistakes. Promise me you'll go easy on me."

"You want me to go easy on you?" he asked, a smug grin taking over his lips as he pulled me down further on the bed so I was on my back.

"Well, I mean," I said breathlessly, just his husky voice making me throb. "Only within reason."

"So, you want it rough, then?" His hand reached between us and his fingers found my opening, sliding two in effortlessly. "Christ, you're already wet." He stroked me, rhythmically thrusting inside me, bringing me an orgasm like a quick, hot, lightning strike. Still in a haze, I heard the condom wrapper tearing open, then seconds later felt Riot filling me, confirming what I'd learned the night before—he fit me perfectly.

He was deep inside me when he laid his weight on me, then moved his hands up my arms, finding my hands and linking our fingers together. Then he was kissing me, his tongue stroking into my mouth as his hips matched the rhythm. The combination of the quiet and poignant kiss, coupled with the deep and slow thrusts of his hips, brought up more than just my arousal; suddenly I was emotionally invested, and I realized he was making love to me.

I clammed up with panic at first, never having made love with anyone before. He must have sensed my tension because his mouth came away from mine, only to move to my ear, whispering, "It's just you and me."

I couldn't be sure what he was trying to say to me in that moment, but it calmed me nonetheless. Regardless of my inexperience with relationships and feelings, I had lots of experience with Riot, talking with him, listening to him, laughing with him, and that was all that mattered. I let myself accept all the feelings that came along with his weight, with his connection. I trusted him to keep me safe, even my emotions. And that, in itself, was liberating.

I opened my eyes and saw him looking down at me, his caramel eyes soft and open, then I leaned up and pressed my mouth to his, trying to reassure him that I was all right. One of his hands came loose from mine and ran down the side of my body, brushing over the side of my breast, causing all kinds of goose bumps to prickle over my skin. His hand reached my waist and slid into the hollow created between my body and the mattress at the small of my back, and he grasped my ass, pulling me further onto him, thrusting himself that much deeper into me.

I cried out at the sudden feeling of being gloriously full, and then moaned when his deeper thrusting brought on a new sensation of being wound tightly. My muscles were coiling, the white-hot burning that hurt so good spreading slowly through me, and I let myself surrender to it.

"Yes," I heard Riot growl, but didn't open my eyes. "This is us, Kalli. This is your body loving mine. Only my body does this to you."

"Oh, God," I moaned, very close to reaching my peak.

"Tell me it's only me, Kalli," he said, grunting and panting above me, his fingers clutching at my ass. "Say it."

"You're it," my mouth uttered before I'd even thought the words, my heart obviously speaking before my mind had a chance to intervene. "It's only you," I said, a little slower, willingly and truthfully. His mouth crashed into mine, the kiss urgent and desperate. His thrusts followed suit, becoming quicker and stronger.

When I finally fell into the glorious release of my orgasm, I heard him follow, grunting and moaning as he came. Then, for a moment, we were both still, the only sound being that of our breaths. When he leaned up and looked at me, he was smiling and I found myself mirroring him, the corners of my mouth turning up.

"I never thought you'd agree to be with me. I had planned to spend months trying to convince you that we should be together."

"Well, if that's how you go about convincing me, I should have held out a little longer." He laughed, which sent ripples of excitement through my body, as he was still inside of me. When he pulled out I tried not to audibly gasp at the feeling of loss, at the emptiness. He stood and walked to the bathroom, and I watched him walk away from me, naked, and then rolled into the pillows, making sure the stupid grin on my face was buried in them.

Chapter Fifteen

Happy Looks Good On You

The weekend went by too quickly, and Sunday evening, while standing at the departures ramp at the airport, I found myself in a stereotypical situation I never could have imagined. But, then again, Riot brought out many unexpected feelings in me.

He was leaving and I was sad. Sad wasn't even a big enough word to encompass what was going through my mind. I was going to miss him.

We'd spent Saturday doing the Movies and Sex plan, and then we'd spent the first half of Sunday driving back up to Seattle, stopping along the way at any and all viewpoints, Riot claiming it was our new tradition to see all the viewpoints we across.

"We've got to stop and appreciate the moments, Kal," he'd said as he was trying to convince me to pull off the freeway at the first viewpoint we passed.

"Appreciate the moments?" I laughed at his cheesiness.

"Yeah, I mean, we're going to spend most of our time apart, so when someone throws a sign at you to literally stop and appreciate the view, I want to do that. With you."

So we did. We stopped and got out of the car, taking in the view and breathing in each other, even taking a few selfies.

We laughed and talked the entire way, but always stopped at a viewpoint.

When we made it back into Seattle, we drove straight to the house because Riot was anxious to see Marcus, which warmed my heart.

When we entered the house it was as if I ceased to exist. Marcus dragged Riot back to the family room and the video games commenced. I flitted in and out of the room, trying not to intrude on their Bro Time, as Riot so eloquently called it, but couldn't resist watching the two of them interact and bond.

"You look refreshed," Nancy stated as I loaded the dishwasher absentmindedly, my thoughts back in Lincoln City.

"It was a good weekend," I said, trying not to blush.

"Happy looks good on you," she said, placing a soft hand on my shoulder, her warm voice comforting me more than ever before.

"Do you think I'm setting myself up for disaster here? Is this a really dumb idea?"

"Love is never a dumb idea, Kalli."

My heart sped up its pulse, blood thrumming through my veins. "I didn't say anything about love."

"No, but you look like you're in love. And that's *okay*, Kalli. You, out of everyone on this green earth, deserve love. You give so much of it away, it's only fair that you find someone to give it back to you."

"But he lives so far away...."

"And?"

"And there's Marcus...."

"And?"

"And this could all blow up in my face, and then what? What do I tell Marcus when he asks about him? Or asks if he can come back to play video games with him?" I ask, motioning down the hall toward the room that held my brother and a man I'd developed so many complicated and wonderful feelings for.

"You're spending too much energy focused on the bad things that could happen. What about all the good things? What if that man in there loves you and Marcus more than anything and only enriches your lives? Are you willing to let that pass by because you might, *maybe*, have to one day tell Marcus that he doesn't have a Mario Kart partner anymore?" She tilted her head to the side and gave me a look that made me feel ridiculous, a look that said, 'You're not that dumb, are you?'

I sighed because I knew she was right. No one had ever made me feel the way Riot did, and I would be stupid to let fear keep me from him. But I knew it would be a tough road; hard to transition from being suspicious of love, wary of love, to letting myself accept the love he offered me.

The drive to the airport had been quiet. There were too many thoughts and feelings floating around in my mind to give them a voice. But Riot's hand was on my leg as he drove. Yes, I let him drive my Rover to the airport. He started begging and whining so I relented. Besides, my body was all a mess trying to deal with the emotions bubbling up inside of me, I wasn't sure I could drive properly anyway.

So, there we were, standing on the sidewalk, people with suitcases passing us by, and I was trying to hold back tears.

"What is this?" he asked softly, his hands brushing over my hair, pushing some behind my ear, a smug grin coming over his face. "You look upset."

"Are you going to mock me now?" I said, sniffling, running my hand under my nose in a very unladylike way.

"Come here," he said, pulling me into his chest, wrapping his arms around my shoulders. "I didn't realize you were such a softie," he whispered into my ear, making me laugh.

"I didn't realize it either." I pressed my cheek into his chest, trying to commit to memory how his arms felt around me, what he smelled like, how his stubble rubbing along my neck made the hair on my nape stand on end. But mostly, I tried to lock into place how cherished I felt when I was with him, how glaringly obvious it was that he cared for me.

He pulled away, but his hand found the back of my neck and squeezed, holding me there. "I had an amazing weekend," he whispered, his face so close to mine. His eyes were on mine and they were full of something, darting back and forth between mine. The air around us electrified, pressure built, and I knew something big was coming. I also knew I was helpless to stop it.

His lips caressed mine, slowly, his hand holding on to the back of my neck with firm desperation. Then his lips moved over my cheek, onto my neck, as he hugged me again.

"God, I love you, Kalli."

His words were hurried, pushed out, like he couldn't contain them any longer. They sounded like a relief, as if he'd been holding on to something painful and releasing the words was an assuagement. He sighed and pulled me even closer into him, his thumb rubbing up and down along the side of my neck.

"I'm sorry, but I love you," he said, this time sounding a little more broken than before.

"You're sorry?" I whispered, not really sure what he had to be sorry for.

"I mean, I'm sorry I just blurted it out here, at the airport, around a bunch of strangers." He pulled back but didn't let go of me. "But I'm not sorry I said it. I'll never be sorry for loving you."

His eyes were on mine again. His eyes were the first thing I'd ever noticed about him. And it was perfect that I was looking into them when I said, "I love you, too."

I could tell he was surprised I'd said it back, but the surprise only lasted a moment before I was in his arms again, being kissed as if he were going off to war. It was overwhelming, but in a good way. I let myself feel everything.

"You make me so happy," he said between kisses, playfully pecking. I laughed because the happiness was contagious and immense. It was everywhere and I made sure I tucked the fragment of time away in my memory, because I knew I wouldn't always be that happy. "I'm going to do everything I can to make you as happy as I am in this moment," he said, his voice lower, more serious.

"Why are you so sure you're the happiest person here?" I selfishly ran my hand over his stubble, wanting to feel it one last time before he got on his plane. "What if I'm actually happier than you right now?" My smile actually hurt, it was so big.

"I don't think I'll ever forget how beautiful you look in this moment, happiness radiating from you." He fingered a tress of my hair, then leaned in and kissed me again, slow and deep. If I hadn't been sure I loved him before that kiss, it definitely would have convinced me. He pulled away and licked his lips, as if he wanted to savor and keep every last part of me he could before we were apart, and my body reacted to the image of his tongue on his lips, tasting me.

"I should probably go," he said quietly, his thumbs brushing over my cheeks.

"Okay," I responded, but felt the sting of the tears I'd managed to push away come back with vigor. The sudden and familiar feelings of being left behind came over me.

"Hey," he said as he pressed a kiss to my forehead. "This isn't goodbye. I'm leaving but I'm not going anywhere, all right? I'll call you as soon as I land and it'll be just like it was before, only better, because now we're together. All right?"

"Okay," I said again, only that time I was definitely crying. I believed him, I did. I believed he loved me and wanted me, but there was that irrational part of my brain that wanted to ruin it all.

He saw me start to lose my composure and leaned forward, his lips pressed to my ear, hand once again behind my neck, and said, "I love being tied to you, Kalli."

The tears came on heavily at his words, streaking down my face, but I managed to keep my crying only to tears. I kept my mouth pressed firmly closed because I knew if I opened it for any reason, only sobs would escape. Riot seemed to understand, pressing a kiss to my forehead, then mouthing the words, "I love you" before turning and walking away.

I watched him until he disappeared, then I got into my car and let the cries I'd been holding in explode out of me. I sat, like a lunatic, crying at the departures ramp at the airport. I probably wasn't the first person to do it, but I was convinced I was the most devastated. When I'd managed to cry until I was hiccoughing, when my face was sufficiently red and blotchy, with the sleeve of my shirt soaked with tears and snot, I was finally calm enough to drive away.

Chapter Sixteen

He's a Gift

Weeks flew by after Riot left me at the airport. Six weeks of phone calls, video chats, Skype dates, and numerous scandalous phone sex episodes. The phone calls were less sexy if I was at home, which I appreciated, but when I was away for work it was almost as if Riot couldn't wait to get me alone on the phone.

Riot had started filming his guest spot on the network crime drama and I loved hearing all about the work and how much he enjoyed it. He was, of course, nervous about his first big role, but it sounded like the director and producers really liked him, so he was hoping for a permanent spot.

"How was your day?" he asked me one night on the phone. I was in my hotel room in Atlanta, Georgia, looking out the window.

"It was all right. I was hoping to walk around the city tonight, but it's rainy and cold. I could walk in the rain back in Seattle, so I think I'll just stay in."

"Good," he replied, and I could hear him falling onto a couch or a bed as he made a slight 'oof' noise. "Wanna watch a movie?"

I'd never been in a relationship before, so I wasn't clued in to how difficult it could be in comparison to relationships where people lived within driving distance of each other. But I could tell that I was nearing the end of my rope as far as how long I wanted to go without seeing

Riot. Even with daily phone conversations and almost constant texting, I was beginning to ache for him.

The last time I'd seen him he'd told me he loved me for the first time, and although he'd said it a thousand times since, I wanted to watch his lips say it in person. I wanted to feel his breath against my skin as he told me he loved me. I wanted to hold his hand and I wanted to sleep in his arms.

"I miss you," I said, still looking out into the rain.

"I miss you too, babe." We were both quiet for a moment because there didn't seem to be much else to add. We were apart and it came with the territory of being together. "I don't have to be on set next weekend. I've got two whole days off from filming, and just a small meeting Saturday morning," he finally said. I could hear the question in his voice. He was letting me know I could come see him if I wanted to, and I did. Of course I did. But we'd had this conversation before—many times, in fact.

"I'm just getting back to Seattle on Thursday evening. I can't come home for twelve hours and then turn around and leave Marcus again." I shook my head even though there was no one to see me do it. I let out a large sigh, irritated with the situation. "This sucks."

"Why don't you just bring Marcus with you? I think he'd love to come to LA. I haven't had a chance to see all the touristy things yet, Marcus would love some of the stuff they've got down here. It would be awesome."

This wasn't the first time Riot had suggested Marcus come with me for a visit and although it sometimes sounded like a great idea, my conscience never allowed it.

I never wanted to be a burden on Riot, and Marcus wasn't exactly a normal seventeen-year-old houseguest. But God, I really wanted to see him.

"I don't know...."

"Come on, Kalli. I miss you like crazy, you miss me, and I'd love to see Marcus. We could go to Legoland. He'd love that. It's been almost two months since I've seen you, and I'm trying to be patient and understanding, but, Jesus, I just want to hold you."

"You're sure it wouldn't be too much of an imposition?"

"Kalli, you're never going to be an imposition. You're in my life and I want to be in yours. That includes Marcus and I wouldn't have it any other way."

His words pushed me over the proverbial cliff I'd been hanging on to by my fingertips. "All right, we'll fly down next Friday morning."

"Wait, really?" He sounded completely surprised by me relenting.

"Yeah," I laughed. "I can't wait."

"Me either. I love you."

"I love you too. But I think I'm going to go take a hot bath and read a book."

"Damn woman, you just told me you loved me. Why would you give me that mental image and then leave me hanging?"

I laughed some more. "Sorry," I said, even though I wasn't. Not really. "I'll call you tomorrow, all right?"

He groaned, making me smile. "You're going to be in so much trouble when I finally get my hands on you," he growled.

"Mmmm," I hummed. "Promise?" I heard him groan in the background, sounding like he'd dropped his phone. When he finally came back to the phone he was whiny.

"Well, looks like we're both going to bathe. Although, I'll be taking a cold shower instead of a hot bath."

Now I had the visual of water cascading down his muscular body and I was the one groaning.

"Okay, we both have to go. I'll call you tomorrow."

"Love you, babe."

"I love you too, Ri."

The next day when I told Marcus we'd be flying to LA soon, he was so excited he nearly broke my eardrum with all his screaming. Days later Nancy sounded a little worn down on the phone.

"Next time, dear, don't tell Marcus news this exciting until it's closer to the actual flight. He hasn't been able to stop talking about the trip and asks every day, multiple times if today is the day." Her voice was loving, but I could tell she was tired.

"I'm sorry this is such a long job, Nance. I'll be home in a few days."

"You know it doesn't matter how long you're gone, dear. Everything is fine, like always."

"All right. Well, I'll be back Thursday evening and then you can take off and do whatever you want. We'll be gone all weekend, and I have the entire next week off, so you go do something. Get away for a bit."

"I might do that, or I might stick around. I'd like to see you for a bit too."

I smiled at her words. Her affection for me was never taken for granted. Sure, she was technically an employee, and I paid her to take care of Marcus around the clock when I wasn't around, but she'd become so much more over the years.

"Well, that would definitely be nice."

"Kalli, let's go! Hurry up!"

I heard Marcus yelling through the house, trying to get me to move even faster than I already was. It wouldn't be his first plane ride, but from the way he was acting one would think he was about to fly in a space shuttle or something.

"I'm coming, give me one minute!" I yelled back. He was my responsibility, but he was still my little brother, so sometimes I reserved the right to squabble with him. When I made it to the front door with my suitcase, Marcus was waiting impatiently. "Can we go now?"

"Calm down, Marky. It's gonna be a while before we even get on the plane."

And that's how the next six hours of my life went.

Marcus was impatient to get to the airport, impatient to get on the plane, impatient for the plane to land, and then impatient to disembark from the plane. Not impatient enough, however, to turn down a tour of the cockpit from the pilots. I smiled watching my little brother look wide-eyed at all the buttons and knobs, laughed along with the flight attendants when he asked if he could talk on their radio, then thanked them for letting him sit in the pilot's chair. It took an extra ten minutes, but the smile on Marcus' face as we walked through the airport, him staring down at the wing pin he'd gotten, was well worth the extra time.

"Marcus, buddy!" I heard Riot yell from at least fifty yards away, shouting down the large walkway of the airport once we'd cleared the security checkpoint. Marcus took off, running at full speed toward Riot, and nearly pummeled him when they finally collided. Marcus wrapped his arms around Riot, and Riot hugged him right back. My eyes misted a little at their reunion, and at Riot's obvious affection for my little brother.

I continued to walk at a normal pace and when I finally reached them, Marcus was pulling away. Riot's eyes met mine and all of a sudden there were butterflies in my stomach.

"Come here, you," he said as he pulled me toward him, his hand finding the back of my neck and his mouth coming down to mine. He gave me a slow and sweet kiss, with just the tiniest hint of tongue, which was appropriate with my brother standing next to us, but also just enough to thoroughly wind me up, to leave me wanting more.

His thumb brushed over the side of my neck as I opened my eyes to look in his caramel ones, feeling relieved to be near him again and still feel that perfect connection with him. His hand came down and took my bag from me, then he linked his fingers with mine.

"Do you guys have checked bags?" Riot asked, looking at me.

"Nope. We packed light."

"Great." He looked to Marcus. "You ready to have an awesome weekend, buddy?"

"Yeah! Kalli said there was a beach and a sidewalk with people's names on it and a place with a bunch of Legos."

"She was right about all of that, and we can see it all if you want."

"What time is your meeting tomorrow?" I asked, turning to look at Riot, still not really believing that he was right next to me. There were definitely strange qualities of being in a long distance relationship with someone; no matter how many pictures of himself he sent me, or how much time I spent trying to remember what he looked like, I always felt like I forgot him a little bit. The realization was both good and bad. Bad in that I never wanted to forget any part of Riot, ever. But good in a way that I got to see him for the first time all over again, marvel at how handsome he was, reacquaint myself with just how much taller he was than me, and I definitely spent a few moments staring at his t-shirt, which did nothing to hide all the muscles under it.

"Early. Seven a.m. It's not exactly a meeting, it's a training session. It's contracted through the network."

"They're making you see a trainer?"

"Yeah. In one of the new episodes there is a shirtless scene, so they hooked me up with a trainer."

At that point a few thoughts ran through my mind. The first being confusion, because, had they not *seen* Riot before asking him to see a trainer? He was already in amazing shape. Second thought was just a twinge of jealousy because he would probably be shirtless with a female. The third and biggest thought was excitement.

"They offered you more episodes?"

He squeezed my hand and gave me an award-winning smile, all white teeth and scrumptious lips. "They wrote me into the cast," he said excitedly.

"What? Riot, why didn't you tell me? That's amazing!" I wrapped my arms around him and he picked me up off the floor, his face buried in the crook of my neck.

"I was waiting to see you in person. I wanted to see your face when I told you, wanted to hug you and see you all excited, just like this."

"I'm so happy for you," I whispered into the skin of his neck.

"Can we go look at the stars on the sidewalk now?" Marcus asked impatiently from beside us.

"Marky, didn't you hear what Ri said? He's going to be on his TV show for a long time! They like him and gave him a big part! Isn't that exciting?"

Marcus' eyes went wide and he looked to Riot. "Is your name on one of those stars?"

Riot and I both laughed at his question and he didn't understand why, so he pouted.

"Ouch, dude, way to bruise my ego," Riot said, gently slapping Marcus' back. "Come on, we'll get you to see all the famous people's stars."

We'd spent the entire day doing every silly touristy thing you could think of in LA. We went to see the stars on the sidewalk, found the Hollywood sign in the hills and tried to take pictures of it in the background of our selfies, and we even rode around on a double-decker bus, taking a tour of famous people's houses. The bus tour was probably more fun for me as Marcus didn't really know who most of the stars were, but he was pretty impressed with the giant bus, so it was a win for everyone. Plus, it gave me a chance to sit and cuddle a bit with Riot.

The last time we'd seen each other we'd been alone for nearly two days straight, allowing us to give in to the need to touch each other. But this time, not only was Marcus with us, but we were out in public. My body was aware of his, knew he was near me, and reacted with an aching need.

We'd gone to dinner at a restaurant outside of central LA, and the crowds were significantly smaller. Riot smartly chose a place that had an arcade and he kept handing Marcus ten dollar bills, trying to keep him occupied as we sat in the booth, neither one of us able to keep our hands from touching one another. It was all innocent, but it was just scratching the surface of our need for each other.

"He seems to be having a good time," I said as I nodded in Marcus' direction. "This was a good pick for a place to eat."

"I may not be the smartest guy you've ever met, but I can make a few informed decisions when it counts."

"So you've got your training session tomorrow morning and then we're off to Legoland?"

"That's the plan," he said, squeezing my thigh under the table.

"This is really nice of you to spend your weekend doing things Marcus would like." His hand stilled and his smile faded a bit. Then, he removed his hand from me altogether.

"You make it sound like it's some sort of sacrifice to spend time with him. I'm not sure how many ways I have to say it, or how many times you have to hear it, but Marcus isn't a burden, Kalli. He just isn't. For some reason, you feel guilty about having him around, like he's something I have to deal with in order to be with you. But he's not. I really wish you'd start thinking better of me than that, and better of Marcus."

I opened my mouth to reply, but no words came out, because there was nothing really to say. Riot was right. Of course he was right. I snapped my mouth shut and tried to figure out the hundreds of different thoughts running through my brain in that moment.

"I'm sorry," I said earnestly. "Really, Ri, I apologize." This time I reached out for his hand, twining our fingers together. "You're right. You've never *ever* made me feel like Marky was a burden. I guess I'm just so used to protecting him that I try to imagine worst case scenarios and prepare for them. I need to be able to fight the battles for him." I exhaled loudly, trying to release some of the tension I'd felt coil in my shoulders in the last few minutes. "I don't know what I'd do if a man I was dating made him feel like he was an annoyance or an obstacle, ya know?"

"Hey," Riot said, tipping my chin up with his finger to look him in the eyes. "You're not dating any other man; you're dating me. And I love you. And I love Marcus because he's a part of your life, an extension of you. You don't have to worry that I'm *tolerating* Marcus. *He's a great kid.* And you've done a great job."

"No one but Nancy has ever told me that," I whispered, my eyes still trained on him, partly because he was holding my chin in place, but mostly because I loved looking in his eyes.

"That's because you've kept him hidden from everyone in your life. If you would talk to Ella or Megan about him, or even introduce them to him, they'd fall in love with him too. He's not a dirty little secret, Kal. He's a gift."

"I know that, Riot. But it's my job to protect him, and letting other people get close to him is just inviting heartache."

He pressed a small kiss to my lips. "You need to give yourself more credit. You wouldn't be friends with the kind of people who could hurt him. Give them the opportunity to know him. Odds are, they'll be better for it. I am."

My heart immediately swelled at his words, my breath catching in my lungs. "How in the world did I get lucky enough to find you?" I whispered, my eyes welling with tears.

"Hmmm, we'll debate later who's the luckiest between the two of us, but in the meanwhile we should probably send Lexi Black a thank-you note." He tucked a lock of hair behind my ear and then pressed another chaste yet electric kiss against my lips. Just then, Marcus returned to the table, hand out, and smile bright.

"Can I have some more money?"

"Please?" I insisted, raising my eyebrows at him for not being polite.

"Please, may I have some more money?"

Riot handed him another ten dollar bill, but kept his hand captured in his as he took it. "This is the last one, buddy. Then we have to head home, all right?"

"All right," Marcus agreed.

"Good man," Riot said, letting his hand go.

An hour later Riot was leading us into his temporary apartment.

"It isn't much, I've only been here for about two weeks," he said nervously as he opened the door. Marcus clomped in, heading straight for the couch in the living room and I swept my eyes over the white, stark, bare walls and nearly empty rooms. The living room had a couch and a tiny, wheeled cart with a TV atop; the dining room had only a small table with two chairs. There were no curtains, no pictures on the walls, no character at all. "The couch pulls out so I thought Marcus could sleep here." Riot's eyes narrowed a little, as if he were trying to communicate something nonverbally. "You can stay on it with him if you want, or…." His voice trailed off and I finally grasped what he was trying to say.

"It's okay, Marcus is a bit of a bed hog. I'll stay with you, if that's all right?" I asked, laughing. I saw his shoulders relax as he exhaled.

"All right." He dropped Marcus' bag on the floor next to the couch, then took my hand. "My room is back this way." He led me down the narrow hallway through one of two doors. The room was tiny and just as bare as the rest of his apartment. He set my bag down on the bed and turned to me, his hands finding my waist. "I'm sorry about that out there. I didn't want to just assume you'd be sleeping with me, and I didn't know what was all right to say in front of Marky."

My hands cupped the sides of his face, completely loving the way he not only thought about those sorts of things, but also that he used my brother's nickname. "You're fine, babe. He doesn't think about those kinds of things. At least, I don't think he does." I rose up onto my toes, trying my damnedest to reach his lips with mine, but he had to lean down to reach me and we both laughed as our lips met each other's.

His arms wrapped around me, lifting me, and we both breathed into the kiss. It was a relief to be in his arms; everything felt better when I was wrapped up in him.

"I'm so glad you're here," he said against my mouth, backing up until his legs hit the bed. Then he sat and arranged me on his lap so I was straddling him.

"I'm happy to be here," I mumbled in response, my body reacquainting itself with his, my hands running up along his arms and shoulders, back down his chest, over his ribs. His hands traveled quickly to my ass and stayed there, making me smile.

"Your apartment is a little sparse," I noted as his mouth moved down my throat, kissing and licking his way to my collarbone.

"This is just some place the studio threw me for a few weeks. I can stay here if I want," he said, then placed more wet kisses back up the other side of my neck. "But then I'd have to give up my apartment in San Francisco."

"I've never even seen your place," I said with a frown.

"I've got a few weeks there still if I choose to give it up. You'll just have to come back soon."

I saw in his eyes he was asking me more seriously than he was letting on. My heart both expanded and hurt at his words. There were times when we were apart where I missed him. It mostly came at night when I had time to lie in bed and think about him and how far away he was, but usually I wasn't spending a lot of time lamenting the fact that we were apart. Perhaps it was because the whole relationship was new, or relationships in general were new to me, but I hadn't gotten to a point where I was upset for missing him.

But as I sat there on his lap, with him, witnessing the look in his eyes, I wondered if he was happy with our situation, or if he was beginning to regret starting a long-distance relationship.

"Is this too hard for you?" I asked, apparently out of nowhere because Riot's eyebrows rose and a confused look came over his face.

"What? You sitting on my lap?"

"No," I said, shaking my head and moving away from him slightly. "This. Us. Is it too hard for you to be with me because of the distance?" I was asking because I was curious; I wanted to know if he was happy and I felt like it was my responsibility to make sure he was. He still wore a confused look. "I mean, like, do you miss being with someone regularly?"

"Are you asking if I miss having regular sex?" his voice was louder and his eyes narrowed even more.

I shrugged.

"Do *you* miss having regular sex?" he asked accusatorily.

"I was never having regular sex," I defended, then climbed off his lap. The motion of getting off him seemed to offend him more than the question and he grabbed my hand, pulling me back toward him.

"Don't go away, just stay here," he said, bringing me right to his knees, which he spread and then brought me even closer. "Why are you asking me these questions?" Both his hands gripped both of mine, holding me close to him.

"You just seem like you missed me a lot," I said, my voice meek and mousey.

"And...?"

"And it occurred to me that you might not have realized what you were signing up for when we decided to be exclusive."

"I was only aware that I was signing up for you."

I rolled my eyes. "You know what I mean." I sighed.

"You don't think I can handle a few weeks without sex? I don't miss sex, Kal. I miss *you*. I don't miss sex with random women, sex with women who are only there because they think I'm somebody famous, or going to be famous, or can introduce them to someone famous. When I think about you, and miss you, I'm not missing the sex. Sure, I think about sex, fantasize about it, but I don't miss sex. I miss sex with *you*. I miss holding *you* while you sleep. I miss that perfect smile that comes across your mouth when you think of something funny, even if you don't tell me what it is. I can't see that on the phone, I can't hold you through the phone. I can't trace the freckles on your shoulders on the phone. I miss *you*, Kalli."

"What if eventually it becomes too hard?"

"What do you mean? What kind of difficulties are you anticipating?"

"What if the phone isn't enough? Or one day you decide you don't want to date someone so far away anymore?"

"I think, eventually, we will get to the point where the phone won't be enough, and I won't want to date someone so far away. I think that's the natural path a relationship takes. Eventually, if you see this working out between us, we'll have to figure out a way to be together." He must have noticed the panic in my eyes, must have felt the breath that stalled in my lungs, because he started shushing me and running his hands over my body. "Don't freak out, baby. That is so far away right now, I'm not trying to scare you."

"I'm not worth all this," I found myself saying. The words surprised even me, as I'd always been a pretty self-confident person. But in that moment, all I could think was that I wasn't worth all the trouble he was going through, all the lonely nights and long phone calls. Eventually, he'd be done with me, anyway, right?

"Hey," he said as he stood, pressing closer in to me. "Listen, you are worth it. You're everything I've ever wanted. And you don't get to decide who I want to be with. If you decide you don't want to be with me one day, we'll cross that bridge when we come to it. I'll fight like hell before I'll let you walk, but like I said, we'll cross that bridge. But you don't get to tell me who I love, or who's worthy of my love. I give my love freely to you, because it belongs to you."

I tried to nod but it was useless with his hands clasping me. "This is all just a little overwhelming."

"What is?" His eyes were worried.

"Being here, with you. It's just so right that going back to being away feels almost cruel, and I don't want to hurt you. I want you to be happy, even if it's without me."

"You stubborn woman," he said, laughing. "Isn't that pretty much the definition of love? Wanting the other person to be happy, even if their happiness doesn't involve you?"

I gave a pathetic nod again.

"Then let me love you, yeah?" he asked with a smile. I couldn't help but smile back, and then his lips bent to mine. It was a softer kiss than we normally shared. He kissed me as if he were afraid I would break or crumble beneath his lips. He was being careful with me.

When he finally pulled away, I whispered, "I should probably go get Marcus ready for bed."

"Okay," he replied, only pulling far enough away to let his hands still linger on my face. "Anything I can do to help?"

"Show me where the bathroom is?"

"Easy. It's the only other door in the hallway," he said with a laugh. He led me out of the bedroom, showed me the bathroom, and then we walked into the living room to find Marcus lying on the couch watching TV.

"You ready for bed, Marky?" I asked, trying to sound upbeat after an emotional conversation.

"Can I watch TV while I'm in bed?"

"I'm okay with it, but you have to ask Riot." Marcus' eyes shot to him, giving him the biggest puppy dog eyes I'd ever seen.

"Listen, you get ready for bed fast and don't give your sister any grief and I'll let you order a movie. Deal?"

"Deal!" he practically shouted as he jumped up from the couch, digging in his duffle bag for his pajamas.

Fifteen minutes later, Marcus was lying on the couch Riot had pulled out into a bed, quietly watching a movie, completely satisfied with his lot in life at that moment.

"Good night, Marky. I'll just be in the room down the hall if you need anything, okay?"

"Night, Kal," was his only response so I figured he was all right. I did a mental check before leaving the living room: Marcus had the water bottle he liked to keep with him at night, the hallway light was on in case he woke up in the middle of the night and couldn't figure out where he was, and he had the one stuffed animal I'd agreed to let him bring, Scruffy the Squirrel, a ridiculous and mangy-looking stuffed squirrel that his dad had given him when he was about three. He'd looked out into the front yard and become fascinated with the squirrels running through it and my mom got so tired of listening to him talk about the squirrels, that my stepfather finally just went out and found one for him. He'd had it ever since and it was definitely one of those childhood possessions that made him panicky to be without. So, Scruffy was tucked up under one of his arms as he watched his movie and I let my fears subside, silently telling myself that Marcus would be okay for the night.

I returned to Riot's bedroom and walked in to find him lying on his bed, looking at his phone.

"Whatcha doing?" I asked, as I reached for my bag.

"Halah sent me a text. Apparently she's at a port and has a good signal, so she just updated all of us that she's still alive and well."

"Still living the good life on a cruise ship?"

"Apparently," he sighed. "What are you up to?" he asked, one eyebrow raised in question.

"Would you mind if I showered? I always feel a little gross after a day of traveling."

"Of course not. I think there are extra towels in the cupboard in the bathroom."

"Thanks," I said, leaning down and placing a small kiss on his mouth, then turning and feeling his hand slap me playfully on the ass. I yelped and then laughed, caught off guard. I shot a feigned look of annoyance over my shoulder, but really just swooned on the inside at the boyish grin across his face.

I took a longer shower than usual, relishing the idea that if Marcus needed anything Riot would be there to help. So I let the hot water work out the kinks I'd gotten in my shoulders from traveling and from being on high alert all day with Marcus in a different city, outside of my comfort zone. When the water started to cool, I reluctantly turned the knob and stepped out of the shower. I'd really steamed up the small bathroom and there was no use trying to dry in there. I wrapped a towel around my body and stepped into the hallway, sneaking toward the living room. As I suspected, Marcus was asleep on the couch, sprawled out across the full-sized pull-out bed.

I turned back toward the bedroom, walking softly to not disturb my brother. When I cracked the bedroom door open, I noticed a soft light flickering from inside. The door opened further and I saw small candles placed all over the room, all lit, creating the soft light, and Riot standing at the foot of his bed wearing only jeans.

My heart sped up as my eyes drifted around the room, taking it all in, including Riot's bare feet. There was absolutely nothing sexier than a man in just jeans with bare feet. Something about it made me feel comfortable. Riot, not surprisingly, also looked sexy in candlelight.

"Come here," he said with an adorable nod. So I walked to him, still grasping the towel around me. When I was standing directly in front of him, he reached up and took my hand off the towel and then pulled it open slowly, his eyes never leaving mine. "You're all wet," he whispered, making my skin erupt in goose bumps.

"I took a shower," I stupidly replied. Luckily, he laughed.

"Turn around," he said through his soft laughter. So I did.

He took the towel and ran it over my long hair, squeezing the excess water out. Then he continued down my back, slowly making small circles with the towel, making sure to wick up every drop of water. When he kneeled to move the towel lower, I gasped as he left a trail of soft kisses starting at the top of my thigh and moving toward my calf. Then he moved to the other leg and kissed his way back up. The towel moved over my ass and he gave me a less than gentle squeeze, causing me to moan.

"Turn back around," he said, his voice low and gravelly. So I did. My gaze fell to him, kneeling in front of me, his eyes dark and filled with lust. He dropped the towel and I tried to rein in the pounding of my heart when he hooked one hand behind my knee and brought it over his shoulder, his other hand grasping my ass and pulling me toward him.

I had to grab the footboard of the bed to keep my balance, but my eyes were frozen on Riot and his mouth as it descended upon me. In all our time together, this was the first time he'd used his mouth on me, and it was glorious. His tongue swept through me, warm and rough, kissing me. His hands pulled me closer to him, and his voice rumbled through me as he gave an appreciative moan.

As his tongue moved over me, my body instinctually tensed, all the muscles tightening, preparing for the onslaught of sensation coming my way. With one hand still on my ass, he moved his other hand to slide two fingers inside me, gently stroking me from the inside as his tongue caressed my clit, taking leisurely strokes over it.

I moved one of my hands from the footboard to his hair, both to stay upright, but also to keep his mouth close to me.

"Riot, oh," I moaned, eyes closed, teeth clamping down on my bottom lip. He replied with a hum right against my clit, sending shockwaves through me.

The combination of his fingers and his mouth sent me over the edge and I cried out as my climax crashed through me. Before I could regain my composure, he'd stood and lifted me onto the bed, splaying kisses up my stomach, stopping to pull my nipple into his mouth.

"You taste amazing, Kal. Every part of you," he said, then sucked the hard point of my breast into his mouth again. I arched into him, offering up every last part of me, wanting him to take it all, knowing he'd give me himself in return. I felt his breath on my lips and opened my eyes to see him, my hand automatically coming to the side of his face.

"I missed you," he whispered just before taking my mouth with his, kissing me deep, letting me taste myself on him. I reached between us and unfastened his jeans, then took great pleasure in sliding my hands down over his ass to push them off, using my hands and feet to rid him of them entirely.

Once he was naked he settled between my legs. I sighed my contentment into his mouth, humming with pleasure at how wonderful it was to feel him between my legs, to feel his warmth pressed up against mine.

"Oh, God, Ri...," I whispered as his mouth moved to my neck, his stubble scraping the skin there, heightening my already soaring nerves, making every single touch that much more intense. "I need you, please," I whimpered.

"Fuck, yes. You've got me," he said harshly, pulling away and reaching for the drawer of his nightstand and pulling out a condom. He wasted no time opening it and pulling it down his length, his movements urgent and speedy.

He leaned all the way back so he was sitting in the middle of the bed and motioned to me with his finger. "Come here, baby," he said, his voice low and a serious look on his face. I sat up and made my way to him on my knees, never taking my eyes off him.

He guided my knees to either side of his thighs so I was straddling him, then pulled gently down on my hips with one hand, while the other guided him into me. I sank down on him and watched as his mouth fell open in awe. By the time I was fully seated on him, we were nearly face-to-face and his eyes found mine.

His hand came up to push my hair from my face, threading through, then landed on the back of my neck as he gripped me firmly and pulled my face to his.

"Jesus, Kalli," he said, holding me still, pulling me down onto him, and forcing me to take him so deep. "God, I love you," he said, his forehead pressing into mine, then kissing me seconds later.

I rotated my hips, grinding down onto him, gasping as the direct friction against my clit sent electricity through my body. "I love you, too," I moaned quietly, rocking back and forth on his cock, afraid to lose the connection, afraid if I backed off him one centimeter I'd never feel that close to him again. "Promise me," I rasped, shamelessly using his body to bring pleasure to mine, throwing years of worry and constant fear away, letting all my walls down. "Promise you'll never leave me." I said the words with both hands clasped to the sides of his face, eyes looking directly into his, voice hitched, breathing ragged.

"Never," he growled, pulling on my hips, matching my rhythm, doing his part to bring me to orgasm. "You're a fucking part of me, Kal." His words sent me over the edge, caused every muscle to contract, squeezing him, then release as a loud moan escaped me and my head fell back.

Mid-orgasm, his lifted me up and placed me back on the bed, positioned one of my legs over his shoulder, and then entered me again, but achingly slowly. He eased in, inch by inch, drawing out my orgasm, filling me completely. Once I'd come all the way down, he pulled out and stroked back in, his eyes glued to where our bodies connected, one hand running up and down my thigh at his side, the other holding on to my waist.

I couldn't watch, the sensations taking over, so I closed my eyes, wanting just to feel him. With my fingers gripping the sheets below me, feeling him pumping in and out, his hands gripping my ass to bring me to just the right angle, and all the sexy groans he was making, my body was in overdrive.

"Fucking Christ…." I heard him mutter as he thrust one last time. When he finally pulled out, he collapsed on the bed next to me, pulling me in to his side, breathing heavy with a sexy grin on his face.

"You look mighty pleased with yourself," I managed after I'd caught my breath.

"Oh, I'm pleased all right. But I'm more pleased with you than anyone else."

"Is that so?" I asked, smiling while trailing my finger in small circles over the damp skin of his chest.

"Baby, I've spent weeks fantasizing about getting back inside of you, but you just blew all my fantasies out of the water. Nothing compares to watching you ride me, feeling your tits up against my chest."

"Tits?" I scoffed, pretending to be offended by the term.

"You don't like the word tits?"

"It's a little objectifying, don't you think? I mean, they're my *breasts*." I waved my free hand over them, trying to emphasize my point.

"Babe, they can be your breasts any other time, but when I'm inside you, they're tits."

"So, I can only call it your *cock* when we're having sex?" I asked, trying not to laugh.

"Feel free to refer to my cock whenever you want." I laughed as he placed a quick kiss against my lips and then hopped out of bed, pulled on some workout shorts, and quietly snuck to the bathroom to clean up. When he returned, he slid back into bed, pulling my back to his front and wrapping his arm around my middle.

"All jokes aside," he said quietly as he twined his fingers with mine at my belly, "I'm really glad you're here. I've missed you more than I could have ever imagined."

My heart swelled at his words, knowing it was perhaps rare to find a guy who was so forthcoming with his emotions, so open to discussing how he felt or what I meant to him. It was becoming more obvious each day I spent with him, either in person or from a distance, that Riot Bentley was not a typical man. It had also become clear to me I was a very lucky woman to have him, so I snuggled in deeper and replied, "I missed you, too."

Chapter Seventeen

Accepting Help

Riot returned from his scheduled workout to an anxious and hyper Marcus, jumping up and down, begging Riot to hurry so we could leave for Legoland. Riot moved at warp speed, showering and dressing faster than anyone I'd ever seen, and in minutes we were in the car, heading south. Marcus was occupied in the car by a tablet and I was happy just to sit in the passenger seat with Riot's fingers laced through mine.

Legoland was a sight to behold and I was instantly nervous about bringing Marcus someplace so big with so many people. I didn't want him overwhelmed, but I also didn't want to become overwhelmed myself. I was so very glad Riot was there with us. Probably for the first time ever I was accepting help from someone who wasn't paid to be there. This was a big step, and it almost reminded me of the days when Marcus and I were a part of a real family. I looked at Riot, whose arm was wrapped around my shoulders as he laughed and said something funny to Marcus, and I let my heart expand just a little.

Any single thing you could possibly imagine, this place had built it out of Lego blocks. It was amazing. There were buildings made of Lego blocks, replicas of actual cars, even Darth Vader and Yoda. Each and every one we passed Marcus would exclaim, "I want to make that!"

"You're going to need a lot more blocks to make that, buddy," Riot said, clapping him on the back and laughing as they admired a life-size locomotive made of Lego blocks.

We saw all the demonstrations, rode the Lego roller-coaster, drank frozen lemonade, and even managed to find a store to buy a lifetime supply of Lego in every color imaginable.

Around lunch time we found a stand that sold hot dogs with every type of fixing one could imagine. Marcus was sold on the idea so we got in line, but my previous bottle of water had me looking for a restroom.

"Marcus, tell Riot what you'd like and then let's go find a bathroom."

"I don't have to go," he said defiantly.

"Well, I do, so please just tell him what you want."

"Kalli, can't I just stay here with Riot? I don't want to go to the bathroom."

I rolled my eyes because I could feel the tantrum coming and my need for the restroom became more evident with every second.

"Kal, I'm fine if you want to go. We'll probably be in this line forever anyway," Riot said, rubbing his hand down my back.

"Are you sure?"

"Definitely, just hurry back," he said with a wink.

"I just want a plain hot dog, nothing fancy," I said, pressing a kiss to his cheek. "Marcus, listen to Riot and I'll be right back." I had the mom finger out, pointing it at his face, as if that would make my words sink in any more than usual.

I followed the signs to the restroom and was met with a huge line and I sighed, trying to keep my mind off my bladder. I pulled out my phone and scrolled through Facebook and answered a text from Megan about helping Ella plan her bachelorette party. Finally it was my turn and I nearly gave a victory cry.

When I returned to the hot dog cart I saw neither Marcus nor Riot. I spun in a slow circle, looking for where they would have sat down to eat, but I still didn't see either one of them. My eyes narrowed and I searched again, but when, on the third pass, I still hadn't seen my brother or my boyfriend, I began to panic.

I pulled out my phone and called Riot, but it just rang and rang and then went to voicemail.

"Marcus?" I called out, still spinning a circle. Where in the world would he have gone?

"Kalli!" I heard Riot's voice above the buzz of the park and turned to see him running toward me, dodging and weaving between people to get to me.

"Good God, Riot. You scared me. I couldn't find you guys. Where's Marcus?"

"I don't know." He breathed heavily. "We were in line and then I turned around to ask him something and he was gone."

"What do you mean he was gone? Where'd he go?" My heart started beating faster and I could feel the prickling of panic start to course through my veins, adrenaline making every one of my senses wake up.

"I don't know," he repeated, obviously frustrated, running a quick hand over his head as he turned, searching for my brother.

"You *lost* him?" I yelled.

"He just disappeared, Kal. I'm sorry," he said, his gaze finding mine, his eyes full of apology.

Just then a park employee walked past us and I snagged his arm.

"Where do I go if I have a lost child?"

"I can take you to the family center," he said immediately, obviously used to dealing with missing children and their frantic parents. He took my elbow and started leading me through the park.

"Shouldn't we stay where we lost him?"

"Don't worry, ma'am. We'll get all the employees looking for him and when we find him, we'll bring him to you. Now, can you give me a description? What's his name? What does he look like? What was he wearing? How old is he?" He was still gently pulling me through the park, walking quickly and making his way through it much more efficiently than I would have, obviously because he knew the park like the back of his hand.

I tried to answer his questions but my eyes kept darting to every head of dark hair I saw, trying to find Marcus, and I couldn't concentrate on describing him.

"His name is Marcus, he's about five foot eleven, shaggy brown hair, and he was wearing blue jeans with a red Lego Movie t-shirt. He's seventeen years old." I heard Riot's voice describing my brother and I was filled with rage I didn't quite understand or have time to analyze at that moment.

The guy walking with me turned his face toward me. "He's seventeen? I thought you said he was a child?"

"He is," I exclaimed. "He has a mental disability and, for all intents and purposes, is just like a seven year old. He looks like a teenager, but he's not. He's just like a little boy." At that, I began to cry. "He doesn't know where I am. He's probably scared."

"Ma'am, it's all right. Listen, most of the time when we find kids, they're having the time of their lives and haven't even realized they're separated from their parents."

I didn't bother correcting him by mentioning that I wasn't his mom. I just nodded and hoped he was right.

He finally brought us into a building and sat us down in chairs while he made an announcement into his walkie-talkie, describing Marcus and his special circumstances.

And then we waited.

After ten minutes I began to pace through the small building.

After twenty minutes I began to cry again.

At thirty minutes I tried to leave and look for him myself, Riot stopping me and making me sit.

Finally, after forty-five minutes, someone's voice came over the walkie and said they'd found him and were bringing him to the family center. It took another ten minutes for the door to open and my baby brother to walk through.

I ran to Marcus and wrapped him in a hug, crying inconsolably, caring not one bit how crazy I looked.

"Marcus, you scared me," I cried.

"Kalli, don't cry. That was awesome! I got to meet Lego Batman! He was super nice and gave me this hat." He pulled away and pointed to his head where he did, indeed, have a new hat.

"Marcus, why did you wander off? You know better than that," I scolded.

"I didn't wander off. I told Riot I was just going to go see Batman for a minute." He looked at Riot, his eyes confused. "I told you. I didn't just leave."

"Yeah, but buddy, I told you to wait until your sister got back. I asked you to stay with me."

"Then what?" I asked, my voice cold and angry. "You just turned your back on him? You dismissed him? You can't do that, Riot. You have to keep an eye on him, you have to make sure he stays with you." I was yelling and I didn't want to be. I didn't want to be in the room or in that building or in that state. I wanted to leave.

"Come on, Marcus. Let's go."

"Kalli, I'm not ready to go. We haven't even seen everything," Marcus whined.

"Kal, we don't have to leave. Let's just calm down and take a breather," Riot suggested.

"Calm down? You *lost* him, Riot." My words and my tone must have communicated exactly how extremely angry I was because both Marcus and Riot stopped arguing with me and simply walked with me out of the building and back to the car.

Once it was unlocked I motioned for Marcus to climb in the backseat and I got in right behind him, needing space from Riot. I could tell he was biting his tongue, wanting to say something to me, but he was smart enough to know I didn't want to listen to him at that moment.

The entire ride back to LA I stared out the window and wiped away single tears as scenarios played out in my mind, scenes in which Marcus wasn't returned to me unscathed, or wasn't found at all. In the back of my mind I knew I was being a little dramatic or unreasonable, but I couldn't argue with the part of my brain that knew if I hadn't left him with Riot, he would never have gone missing.

We arrived at Riot's apartment and I quietly asked Marcus to pack up his bag.

Kalli, your flight isn't even until tomorrow," Riot pleaded quietly. "Please, you don't have to leave."

"I'm too angry to stay here right now. I just need some space."

"I'm not ready to go!" Marcus complained.

"Come on, Marky. Don't do this. I just need you to pack your bag." I turned to Riot. "Can you call us a cab, please?"

"You won't even let me take you to the airport?"

I shook my head and walked back to his bedroom, but I heard him following me. "Kal, please, you have to believe

how sorry I am about Marcus. It was an honest mistake.
He just disappeared."

"An honest mistake?" My voice rose with my anger.
"An honest mistake? Do you have any idea what could
have happened to him, Riot? Any number of things could
have happened, and I'm just lucky that someone found him
while he was still safe and unhurt."

"God, I know that. You don't think I know that? I was
just as freaked out as you were." His hands swiped
furiously through his hair, his agitation evident.

"No! You don't get to pretend like you have even one
tenth of the love for him that I do. I've been there for him
his whole life. His *whole life*. You can't crash into our
lives and possibly care for him as much as I do after a few
months. If it weren't for you, he never would have gone
missing to begin with. It's your fault."

I watched as my words hit him like an arrow slicing
through the air, connecting with the red circle, splintering
its target.

"It was an honest mistake," he said, his voice a
whispering ghost of what I was used to—empty and sad.

"Yeah, well," I said as I threw my clothes into my bag.
"It's a mistake I never would have made. Coming here,
obviously, was one though." From the corner of my eye I
saw his mouth open to say something, but then it closed
and his head hung low.

There was one tiny part of me that immediately regretted
saying those harsh words, but the majority of me felt
justified and too angry to even consider it being out of line.

When I was sure I'd packed all my stuff I sat on the couch with Marcus, waiting for our cab.

The cab came and honked, Marcus grumbled about having to leave, and Riot refused to let us carry our bags. I wouldn't look at him as he took mine from my hand, anger still coursing through my veins. I climbed into the back of the cab, not giving him a second look. I did notice him hand a hundred-dollar bill to the driver to cover the ride, and the nastiest part of me thought it was the least he could do.

We managed to make it onto a flight that left at dusk, and as the plane climbed into the sky, I couldn't help but feel I'd left something behind.

Chapter Eighteen

Fear of Being Left Behind

Three weeks passed and I hadn't spoken a word to Riot. When we arrived home from our flight there were flowers waiting for me with an apology note, but I was still too angry to appreciate them. Not hearing from me, however, hadn't deterred him in the slightest. Flowers arrived three times a week, always with a sweet note, begging me to forgive him, explaining he missed me, urging me to just call him.

I received a text two times a day; once in the morning, once around bedtime, all from Riot, mostly telling me that he loved me, trying to convince me to call him. Some of them were funny, some of them were normal texts one would send to one's girlfriend, just telling me about his day. It was emotional warfare.

At first, I was legitimately angry with him. Perhaps ridiculously so, but I felt it was justified. But a week passed, the flowers came, the texts continued, and my anger waned.

Nancy had gotten the low down on what had happened, but she got her information from Marcus, as I didn't have anything to say about the matter. Until, one night, about ten days after we'd come home early from California, she cornered me as I did dishes.

"When are you going to forgive that poor man?"

"What are you talking about?"

"You know what I'm talking about. Don't play dumb, Kalli; it's not becoming."

I rolled my eyes, knowing she couldn't see me. "I'm not sure I haven't forgiven him," I said quietly.

"Then why haven't you called him? Why are the Please Forgive Me flowers still arriving like clockwork?"

I shrugged. "I'm not sure we have anything to talk about."

"Kalli, for as long as I've known you, you've never been a particularly stubborn person. Strong? Yes. Opinionated? Definitely. But not stubborn, and not to the point of throwing away something wonderful."

"You weren't there, Nancy," I said quietly as I turned off the faucet. "He was just gone. Vanished. Anything could have happened to him."

"And it could have happened to anyone," she said quickly. I felt those words in my bones because I knew they were true. I'd lost him before, taken my eyes off him for just a moment only to realize he was gone. I knew it wasn't Riot's fault that Marcus had wandered away.

"I know," I whispered. "I overreacted."

"Good, well at least you can admit that much. But I want to know why."

I shrugged again, and moved to sit next to her at the small table in the nook of our kitchen. "Everything with Riot happened so quickly, or at least, it felt like it did. Every time we saw each other it was frantic and fast and full of so much emotion. By our third actual time seeing each other I already felt like I couldn't breathe without him. But when we lost Marcus, I was beside myself. Even after he was found safe and sound, I couldn't help but think about the what ifs. What if we hadn't found him? What if he'd been hurt? And the biggest one was what if I'd never met Riot? What if I hadn't let myself fall in love with him? We wouldn't have even been there." I paused, looking down at the tabletop, picking at my cuticles. "I was *so angry* at him, Nancy. But as that rage subsided, I knew I was really angry with myself for putting us in that situation. We shouldn't have been there, I shouldn't have left Marcus with Riot, it never should have happened."

"But it did, Kalli. It all happened. And now, the only thing that's really wrong is that you're unhappy." She reached across the table and put her hand over mine, stilling my nervous fingers. "Marcus is *fine*. He's happy, he's healthy, and he's okay. When will you stop punishing yourself for living your life? He doesn't want you to be unhappy. And if he could understand why you're doing this, why you're keeping yourself from Riot, he'd tell you to stop. He'd want you to be happy."

"But, that's not my life, Nancy. Marcus isn't normal and he can't understand. He'll always be this way, and I'll always need to put him first, and that's what I'm doing."

"Punishing yourself is not the same as putting him first."

"It never would have worked anyway," I say, pulling my hand from hers, trying to end the conversation, trying to put a nail in the coffin, because I wasn't ready to resuscitate my relationship with Riot.

The next week I put on a front and went out to celebrate Megan's last night of being an unmarried woman. Ella was sporting a cute little pregnant belly and looked stupidly happy, and I tried my hardest not to be angry about it. Megan, of course, was elated and drunk, having a blast. I could tell Ella was a little uncomfortable being that we were the only women there over twenty-five and she was most definitely the only pregnant woman. But I sat next to her and watched the drag show commence, entertained by the song and dance, my mind not fully invested and wandering every few minutes to what my heart was consumed with: Riot.

Just when we thought the show was over, Megan wouldn't let us leave, and after a minute we realized why. Male strippers. This was the part of the bachelorette party where I should have been having the most fun, should have been tipping and drinking, careless and worry-free, but the most I could do was plaster a fake smile on my face and wait for it all to be over.

I didn't want to be a downer on Megan, although she was so drunk she probably never would have noticed had I spent the duration of the show sobbing in the corner. But I tried to pretend as if everything was fine for the sake of my friend.

It was in moments like those I regretted not being open and honest with the only two friends I had. The problem with secrets was that since I kept one, I was always keeping others. One lie turned into two and they multiplied, burying me. I wanted nothing more than to turn to my best friend and tell her about Riot, and have her tell me what I should do about it. But if I did that, I'd have to tell her about Marcus, and then I'd have to tell her everything, not to mention it would hurt her tremendously if she knew I'd kept such a large part of my life from her.

No, it was better to keep my problems to myself.

Finally, when the men were done shaking their goods, Ella announced she was ready to leave and I inwardly sighed with relief. We hugged and kissed Megan goodbye and I hoped her friends had a good handle on her and wouldn't let her go home alone or do anything stupid.

"You feel like walking or catching a cab?" I asked Ella, noticing how tired she looked.

"Cab. Definitely," she replied, sighing loudly. We walked to a corner and hailed a cab pretty easily, which I was thankful for. "Hey, were you okay back there?" she asked once we were in the cab. "For a single lady, you didn't seem to be enjoying the show very much." She was looking at me with her concerned face, head tilted, eyebrows furrowed.

"Sure," I said, reaching over to gently pat her leg, trying to convince her I was fine. "I've just got some things on my mind."

"Things?"

I shrugged, looking down at my hands as they worried the hem of my dress. "I met somebody." My heart thundered in my chest, wanting to tell Ella everything, but I knew if I opened up completely I would lose all the composure I was just barely clinging to. I wanted to tell her, but I wasn't sure how.

"Oh?" Ella tried to contain her excitement, tried to play it cool as if she wasn't planning double dates in her mind. I felt a tiny smile come over my face as I pictured Riot and Porter drinking beers together, becoming friends. But then I remembered that wouldn't ever happen and the smile faded just as quickly as it had appeared.

"Yeah, but he's gone. It wasn't a big deal." More lies.

"Wasn't it? It kind of seemed like it was a big deal."

"I thought it was what I wanted. I told him that it had to be casual, like a one-time thing. He was okay with it, at first, but then when it was time for him to go, it all just kind of blew up in my face." I shrugged again. That wasn't totally a lie, it was how we'd started, and it was the closest to the truth I could come without mentioning Marcus.

"How?"

"He told me he wanted more. I told him I didn't."

"But you did, didn't you?"

I nodded and wiped a tear that escaped down my cheek.

"Oh, Kalli," she said as she pulled me closer to her, hugging me. "Who was it?"

"It doesn't matter," I said as I sniffled.

"It kind of does," she countered.

"I can't tell you, though. I'm sorry. I worked with him and if it got out, it wouldn't be good for him." More lies.

"You know I'd never tell anyone, Kalli. You're my best friend. We should be able to tell each other these things."

"It's okay. I'll be fine."

She placed her hand on my shoulder and gave it a squeeze. "It's okay if you're not. You know that right? You don't have to be fine all the time."

I couldn't say anything back, couldn't find the words to explain that if I wasn't fine, everything in my life would come crumbling down around me. There was more on the line than my happiness, more important things to consider. But I couldn't tell her any of that.

We made it to the hotel and before we split to head to our individual rooms, she reached out to hug me and I let her. I wasn't strong enough to resist the comfort she offered. I was so bad at soothing myself, I needed someone else to do it for me.

"I love you, Kalli. You're like a sister to me. You can always count on me." Her words did nothing short of cut me open. I didn't know what it felt like to have someone love me that way. Love, in my experience, was a hardship, a responsibility, something we carried around on our backs. But Ella spoke of love like it lifted her up and I couldn't understand. How could our views of love be so different? Why couldn't I let love heal me instead of hurt me?

She released me and I gave her a weak smile, then headed to my room. I made it as far as just inside the door and when it closed behind me I lost the composure I'd been gripping so hard all night. My back slid down the door, slowing making my way to the floor as tears came hard and hot, streaming down my face.

I cried for what seemed like hours, trying to be quiet, not wanting to disturb the people in the room next to me. At some point I picked myself up and moved to the bed and I must have cried myself to sleep, because suddenly I opened my eyes and there was sunlight streaming into my room through the window.

I groaned and rolled away from the light, throwing my arm over my eyes, realizing I was still wearing my dress from the night before. I didn't feel hung over from alcohol, but I did feel exhausted from crying.

My phone buzzed from inside my purse across the room and my stomach bottomed out, knowing it was a text from Riot. I usually tried to ignore them until I absolutely had to use my phone, but something about the devastation from the night before and the fresh hurt still making its way through me compelled me to read it right away. I ambled out of bed and found my phone, swiping the screen.

More than anything this morning, I wish that you were here. I know if you were just in front of me, I'd be able to convince you we should be together, that I love you more than anything.

My first thought after reading the text was that I wished I was with him as well. I wished everything was simple and I didn't always feel like I had to keep running away, that I could stop and stand still just long enough to let him grab hold of me.

Suddenly, just like the sunshine filtering through my window, a light came on and a door inside my heart opened that I'd never unlocked before. The only way I'd ever stop running away was if I started running toward him instead. The urge to go to him became overwhelming, a new wave of adrenaline coursing through me, my mind flipping through ways to get to him.

My fingers shook as I got online, looking at flights to LA. They trembled as I called Nancy, asking her if she was fine with Marcus for another day or two. Once I told her where I was headed she gave me her blessing and told me she was proud of me, which made the tears start again, only this time they were happy.

The next flight left for LA in two hours, which didn't leave me a whole lot of time, but I booked the ticket and scrambled out the door, making it to the airport just in time to board my flight.

I was in the comfortable clothes I'd packed to drive home to Seattle in, not my most flattering outfit, and I'd only managed a quick shower, throwing my wet hair up in a messy bun, but I couldn't bring myself to care about my appearance. My instincts were telling me to get to Riot as quickly as possible.

I felt nothing but excitement in the air. The flight was long, only because my leg was bouncing the whole time and I had nothing to distract me from the thought of seeing him again.

The plane landed and I nearly ran to rent a car. Thirty minutes later I was on the road, hoping I remembered the way to Riot's apartment. It wasn't until I was stuck in traffic, sitting on the freeway in LA, that I began to doubt my plan. I couldn't help but think I should have called him first, or even sent a text. My heart thundered in my chest trying to picture his reaction to me showing up on his doorstep. I had every reason to believe he would be excited to see me, but the doubt lingered. The fear of rejection tried to seep into me, but I did my best to push it back.

When I finally made it to his apartment building, I parked and killed the engine, staring at his door, willing some sign to show me I was supposed to be there. Of course, there was nothing; that would have been too easy.

I took a few deep breaths, and tried to tell my stomach it wasn't the time to become queasy.

I stalled in front of his door, building the courage to knock, trying to form some sort of script in my mind, not wanting to see him without something substantial to say to him.

Before I could gather myself enough to knock, the door opened and I saw him. My eyes took him in and my whole body sighed with relief at the sight of him.

He was obviously surprised to see me; his face moved quickly from confusion, to shock, to disbelief and then to caution.

"Kalli," he said softly, just breathing my name.

"Hi." There went all my plans for a good opener.

"What are you doing...? How did you—"

"Were you leaving?" I asked stupidly, motioning toward the gym bag in his hand. "I can come back later," I offered. I started to turn back toward my car, just making it a fraction of an inch before his hand was on my arm, stopping me.

"What are you doing here?" His voice was back. He sounded less surprised and more curious. His hand was warm on my skin and I tried not to think about how soothing it was just to feel his skin against mine.

"I'm not really sure. I just woke up this morning and kind of thought I wanted to see you." Inside, in my mind, I was berating myself for taking the safe route, for skirting around the enormity of how I'd felt that morning when I woke up. I gathered every bit of courage I could and pushed out words I never thought I would say to anyone. "That's not true," I said, the words tumbling from my mouth. I sucked in a deep breath and then I just let the rest of the words I'd kept inside of me for so long fall out.

"I woke up this morning and I realized I'd made a mistake. I've let the fear of being left behind rule so many parts of my life. I never wanted to give anyone the opportunity to leave me, so I never let anyone close enough for it to matter. Until you." I swallowed hard, realizing that saying the words in theory was easier than in practice.

"That last day we were together, when Marcus and I were here visiting—"

"Kalli, you'll never know how sorry I am about what happened," he said, interrupting me, pulling me into his apartment and closing the door behind me.

"No, Riot, please, just let me talk." He nodded and I continued. "When we were here, it was the first time I'd felt like a part of a family in so long. I was happy and had the overwhelming feeling that we belonged together like that, with Marcus. It was as if everything was so *right*. The instant something went wrong, I got scared. When Marcus disappeared I got a taste of everything falling apart around me and I ran." I swallowed hard, knowing the next words were important. "I took my fear and turned it into anger and aimed it right at you."

My eyes found his and I pleaded with him, "I'm so sorry for everything I said to you that day. It wasn't your fault. It wasn't anyone's fault. It was just an accident and it could have happened to anyone." I inhaled, trying to keep back the tears I felt welling in my eyes; I wanted to get through the words. "I shouldn't have pushed you away, but in the moment it was the only way I knew how to deal with all the emotions. Running away is my default. You know, never standing still and all."

"Is that why you came all the way to LA? To apologize?"

"Well…" His question caught me off guard. Yes, I went there to apologize, but I also was there to finally be with him, to throw away everything that had kept us apart in the past. "Nothing else matters if you don't forgive me."

"Of course I forgive you," he said, finally moving to me and pulling me into his arms.

My breath left me as his arms wrapped around my shoulders, all the tension of the last month falling away. His hand landed on the back of my neck and I melted. I'd never belonged anywhere more than I belonged in his arms.

"I wasn't ever going to give up, Kal, but I was starting to think you were gone for good," he whispered in my ear, his fingers gently squeezing my neck.

"I never thought I'd come back either," I said against his chest. "There are a lot of things that keep me from being happy, but the biggest one is just me. I have to let that go, let go of the fear of losing love, or having love taken from me." I pulled back from him just far enough to look up into his eyes. "Love is supposed to make us feel good, not make us afraid." I closed my eyes and took in a deep breath, then open my eyes to stare into his caramel ones. "I'm so tired of being afraid."

"I'm never going to leave you, Kalli," Riot said, his hands on the sides of my face, thumbs brushing over my cheeks. His voice was soft and sincere, and it was the first time I'd ever truly believed him as he said those words. I took in a breath and it might have been the easiest breath I'd taken in over twenty years. The tears came, but they were happy tears.

"I believe you," I whispered through the pinch in my throat, smiling despite the tears.

He leaned down to me, pressing his lips against mine and everything outside of us and our kiss fell away. He moved slowly against my mouth, as if he were testing the waters to see what I was comfortable with, how far I wanted to take the kiss. I wanted everything from him, wanted to feel him against me, inside me, around me.

"I need you," I mumbled against his mouth, and with a growl he picked me up and carried me to his bedroom. He never let me go as he walked me to his bed and gently laid me down, pressing his long body all along mine, covering me, holding me down with his weight.

I pulled on the back of his shirt, wanting to feel his skin against mine, and he eagerly pulled it off the rest of the way, then pulled mine over my head as well. We went through the motions of removing our clothing, never breaking contact, never taking our lips off each other. If his lips were on my shoulder, mine were on his neck. If his hands were on my waist, mine were on his back. We were connected at every juncture, possibly afraid to let go, but definitely happy to be reunited.

His lips found my neck while his hand found my breast. I gasped at the combination of sensations as his teeth grazed my skin and his fingers tugged on my nipple. My legs drew up around his waist and he slid into me effortlessly, as if our bodies were just waiting to be reunited.

He groaned around the skin of my neck once he was fully seated inside of me, and I couldn't hold in the cry that left my mouth. He was everything I needed in that moment. I was full of him and love and light. I was grounded in that moment, tied to him, embracing everything that being with him gave to me.

His hands came to rest on the sides of my face and his mouth brushed over mine, kissing me softly as he pumped in and out of me, slowly gliding, not hurried or frantic, but slow and smooth, enjoying every single moment. His kiss matched the movement, taking long and slow swipes through my mouth, nipping at my bottom lip, humming in satisfaction as he stroked into me.

Eventually, his pace quickened and his thrusts became more forceful. My climax started building and with every drive I was pushed a little closer to the edge. My cries rang out, and one of Riot's hands came to the back of my neck, holding me still, while the other reached between us. The pads of his fingers began circling my clit and I was lost. I felt his breath on my face as he demanded, "Come for me, Kalli," and I did.

I came hard, loud, and long. And it was glorious. It wasn't just a release of a sexual nature, but also a release of all the bullshit I'd been carrying around with me for years.

I hadn't known it before that moment, but Riot had always been the key, and I was finally unlocked.

"I love you," I managed to rasp out while coming down from my incredible orgasm, watching his eyes as he continued to slide in and out of me.

"I love you too," he responded just before he buried his face in my neck and found his own release.

It was hours later and the afternoon sun was sinking lower in the sky as we laid in his bed enjoying each other. I watched as the light slowly dwindled, his fingers making slow and lazy circles on my back, my front draped over his chest. His caramel eyes stared at me, crinkled at the very corners with a slight smile. His other hand came up and he ran his fingers very loosely through my hair, making my eyes close.

When I drifted off to sleep in his arms, it was possibly the first, and definitely the last, moment I had of true contentment.

Chapter Nineteen

Slipping Away

I woke up to darkness, a little confused as to what dragged me from sleep, but felt Riot's arm wrapped around me, holding my back to his front, his feet tangled beneath the sheets with mine. Then I heard the faint buzzing from the living room through the thin walls of his apartment.

Even though it might have been easy to fall back asleep, there was a voice in the back of my mind telling me get up and find my phone, and the voice instructing me to do so sounded panicked and urgent. Even though my body was still trying to fully wake up, my heart started thundering in my chest and my hands were shaking as I pulled the covers back and slid out of Riot's bed.

I found my purse where it had been dropped yesterday as Riot carried me into the bedroom and saw a light flashing inside from my phone. I pulled it out and swiped the screen and my heart jumped into my throat when I saw I had over twenty missed calls and just as many text messages. All from Nancy.

My fingers trembled as I pressed the phone icon to return her call, and it seemed like it took forever for the call to connect. Finally I heard ringing, and a few seconds later I heard Nancy's frail and frantic voice.

"Kalli?" She said by way of greeting, and I could tell she was crying.

"What's wrong, Nancy?"

"Oh, Kalli," she sobbed. "You need to come back to Seattle. It's Marcus."

"What happened? Is he all right?"

"No, he's not all right. He's in the ICU at Seattle Children's Hospital and you need to get here as soon as possible." I heard her continue to sob, my mouth slack, pulse frantic. I heard muffled noises and then Bob was on the line.

"Kalli," he said softly. I could hear Nancy in the background still crying and I could find no words. "We took Marcus to the park to ride his bike after dinner. He'd had sort of a rough day and Nancy thought if he got some of his energy out he'd calm down and sleep better. But when it was time to leave he didn't want to go. He started to become slightly combative and when we tried to convince him to calm down he took off on his bike, not stopping at the sidewalk and rode right into the street."

I knew where the rest of the words were going to take me. I knew exactly the words Bob would say, but I wasn't strong enough to hear them, so I dropped the phone and just started saying, "No," over and over again. My voice got louder as my panic took over, my fear and grief overshadowing my awareness of my volume.

Riot was at my side, asking me what was the matter, and when he finally picked up the phone, he heard the words I couldn't take in, and I watched as his face paled in the moonlight, as the pain filled his eyes, and I knew for sure Marcus was slipping away.

Without much help from me, Riot took us both to the airport and got us on a flight back to Washington. I was practically catatonic. I knew once I opened the gate to my emotions, I'd drown in them. Riot tried constantly to comfort me by touching me, holding my hand, but I pulled away. Any emotion was unwelcome, even if it was love. Perhaps especially *because* it was love.

I was both anxious to get to Marcus, but also dreading it. I couldn't be sure what I would find when we got to the hospital, but I knew it wasn't going to be a few scratches and bruises. It was more substantial than that; more devastating.

The plane landed and I let Riot get us a cab to the hospital and then soon I found myself walking into the pediatric ICU. I gave them my name, then gave them Marcus' name, and was taken to his room.

I first saw Bob standing outside the room in the hallway, leaning back against the wall, head hanging low, body looking tired. When he heard our footsteps approaching he looked up and our eyes met.

"Kalli, thank God you're here," he said stepping toward me. I held out my hand, motioning for him to not come too close.

The nurse turned to me and said, "This is Marcus' room and he's resting comfortably. I've alerted the doctor that you're here and he'll be by shortly to answer any questions you have." She looked back and forth between Bob, Riot, and me, and then added, "There're only two visitors allowed at a time." With that, she gave a sad smile and returned to her station.

"Nancy's waiting for you in there," Bob said, quietly. I nodded and then walked toward the door, pushed it open slowly, and walked inside.

I was greeted with all manner of beeping and machines, the glow of computer screens illuminating the room, and the sight of my baby brother lying in an uncomfortable-looking bed, nearly unrecognizable.

His face was swollen, with gauze wrapped around most of his head, leaving only the oval of his chin to his forehead visible. He still looked like the boy I loved, just broken.

When Nancy turned to look at me, I saw all the heartbreak I'd heard on the phone, and when she stood, walking toward me, I couldn't keep her at bay. Didn't want to. I let her hug me and cry into my shoulder and listened to her tell me she was sorry over and over again.

"He rode his bike into the street and in a flash he was hit by the truck," she sobbed. "It's my fault. I shouldn't have had him out that late. The sun was setting and it was starting to get dark. We'd been arguing with him, trying to get him to come home with us, so I'd unbuckled his helmet." She let loose a round of sobs, gut-wrenching cries that I'd only ever heard from myself when I learned my mother had died. The kind of cries where one lost a part of one's soul. "I'm so sorry," she said through the sobs.

For a few minutes we just stood there, holding each other, and I wasn't sure who was getting more comfort from whom. I was holding on to her because she was all that was keeping me upright, but I felt like she would collapse without me, too. There was nothing for either one of us to do except be with the other, so that was what we did.

Finally, a man in a white lab coat came in and introduced himself as Marky's doctor, said he was a pediatric neurologist. Once all the introductions were made, he wasted no time at all telling me something I never thought I'd hear.

"Your brother has suffered a major head trauma and, unfortunately, there doesn't seem to be any brain activity."

The tears came hot and hard, stinging my eyes as I listened to the man tell me something I never wanted to know.

"Now, usually, in cases like these, we'd give the brain some time to heal, let the body calm down a little before making any rash decisions about care, but your brother isn't lucky enough to be afforded that luxury. You see, along with his brain damage, he's had significant internal injuries as well. His body is shutting down."

I looked over at Marcus, lying so peacefully in that bed, trying to see what the doctor was telling me, trying to find something I could hold on to that was tangible. Sure, he looked banged up, but surely, *surely*, he could wake up from this. We'd dealt with obstacles before; we could handle this as long as we were together, as long as he was here for me to take care of.

"I'm sorry to tell you there's probably only a matter of hours left." The doctor said the words with such finality, such irrevocability, but I shook my head regardless.

"This can't be the end," I managed. "He's so strong, he's been through so much already, I know he can pull through."

"I wish there was something we could do. I know this must be difficult."

His words sounded sincere, he was doing everything he was supposed to be doing, but I couldn't help but think his sympathy was rehearsed. My mind wasn't thinking logically and was only trying to find a reality in which Marcus lived.

"I want a second opinion," I said, flatly.

"I can put in a call to our other resident neurologist, but I'll warn you, Marcus might not make it long enough for someone to see him. I think it's best you use this time to be with your brother. I'll put the call in right away."

The doctor left the room and I turned to Nancy. "They're wrong. I know he'll be fine."

"Sweetie," Nancy said in her best mom voice. "Why don't you just sit with him and talk to him. He needs to hear your voice right now."

I looked anxiously at the chair Nancy had been in, which was sitting at Marky's bedside. It looked too much like a scene in a movie, too much like loss and heartache, but deep down inside I knew he needed me to be there with him. I didn't want to believe this was the day I'd lose my brother, but I'd be damned if he felt like he was alone when the time came.

So I sat down and reached for his hand, trying to block out all the wires and beeping that surrounded him, and just tried to focus on Marky. My little brother. The boy who'd brought so much happiness to my life for the last seventeen years. The very last piece remaining of my life before destruction. His hand was warm, but limp, and it lay heavily in my own.

"Hey, buddy," I said, more tears trailing down my face. I couldn't find the right words in that moment, couldn't figure out what you were supposed to say to the most important person in your life as they slipped away from you. So, I just started at the beginning.

"The day you were born was the most magical day of my life. All throughout Mom's pregnancy I was so anxious to meet you, so excited to hold a little baby." I used my other hand to wipe my nose and then laughed a little when Nancy was suddenly beside me with a tissue. I gave her a weak smile, but then turned back to my brother.

"Mom wouldn't let me in the hospital room because she thought I would be scarred by seeing a birth, but I sat just outside the door, waiting to hear you cry. When you finally made your grand entrance, you were squawking and wailing, and you were loud." I smiled at the memory, remembering the hard floor under me and the nurses who kept walking past the room, giving me curious glances, unaccustomed to girls sitting on their floors.

"I heard you cry and I immediately jumped up and burst into the room. You were lying on Mom's chest and just *crying*. I made it to you and Mom and saw the look of amazement on her face. Your dad was there, right by her side, smiling with tears in his eyes, obviously so excited to meet you."

My voice cracked again and I looked down into my lap, remembering the best day of my life. "He looked at me too," I cried. "He looked at me and said, 'You've got a baby brother. We're all a family now.' And it was true," I sobbed. "You brought us all together and you gave me something I'd never had before. Unconditional and pure love. You united all of us and I'll never have enough ways or words to thank you for that, Marky."

In the back of my mind I heard the door open and close, and knew Nancy had left us alone, but I couldn't look away from my brother.

"For seven years you were the brightest light in all of our lives, and I know Mom and Dad were so in love with you. They'd be so proud of you, and I know they're going to be waiting for you, they're going to be there to take care of you, Marky." I lost all sense of composure, unable to see through the fat tears spilling from my eyes, unable to speak for the loud sobs coming from me. I was drowning in so many things I couldn't have put my thoughts in order had I tried.

I would be lost without him. No purpose, no reason, no existence. He was it. He *had been* it for so long, I couldn't fathom moving forward without Marcus. And also, there was a part of me, and I couldn't measure how big a part of me at that moment, that wanted to go with him, wanted to protect him through the scary and unknown. I wanted to be there to see my mother on the other side. I wanted to know with certainty that he would be safe and cared for.

"I know you can hear me, Marky," I said through the sobs. "Mom is waiting for you. You don't have to be afraid."

I swallowed hard, waiting for my tears to subside, waiting for some sort of calm to wash over me, but it never did.

"I love you, Marcus. And I'm sorry I never told you before now. I'm sorry I couldn't say the words, but I know you felt it. I love you more than anything. Don't be afraid."

All my words were filled with tears, said between halted breaths, pushed out with cries. But I never left him. I stayed by his side, telling him I loved him, until finally, the beeping slowed and his chest stopped moving.

When I watched him take his last breath, his chest barely rising, then falling, I willed my heart to stop right along with his, for someone to let me go with him.

Chapter Twenty

My Most Prized Possession

I heard the door creak open, pulling me from the heaviest and most exhausting sleep I'd ever experienced. Every time I slept it was almost like it drained more energy from me instead of recharging my batteries.

It had been three days since Marcus passed. Three of the longest and most agonizing days I could remember. After all the beeping had stopped and I was sure Marcus was gone, I stayed in his room holding him, hugging him. Nurses came in and declared him dead, quietly noting the time of his death, and I just rocked him back and forth.

At some point Nancy came in and I let her hold him, then we held each other. The staff was very accommodating and let us stay a few hours, but eventually they told us they had to take his body away.

I kissed his forehead and told him I loved him, and then somehow found the strength to leave him behind. Everything after that was a blur to me. I know Riot was there, but I couldn't talk to him, didn't have anything to say to him.

Somehow I got home and I went to bed. And there I'd stayed until someone creaked open my door. One of my eyes opened and I saw the silhouette of a slender woman in the doorway, but when she turned I saw her belly was rounded and I knew it was Ella. I blinked, trying to make sure I was really seeing her in my room, confused because she'd never been there before.

She closed the door behind her, but didn't flip on the overhead light. Instead, she came to my bed, sitting on the edge, and turned on the small lamp on my bedside table.

"Kalli?" she whispered, trying to wake me gently.

"Ella, what are you doing here? How'd you get here?"

"Well," she said, tucking some hair behind my ear, making me inwardly cringe because I knew my hair had to be a greasy mess. "Riot looked up Tilly's restaurant on the Internet, called her, got Porter's phone number, and here I am." Her voice was soft, so maternal. I had a brief moment of admiring how good of a mother she already was. "He's worried about you, Kal. We all are."

"We?"

"Megan's here, so is Porter. Although, he's not *here* here. He's back at the hotel. He didn't want to crowd you." She paused, just looking at me. "And Riot's still here."

My breath caught. "I can't see him, Ella. I just can't. Please, tell him to go back to LA."

"He just wants to talk to you," she said, trying to soothe me by running a hand down my arm. I couldn't say anything more; I knew if I tried to say anything about Riot I would burst into tears, so I just kept my mouth shut. "Can you tell me about your brother?"

My brain flooded with images of Marcus: him as a baby, watching him sleep wrapped in a light blue blanket, watching him learn to walk, riding a bike for the first time. I tried not to picture him in the hospital bed, tried to keep my mind from torturing me that way, but it was inevitable.

I didn't know if I'd ever be able to think of Marcus again without remembering rocking his cooling body in a hospital bed.

"I'm sorry I never told you about him," I managed, my voice a low whisper.

"Shhh," Ella shushed me. "You don't owe me an explanation or an apology, Kalli. You're my best friend, and one of the best things about our friendship, the thing I value so highly, is that you take me completely at face value. You never asked questions, never pried, you were just there for me when I needed you most. If you felt like you couldn't tell me about him, I accept that. But, if now, you feel like telling me, I'm ready to listen. Let me return the favor, Kalli. Maybe talking about him will help."

Just before I opened my mouth to try and explain everything, the door opened and I saw Megan's face poke through.

"Can I come in?" she whispered. I nodded and she came into the room, carrying a mug, walking to me and setting it down on the bedside table. "It's just tea. I thought you could use something warm in your belly."

"Thank you," I said, but didn't move to touch the mug.

"Kalli was just going to tell me about her brother," Ella said to Megan, but her eyes were on me.

"Can I stay? I'd love to hear about him." Megan's voice was soft and curious, and nothing but sweet. I nodded again and she sat at the very end of the bed, allowing me to see her and Ella. In that moment I noticed how similar they were. Both were beautiful in a natural kind of way, as if they rolled out of bed pretty. But they were both supremely compassionate and warm-hearted.

"Marcus was my baby brother," I started, the tears immediately welling in my eyes, the words rough and strained. Megan's hand found my foot, gently squeezing it, while Ella's hand continued to stroke my arm. "He was born when I was thirteen and he was perfect. He was my most prized possession," I said, wiping away a tear. "When I was twenty and away at college, my mother, stepfather, and Marcus were in a car accident and Marcus was the only survivor."

I told Megan and Ella all about Marcus' struggles, his medical issues, but I also told them about his light and his spirit. Hours passed as I told them stories about him, funny things he did, adventures we'd had. I explained to them about how Nancy took care of him while I was away, which was why I was always quick to leave after a job. Then I told them that while I was away he was in another accident, but that he didn't live through it.

They didn't ask for specifics, which I appreciated, and I figured someone else had filled them in enough they weren't particularly curious. I wiped the tears that had fallen and blew my nose, using a box of tissues that I assumed had been put in my room during my three-day coma.

"So, how does Riot play into all of this?" Ella tilted her head to the side, obviously curious about him and our relationship.

I took in a deep breath and then exhaled loudly, trying to find a way to put words to what was between Riot and me.

"Riot was, well, a mistake," I said with a rush of breath. "I let my guard down with him, let him into my life, let him into Marcus' life, and then it all just collapsed around me."

"Why do you think it was a mistake?" Megan asked.

"It's hard to make the dots connect in my brain, let alone explain them to someone who wouldn't understand," I said, trying not to come off as angry, but I could feel something brewing right in the hole where my heart had been three days ago.

"Can you try?" Ella asked, softly. "He's out there Kalli," she said, motioning to the door of my bedroom. "He hasn't left this house in three days and he's worried sick about you."

"He just needs to go. I'll never be good for him. I'll never get past this. I just can't."

"Tell us why, or at least try, Kal." Megan's voice matched Ella's, soft but insistent.

"Every single person I've ever loved, or who has ever loved me, has gone away. So, even if I let him stay, eventually it would end and I'd be alone anyway. Plus," I said, the tears coming more rapidly. "If I hadn't gone to see him, if I'd come home like I planned, Marcus would still be alive."

"Sweetie, that's just not true. You can't let that weight sit on your shoulders," Ella said, a new level of concern in her voice.

"It is true. He ran from Nancy, he was upset that I wasn't home like I said I would be, that's why he was being unreasonable. If I'd come home we would have probably stayed in and played Monopoly, or watched a movie, like we always did. But odds are he wouldn't have been on his bike or gotten hit by that truck."

"It's not your fault," Megan said. "Bad things happen, you can't take responsibility, honey."

"Bad things happen *to me*. My life has been one bad thing after another, so," I said, wiping my nose again, "I'm not putting myself in a position of losing again."

Ella's lips were in a straight line and I could tell she had more to say to me about it, but was thinking better of it. We sat in silence for a few minutes, and every once in a while I could hear Riot's deep voice from the living room and Nancy's sweet one responding to him. My eyes closed and somewhere deep inside me I tore out the last part of Riot that had taken hold of me.

"I can't hear his voice anymore, Ella. Please tell him he needs to go."

"I don't think it's going to be that easy, Kal. He's pretty convinced you'll want to see him, that you'll let him back in."

"I won't," I said with strength I didn't have. "I can't," I said in a whisper.

I closed my eyes and turned away from her, not wanting to hear or say anymore words. Eventually, I felt both her and Megan's weight lift from the bed, and heard the door open and then latch shut again. A few quiet moments passed, but then the yelling started. Riot's loud and gravelly voice shot down the hallway.

"She can't just push me away!" he screamed. I wasn't sure if he was yelling just because he was angry, or if he was trying to make sure I heard him. It didn't matter. The sound of his voice filling my room did nothing to change my mind. If anything, it solidified my resolve.

It was better to let him go now. He deserved better than me, better than someone who would never be able to let him all the way in. And I didn't deserve anything.

"Kalli!" he screamed. I grabbed my pillow and held it over my head, trying to muffle the sound of his screams. I heard him coming closer to my door, then I heard a commotion, Bob's voice telling Riot to calm down and give me some space.

"Kalli, you can't just ignore me! You can't just pretend I don't mean anything to you, like I don't love you!" He was screaming and sobbing at the same time, and even though I didn't want to cry anymore, I couldn't help the tears that poured out of me. "I lost him too, Kalli." I heard him fall to the ground outside my door, murmuring how he'd loved Marcus too, how he would miss him.

Then I heard him right up against the door, just on the other side.

"His death isn't your fault, Kal, baby. It's not. But if you push me away, if you give up on us, that *will* be your fault." He was quiet for a moment, apart from the cries I heard coming quietly from him. "I'll never leave you," he sobbed.

I listened to him crying on the other side of my door for a while, eventually removing the pillow and absorbing the sound. A part of me wanted to hear him cry, was comforted a little by the fact that he was upset about losing me, but not enough to change my mind or open the door to him.

I was very aware of the fact that if I opened the door, if I let him touch me, I'd lose my ability to keep myself from him. No, he needed to go.

"Go away, Riot," I whispered into the empty room, knowing full well he couldn't hear me. But I repeated myself, each time getting louder and louder.

"Go away, Riot."

Louder.

"Go away, Riot."

Louder.

"Go away, Riot!"

Louder.

"GO AWAY!"

I was screaming, could feel the oxygen burning in my lungs, the blood rushing to my face.

"GO AWAY! GO AWAY! GO AWAY! GO AWAY! GO AWAY! GO AWAY! GO AWAY!"

I screamed until I nearly fainted, until there was nothing left in me to push out, until every part of me was empty. I literally screamed myself to sleep.

When I woke, I left my room and was welcomed by an empty and dark house. Empty, that was, except for Nancy, who was sitting on my couch. She looked just as ruined as

I felt. We looked at each other for a moment, words unnecessary; we were both irrevocably broken. After a beat or two, I opened my mouth to speak, surprised by the sound of my harsh and strained voice.

"Is he gone?"

Nancy just looked at me for a moment. Then, in words I'd probably remember for the rest of my life because they felt heavier than anything she'd ever said to me, she answered.

"Yes, dear girl. He's gone."

Epilogue

Riot

I straightened my tie in the mirror, trying to fix something that was unfixable. There was nothing wrong with my tie. There was something wrong with me, but it wasn't something I could adjust to make right, or wiggle back into place. *She* was missing from me. So much hurt had drifted through my life in the last week, but nothing had hurt worse than hearing her, broken and weak, screaming at me to leave, to go away.

I sighed, giving up on my mission to fiddle with my suit. It wasn't a fashion show. It was a funeral. No one would care if my tie was slightly crooked.

It had taken me three days in Kalli's house to realize that my being there was just hurting her more, adding to her pain. It took every ounce of strength I had to leave her there, and honestly the only reason I could walk away was because she so desperately wanted me gone.

My phone rang and I saw it was my agent again. After I'd jumped on the first plane to Seattle, I'd had to explain to the studio why I wouldn't be back for filming the next day, or the next week for that matter. Usually, this would mean a cut from the show I was working on. The studios don't wait for anyone, especially a newbie like me. But luckily, the writers were invested in my storyline and the producers found a way to work around my absence, filming scenes without my character. My agent was calling to remind me that if I wasn't back at the soundstage tomorrow morning I would be replaced.

I silenced the ringer, sending him to voicemail, and then shoved my phone in my pocket, grabbed my keys and bag, and headed to the lobby of the hotel to check out.

Forty-five minutes later I was walking into Marcus' funeral, which had started a few minutes prior. I knew Kalli wouldn't want me there, so I purposefully came a few minutes late, hoping to just sneak into the back of the church unnoticed.

The front of the church was filled with flowers, all surrounding a pedestal with an urn atop it. Next to the urn stood a large picture of Marcus, his face shining with a bright smile, sitting on an easel. He looked just like a seventeen year old young man, but also so much like a child. Perhaps it was because I knew him, because I understood that even though he looked like he was nearly an adult, he was so innocent and pure, so childlike.

A small smile came over my face as I also thought about how stubborn he could be, how he was a sore loser and a gloating winner, all our games of Monopoly coming to mind. He was an expert Mario Kart driver. He was so much more than that picture or even that urn could hold. And I felt lucky I'd had the opportunity to know him, even for such a short while.

My eyes drifted to the front row of pews and I spotted Kalli's auburn hair. My heart lurched at the sight of her, my eyes begging to see her face, my arms aching to hold her, to comfort her. Her shoulders were low, sagging, and every once in a while I saw them shake, and I knew she was crying.

To Kalli's right sat Nancy, and next to Nancy was Bob. On the other side of Kalli was Ella and I was at least relieved that her friend was there for her. I saw Porter, Megan, and who I assumed was her fiancé sitting next to her as well. My body relaxed a little seeing Kalli surrounded by people who cared about her. Even though she wouldn't let me near her, wouldn't let me love her in the way I wanted to, at least she had a support system. She had people she could lean on, if she allowed herself to lean on anyone.

I shook my head at her stubbornness, thinking of how it must have been a family trait. Next a wave of sadness came over me with the realization that she had no family left. After the sadness came the longing, because I desperately wanted to be her family. I had, in fact, thought we were halfway there, working toward becoming a family, when tragedy struck, sending Kalli back down the rabbit hole.

For whatever reason, Kalli decided to shut down after Marcus passed, to deny herself the opportunity to be cared for. I couldn't fault her for the way she grieved. Grief was grief, and whatever she felt, however her mind processed her devastation, well, I couldn't argue with that. Sure, I had a moment of my grief, where I felt the loss of Kalli as well as her brother, where I came to terms with the fact that she wasn't going to allow me to comfort her or even *be* with her, and I might have lost my composure. But in the last couple of days, I'd come to terms with my role in Kalli's life.

I would simply wait.

I would hold on to the fact that I knew she was mine and that she would eventually feel those ties that bound her to me, those ropes that tethered us together, and come back to me.

The service ended and I made sure I was one of the first to leave the church, intent on not being seen by her. But I did find a tree at the edge of the parking lot to lean against, waiting for just a glimpse of her face before I left. I needed something to hold on to, something to take with me. I was leaving her, putting so much faith in our connection and trying to remain optimistic that soon she'd realize she needed me, or at least wanted me, again.

There weren't a lot of people at the service, so it didn't take very long for everyone to leave, and Kalli was one of the last, as I suspected she would be. When she came out of the church and walked into the pale gray light cast down by the clouds in the sky, I nearly gasped at the sight of her and had to force myself to remain in my spot, fighting the urge to run to her.

Her skin was ashen, eyes lightless, and she was frail. She hadn't had any weight to spare when I met her, and she had lost at least five pounds, if not more, since I'd seen her last. Where she was soft before, she was sharp. All gentle curves were gone and replaced with corners and edges. I had an unexplainably strong urge to hold her and feed her.

I watched as she got into a town car, helped in by Ella, and my eyes strained to see every last part of her before the door shut. I knew that was the last glimpse of her, the last time I'd see any part of her, until she decided to come back to me.

Ella watched the town car leave the church parking lot and then turned and looked right at me. She said something to her husband and then walked over to me. I couldn't help but notice the belly she led with, one hand softly caressing her unborn child as she made her way toward me.

"You came," she said, still a few steps from me.

"I know she didn't want me here, but I couldn't stay away. I tried to be discreet." I stood up straight, pulling my body from the support of the tree.

Ella shook her head. "I don't know if she would have noticed you anyway. She's pretty out of it still."

It hurt to hear those words. I wanted so badly to just hug her, and then shake her, and then hug her again. "She hasn't been eating," I said.

"No," Ella sighed. "We've tried, but she can't keep anything down. She's too upset most of the time."

I ran the back of my hand under my chin, trying so hard to fight every instinct I had to take care of her. "Are you going back to Oregon soon?" I needed someone there to take care of her for me.

"I'll be here for a few more days. Porter and I both took some time off." She took another step toward me and put her hand on my shoulder. "We'll watch over her, Riot. I know this must be hard for you."

"She'll come back to me," I said, my voice low but sure.

"I hope so," she replied, but didn't sound convinced. I couldn't blame her; she'd only seen us at our worst, never at our best. Only Kalli and I knew what it felt like when we were together, when our bodies were so relieved to just be near each other. She'd never seen the way Kalli looked at me as I hovered over her, filling her, kissing her. Only I knew what Kalli looked like when she forgot, even if for just a moment, how much she'd lost.

Ella gave me a slight nod, but then headed back to her husband who was waiting at their car for her. I watched the parking lot empty, knowing everyone was headed to Kalli's house for the wake, but I knew I couldn't go there. I sighed, then headed to my car and continued on to the airport to catch my flight to LA.

All I could hope was that, eventually, Kalli would accept the fact that she was mine. I would be waiting for her, standing still, until she decided to find me.

I hope you'll look forward to reading the conclusion to Kalli and Riot's story

Never Tied Down

Coming Soon

Acknowledgments

The first thank you goes to the readers. Thank you so much for continuing to read my stories and sharing your heart with them and me. If one person reads this story and feels anything, then I know it was all worth it.

To Hang Le, thank you for the amazing cover that so totally encapsulates Kalli. It is sad and soft and beautiful, just like I imagined.

To the ladies at Hot Tree Editing, thank you for helping me make the book the best it could be.

Sabine, Sarah, Kelly, and Andrea – Thank you for reading the book in its bare bones form. I always appreciate the early readers. And Sabine, thank you for giving me Kalli's last name! I was stuck before, and now it all makes sense.

To Becca, Riot is yours - let it be known! Thank you for everything you've done for me; he's the least I could do for you. I love you endlessly and I am so grateful to have found you (first, I might add. I was first. Me. She's mine!).

To Enticing Journey Book Promotions, thank you for helping me spread the word, and to all the blogs who have EVER even mentioned my name or my books – THANK YOU! You don't get the recognition you deserve, but I am so thankful for all of you.

Thank you, of course, to my family. I am so blessed to have a supportive family who is always encouraging and proud. I love you all.

Please feel free to follow me on any and all media platforms!

http://www.facebook.com/AuthorAnieMichaels

https://twitter.com/Anie_Michaels

Shoot me an email!

anie.michaels@gmail.com

Sign up for my newsletter to stay up to date on exciting news and new releases!

http://eepurl.com/-DPjn